THE SUMMER MY GRANDMOTHER'S YARD TRIED TO KILL ME

Written By
HARRY HARVEY

The Summer My Grandmother's Yard Tried to Kill Me
Cover Design & Illustration by Femi Ford
Art Direction by Tom Haag
This edition published in 2021

Xander Books is an imprint of

Winged Hussar Publishing, LLC
1525 Hulse Rd, Unit 1
Point Pleasant, NJ 08742

Copyright © Xander Books
Paperback ISBN 978-1-95042-349-1
E-Book ISBN 978-1-950423-66-8
LCN 2021939987

Bibliographical References and Index
1. Fiction. 2. Middle Grade. 3. Adventure

For more information on Winged Hussar Publishing, LLC, visit us at:
www.wingedhussarpublishing.com
or www.whpsupplyroom.com

Twitter: WingHusPubLLC
Facebook: Winged Hussar Publishing LLC

Acknowledgements

First and foremost, thank you to Zmok Books for taking a chance on this middle grade novel. I am forever indebted to Vincent Rospond, publisher, and Brandon Rospond, editor, for believing in this quirky story and for their patience and advice.

My deepest gratitude to the generous and talented creators of the fantastic cover! Tom Haag did the art direction and Femi Ford did the cover design and illustration.

I appreciate the time school psychologist, Robert Kehoe, and POAC Autism Services director, Gary Weitzen, took to educate me about autism spectrum disorder, and for the work they have done, and continue to do, for the ASD community.

Heartfelt thanks to Emily Daluga, my mentor at The Rutgers University Council on Children's Literature One-on-One Plus Conference. Being invited to the conference and Emily's down-to-earth critique was a great kick in the writing pants. Also, let me tip my hat to my Manasquan High School family—a source of endless stories and super supportive friends.

This book would never have gotten to where it is without the help of my incredible SCBWI-NJ critique group: Michele Prestininzi, Jennifer Mary Grolemund, Barbara Messenger, Jennifer Glackin, and Cheryl Miller. Answering your questions made every chapter better.

My appreciation to the editing powers of Jenny Martinez-Nocito and the critique from her very literary daughters, Lina and Ella. Your notes put the sprinkles on top of the cupcake.

Gratitude to the best neighbors ever—where everyone tells great stories by the pool. Could I have been luckier to move in across the street from a real editor? Mary Raftery encouraged and helped me from day one! Ray Pell, you got the ball rolling.

Finally, the biggest thanks to my family. Ethan, you inspire me without realizing it. And, love to my wife Robin, who has supported my creative side since we first met, and after reading the first draft said, "I love this ending!" Couldn't do it without you, Camerado.

Chapter 1

I was on the verge of a full-blown, tears-streaming, snot-flowing breakdown.

Pinned against the ground, those snake-like creepers had me. I tried to rise but the green devils tangled up my arms and legs. They slithered over top of me, crisscrossing again and again. When one touched my skin, I got the heebie-jeebies.

Wrapped up in green, I screamed, "Help!"

Then the squeezing pressure around my throat was too much. I could hardly breathe. I heard that monstrous thing slither away. It had Gram. She was too old to fight back, and I was helpless to save her. The thing made that weird sound when it moved, a cross between a strange whistle and the howl from The Wolf Man, 1941, a Universal horror classic.

But you know what grated my cheese the most about dying? I hadn't even kissed a girl yet! I could have, too. I know it sounded crazy, but I really think I could have.

Everyone says when you're about to check out, time slows down and your life flashes before your eyes. Guess what? It didn't happen to me that way. I mean, time slowed down, way down. But my life didn't flash before my eyes. My summer did. Up until this day, it had been the best summer of my twelve-year-old life. Now, I was in the dark. I was giving up. Worst of all, I was crying. Crying! How did this happen?

Chapter 2

It started the summer before. I sat on a spongy mat that had a funky smell, wearing black sweatpants. I was at a two-week enrichment program called Karate Kamp. It bothered me that it was spelled wrong, but that was how Master Jeffrey spelled it on his flyer and website. The master stood before us in his dark green karate pants and white karate shirt, a black belt tied around his waist.

"Karate Kamp will give you the basic fundamentals in the Japanese art of self-defense," he said, holding a white belt in his hand. "Basics you can learn, if you practice hard."

I was there for the standard stuff my parents always signed me up for—try to make a friend, try to lose some weight, and try not to cry.

"Karate," Master Jeffrey continued, "is a skill you must use for self-defense only. Never to become a bully."

No problem there. I was the kid getting bullied at school. I would love to use this Japanese art on my bullies, but I didn't have the guts. I wiped my glasses on my new Karate Kamp T-shirt, which I wore under protest. My mom would not, under any circumstances, let me wear my Creature from the Black Lagoon, 1954, T-shirt.

"You will begin as a white belt, the lowest rank," Master Jeffrey explained, showing us the belt. "But, if you work hard, at the end of this camp, you will earn a yellow stripe and begin a journey that years from now may end with a black belt."

Years? Wait a minute. I was promised fighting skills, weight loss, friends, and a trip with Mom and Dad to Red Lobster when this whole thing was over—in two weeks! I was nervous. Not 'I think I am going to cry' nervous, but enough that I started doing one of my other things. I raised my hand and said, "Question."

"You have a question?" Master Jeffrey asked.

"Indeed, Sensei."

"Let's have it, Peter. And there's no need to call me sensei."

I heard Master Jeffrey, but I couldn't resist calling him that. In martial arts movies, the student always called his master 'sensei.' Movies were my passion.

"Have you seen any of Bruce Lee's films, Sensei?" I asked.

"Um… Yes… I own the box set. Now, if we could continue. Physical fitness is—"

I raised my hand again.

"Yes?" Master Jeffrey said, annoyed.

"Follow-up question, Sensei. Which Bruce Lee movie is your favorite?"

Master Jeffrey rubbed his chin. "I think my favorite is… Way of the Dragon."

"Released in 1972," I interrupted. One of my recent movie obsessions: kung fu flicks.

Master Jeffrey added, "I like that one because Bruce fights—"

"Chuck Norris!" I blurted out.

"Correct. A great fight at the Roman Coliseum. And as you may or may not know, young man, Chuck Norris studied karate, which we will do now if you stop interrupting. Understood?"

"Crystal clear, Sensei." Master Jeffrey's Bruce Lee knowledge relaxed me. Maybe this whole thing wouldn't be so bad.

As the days at his camp progressed, I got to know a girl in the class—Bernadette. She was in the same boat as me, sort of. She told me she was there to lose some weight, but I don't think she had a problem fending off bullies. Her "Ki-yahs!" were loud. She had a big smile that lit up the dojo. Perhaps because her head was bigger than anyone else's.

Amazingly, we had many semi-romantic moments. Here were my top three in descending order: 3) "Sure is hot in here." 2) "Do you think the mat smells funny?" 1) "Are you signing up for week three?" I would if she would. This was the most conversation I'd had with a girl ever. These lovey-dovey tidbits had me so smitten, I caught myself writing her name in my summer math workbook. 'Peter Mulligan + Bernadette.' I didn't know her last name.

Chapter 3

On the final Friday, before we received our yellow stripes, Master Jeffrey decided to reward us with sparring. We wore boxing gloves, soft foam helmets, and foot pads.

Except for Bernadette: her lovely head was too big for all the kid-sized helmets.

Each Karate Kamper had a round with a classmate assigned by Master Jeffrey. I waited. I was sweating. I worried who I would fight. Most kids were smaller than me, but some were pretty quick. I thought I could take Rachel. Every time she side-kicked, she lost her balance. But she was paired up with Alan.

I would be last and so would... Jeez Louise! We were the main event! In this corner, weighing too much for an eleven-year-old, a terrified Peter Mulligan versus the enchanting Bernadette! Oh no!

I was definitely not ready to rumble! Actually, the only thing rumbling was my churning stomach pushing a wave of fear up my body and into my eyes for a good cry. But, I didn't want to cry in front of her. Usually, I didn't have this much pride. I didn't care who saw me blubber. Most times, I couldn't even control it. But not in front of Bernadette! Thinking quickly, I planned to take the gentlemanly (or cowardly) way out and take a dive (which means, for you non-boxing fans, fake being knocked out).

Master Jeffrey yelled, "Spar!"

Bernadette and I approached each other, her big smile beaming.

"Come on, Peter, let's do this!" she said, punching her gloves together.

She was so excited. There was no way I was going to punch, chop, or kick her. As soon as she got close to me, I fell to the mat.

"Peter, what are you doing?" Master Jeffrey said, staring down at me.

"Taking a dive, Sensei. Bernadette wins."

"A dive? Get up, Peter! She didn't even hit you."

I got up. We circled each other. Bernadette attacked. Without my glasses, I only saw blurry bits of red glove flashing before my eyes as she punched the crap out of me. I took my second dive. The mat did smell funny. The cleaning solution had a hint of vinegar.

"Peter! Come on, son! Get back up and get in your proper stance."

Slowly, I stanced.

"Okay, Peter. Just try to spar a little. There's nothing to be afraid of. She won't hurt you."

It wasn't the sparring I was afraid of. It was just... I didn't know where to aim. I couldn't hit her head, she had no helmet. I couldn't hit her chest area, of course. I didn't want to hit her at all. I liked her.

"Just throw a punch, Peter. It doesn't have to connect. I'm sure she'll block it."

"Oh, I'll block it," Bernadette said, smiling.

"See?" Master Jeffrey said. "Don't worry."

"Where?" I asked.

"Aim for her shoulder. The whole point is to try." He grabbed my glove and demonstrated. "A little jab. Like this." Humiliating.

"Yeah, Peter, don't be scared," Bernadette reassured me. "I'm too fast for you." She commenced bouncing on her feet. "You won't hurt me."

"All right, you heard Bernadette," sensei said. "Let's fight, I mean, spar. Go!"

I held up my gloves. This time, Bernadette hit me with every punch we learned: straight fist, back fist, and I didn't see this one coming: a hammer fist. It hurt, too. I stood there, taking it.

"Hold it!" Master Jeffrey called.

I dropped my arms and tried to catch my breath. I was exhausted. I should have quit right there, but I didn't have the guts. Master Jeffrey put his arm around my shoulder.

"Okay, Peter, that was better. But you've got one more thing to do. Throw one punch. It doesn't have to land. It doesn't have to look good. You just have to try it. That's what Karate Kamp is all about: one good punch."

"I thought you said Karate Kamp was about the Japanese art of self-defense, Sensei?"

"You don't have to call me— Look, for every student it's different. For you, it's about this. One good punch, okay?"

"I don't know."

"You can do it," Bernadette said.

11

That was awfully encouraging of her. Was she flirting with me? According to every romantic film I knew, I think she was! I considered that maybe, just for her, I might throw one punch. Maybe.

"Begin!" Master Jeffrey commanded.

Bernadette unleashed her fists of fury.

"Come on, Peter, try!" Master Jeffrey shouted. "Just one punch. One punch and that yellow stripe is yours. You can do it. Just one punch!"

The class of eight took up the chant. "Just one punch! Just one punch!"

"Come on, Peter!" Bernadette yelled.

The chant, the flirting, disappointing her, the pressure, it got to me. I still didn't want to, but I closed my eyes and threw just one punch straight ahead. I felt it connect. Hard. I heard a strange noise, like when you watch a monster movie. The scene where someone hid in the woods and stepped on a stick by accident. That sort of noise and a gasp.

I opened my eyes and Bernadette's face was covered in blood. Oh no! What had I done? Something horrible... The kids in the room screamed. She was crying! Master Jeffrey ran to her. Her poor face, the blood. I started to cry! I cried so hard, I couldn't catch my breath. Then, the room spun and I passed out. No dive this time. For real. Knockout.

Later, my mom and dad told me what happened. Master Jeffrey said that my straight jab shot out just as Bernadette moved in. I threw it too high as well. It was karate's perfect storm: Bernadette moving forward with all her weight, my right hand going out with all my weight. Bam! Too much force generated. It broke her nose.

I did not sign up for any more weeks.

Chapter 4

After I accidentally broke Bernadette's nose, that story followed me to Stone Hill Elementary and stuck with me all through fifth grade. I had no clue how. She didn't even go to our school. Anyway, I was known as "The guy that broke his girlfriend's nose!" or "Don't get Peter mad, he might Bernadette you!" or "Facebreaker!" There were lots of variations. I felt such guilt and anger about it, just hearing her name for a while made me cry.

For most of the fall, that happened: whenever a classmate said it, I cried. At first it was gushers (tears, snots, can't catch my breath), then waterworks (steady tears but in control), and finally, the leaksies (red face and wet eyes I wipe away). It happened way too much for a fifth grader. The Bernadette thing died down, but it got so whenever someone picked on me, I got upset and I would easily cry.

By now, my fellow Stone Hillians were really good at teasing me. They weren't just bullies. They were ninja bullies. They called me "crybaby" and "fat-face," slapped books out of my hands, made fun of my monster movie T-shirts, dropped boogers or chewed gum or other disgusting things in my food in the cafeteria, and they never got caught! Perfect timing. Never when a teacher was looking. When I complained—I was the weirdo! Jeez Louise!

I meant no harm. I didn't purposely annoy people with my issues. I simply couldn't help it. And I couldn't help what happened that day. My parents called it 'the incident.'

It was late May, a little before lunch. We were taking the super-important Academic Preparedness Exam—a state standardized test which everyone called the APE. Terrible acronym. But it was a big deal. We'd been APE-prepping for months. There was only sixty minutes left of this four-and-a-half-hour test. I was working hard, feeling anxious, scrolling through the test on my school-issued tablet.

Then, my classmate leaned over and whispered, "Hey, chub-butt, get a new T-shirt." I sported my Frankenstein one, which I must confess, I wore once a week. I really liked it. "Don't you have any other clothes?" He pointed to the monster's face. "That what Bernadette looked like after you busted her nose? You're such a weirdo."

That was the first time someone mentioned her name in months.

Something inside me snapped.

I wish I could say 'snapped' meant that I got up, jumped into a Karate Kamp stance, grabbed that kid, and threw him across the room! But I didn't have the guts. What 'snapped' really meant was I started to cry. At first, it was a leaksie. I wiped my eyes. I sniffled. My teacher sighed and walked to my desk.

"Peter, are you okay?"

I wiped again and again, but the tears kept coming. The class noticed and turned their heads my way. She noticed them noticing.

"Peter, please get a hold of yourself. We're in the middle of the APE," she said, firmly.

I tried, but I couldn't stop. The class laughed. The waterworks began.

"If everyone could just ignore Peter and please keep testing," my teacher said. "We have fifty-five minutes to go." No one got back to work. "Peter, you have to stop. Please! These APE scores are very important!"

I couldn't stop.

She frowned. She glared at the kids near me. "What happened back here?"

My classmate confessed. "I mentioned Bernadette."

"Oh no," my teacher gasped.

Oh yes. When he said it again, the dam of pent-up emotion burst. The waterworks overflowed into a full-on gusher! The rest of it I remembered in bits and pieces.

The next thing I knew, the principal, in a serious black suit, stood over me.

"Peter J. Mulligan," he whispered, sternly in my ear. "I think it's time you end this show. This is the APE, young man. The APE! Do you know how important this is? Now, stop crying and finish that test."

I kept gushing.

"Should we get the class to leave?" my teacher asked the principal. "Once he gets going, it can be bad."

"And waste a whole morning of testing?" he answered in a low voice. "We'll have to cancel the whole class's scores. I'll have to fill out an

APE-Disruption Report. It's a paperwork nightmare! We have to get him out and cancel his scores." He leaned down. "Let's go, Mr. Mulligan. Now."

"I'll... be... fine," I managed to get out between gasps for air.

"You are not fine! Let's go," he said. He stared at me, waiting. He turned to my teacher and whispered, "Did someone mention Bernice?"

"Bernadette!" I cried out. The gusher swelled into an emotional tsunami. Without thinking, I gripped the desk and kept right on going: tears and snot flowing.

It was a full-blown incident.

And the APE clock was ticking.

Chapter 5

The principal shut my tablet and snatched it off my desk. "Please keep working, children!" he said to the class. He raced to the front of the room and picked up the phone.

In a minute, Miss Nunzio, the school social worker, arrived. I knew her well. I'd visited her once a week since kindergarten. Speaking softly, she tried to calm me down. "Please, Peter. You can come to my office and we'll talk about it."

Miss Nunzio handed me tissues, but I ignored her. I let the mucus pour on the desk. When a snot string bothered me, I wiped it across my arm.

Thinking quickly, Miss Nunzio sent for Dr. Carlos—my therapist. He happened to be sitting in her office on a consultation. "Peter, why don't we find a healthy way to deal with this?" whispered Dr. Carlos. "We can go to my office and role play." Though I enjoyed a good role play with Dr. C, it couldn't solve everything. I shook my head.

"Okay, students, you keep APE-ing," the principal said nervously. "We'll handle this, you handle those word problems, okay?" He ran to the phone and made another call in hushed tones. He tried not to disturb my classmates, but I felt the kids staring at me.

Then, things got weird. Who'd he call? Not Ghostbusters, 1984. I had the T-shirt. My mom and dad. We lived nearby. The principal briefed them on the APE and the situation. They promised me everything.

"Red Lobster tonight, okay, bud?" my dad said quietly. "Just get up and come with us."

"How about the movies, Peter?" my mom asked. "I'll let you have an extra-large popcorn with extra butter. As much butter as you want. Please."

In desperation, my mom texted Chad, the last person I would have called. He was my personal trainer. For the last two months, my mom forced me to work out with Chad. Believe it or not, he showed up. The gym was a block away.

"Come on, dude," he said. "We'll skip planks for a week, okay? I know you hate planks."

Not doing planks did not snap me out of it. My classmates sat in stunned silence. No jokes. No insults. No one working on the APE. Nothing. I was freaking them out.

Suddenly the principal, sweat beading on his forehead, got an idea. "Perhaps, with your permission, Mr. and Mrs. Mulligan, we could... under the circumstances... slide him out?"

The classroom floor was vinyl tile. My teacher made us slide desks to make groups all the time. Only problem: I was fifth row, last seat, in the back. Could they make it the whole way? They discussed it. Dr. Carlos delivered the ultimatum. "Peter, if you won't leave, we are going to slide your desk, and you, out of the room. Will you please get up and leave with us? We only want to help you."

I should have been helpful. I should have gone along like I always do. But with the tsunami flowing, I did the opposite. I hunkered down. They had no choice. To make it tougher, I planted my feet and pushed my overweight self as low as I could. Being chubby was about to pay off. I guess in some strange way, I finally stood up for myself, by sitting down and crying this one out. Every ninja bully could see how I felt. The adults positioned themselves around me: Chad, Dr. Carlos, Miss Nunzio, Mom and Dad, and the principal.

"Keep working, people," the principal ordered the class. "You're almost finished. There's nothing to see here. But, could these two rows make a path, please? Thank you. Keep APE-ing."

My classmates parted their desks like Moses parted the Red Sea in The Ten Commandments, nominated for Best Picture 1956. Great flick.

"Peter, please," my mom begged.

I just kept blubbering.

"On the count of three then," the principal said. "One, two, three."

They heaved. I planted. My sneakers squeaked across the floor. They moved me about six inches or so.

They did it again. It took a good five minutes of push squeak, push squeak, until they finally hauled me out of the room and shut the classroom door.

They took a break. They asked me to get up. I ignored them.

They pushed and squeaked me down the hall. I could hear teachers telling classes to stop work and pass forward all APE identification tickets.

The principal heard it, too. With a smile, he wiped the sweat from his brow.

They stopped at the elevator. They were breathing really heavy. They took another break.

"Please, Son," my dad asked, "will you stop now?"

Too upset, I didn't answer. On the count of three, they lifted me into the elevator. Inside, I stopped crying and just held onto the desk, my knuckles white.

Finally, they pushed and squeaked me to the school's main entrance. They summoned secretaries to hold open the double doors. As they prepared to lift me down the three front steps, a cool breeze blew through the door. Outside Stone Hill Elementary, it was May—a beautiful afternoon, sunny and cloudless. I inhaled and exhaled. It was over. I was all cried out.

So, I got up. They looked at me, astonished. I wiped my face. Gross. I wiped my glasses on my T-shirt. I turned to them and said in my best Southern drawl, "Why, thank you." I cleared my throat. "I have always depended on the kindness of strangers."

That famous line came from a film called A Streetcar Named Desire, 1951. Vivien Leigh, who delivered the line in the movie as Blanche DuBois, won the Academy Award for Best Actress. After Blanche said it, she was led away by a doctor to a mental hospital. Not so dramatic for me. After I said it, I went to my parents' car and sat in the backseat.

Chapter 6

I didn't remember everything my parents said during that tense car ride. They were angry, embarrassed, disappointed. I felt that way, too. I did remember the conversation my parents had later that night. At least the snippets I could make out while I was in bed.

I was under the covers. It was around eight-thirty—my bedtime. This was on Miss Nunzio's recommendation. She thought ten hours of sleep would help me control my emotions better. I'd been doing this since I was eight. Even with my room-darkening curtains drawn, it was bright in there because it was still light outside.

My bedroom was either the lamest or coolest ever, depending on your opinion of classic movies—mostly horror. Aside from a dresser and small bookshelf, filled with my movie character Bobbleheads, my poster collection covered every inch of the walls and ceiling, I thumbtacked them myself. Well, my dad helped me with the ceiling ones because we needed a ladder. They weren't vintage or original, but they looked great to me.

Some people count sheep when they can't sleep. Not me. I counted my posters, one at a time. I studied each one and named the title, release date, and my favorite line. In that order. It was soothing.

"Frankenstein, 1931," I whispered mad scientist-style. "It's alive! It's alive!"

My parents had just tucked me in and had left the door open a crack because I get creeped out in the middle of the night. I could hear pieces of their conversation downstairs.

"—so he can't go back," I heard Mom say.

"I know," sighed Dad.

That was fine with me. I never liked Stone Hill Elementary anyway.

"Dracula, 1931," I whispered in a vampire voice. "Listen to them. Children of the night. What music they make."

"Are you serious?" Dad asked. "Johnson Island, alone, with my mother?"

"What choice…" I partly heard Mom answer. "…summer won't kill him."

Whoa. Wait a minute? Johnson Island? With Grandmother? There was no way my parents would go through with this idea. It was an island in the middle of nowhere. You took an hour ferry ride just to get there! The ferry was like three hours away from our house. Dad grew up on Johnson Island. After he met Mom at a Grateful Dead concert, he never went back. The first time I even knew he came from the island was when my grandfather died last year. My parents went to the funeral. They didn't take me because they said I might get too emotional, which was probably true.

"King Kong, 1933," I whispered, then in my old-time tough guy talk. "Oh, no, it wasn't the airplanes. It was Beauty killed the Beast."

"It's not like we haven't…" I caught Mom saying.

"You're right," Dad agreed. "We've tried everything to help him."

It was true. Aside from Karate Kamp, they had signed me up for every sports team you could think of, but when a nine-year-old told his Little League teammates in a British accent—"My apologies for striking out, gentlemen. I shall try harder. You have my word."—it didn't go over well. My theater teachers hated my imitations, too. When I said my lines like Cary Grant or Tom Hanks or Lucille Ball, they were not happy. But my Lucy impression was spot on! I cried or movie-ed my way out of every activity: art, music, science, writing; you name it, I tried it.

"Godzilla, King of the Monsters! 1956." Then in my dubbed-over, Japanese doctor voice I said, "Godzilla should not be destroyed, he should be studied."

"—about the therapy?" Dad asked. "Do you think everyone will—"

"What about it? Is any of it working?" Mom replied. "It didn't prevent today, did it?"

There was a long pause. "No."

"It will be a break for him. For us. It'll give us time, too."

Time for what? I missed that. Then, I couldn't hear them anymore. They must have gone to the back porch. I counted my posters three times before I finally fell asleep. I got their full plan in the morning.

"With Grandmother?" I said, watching Mom pick the strawberries out of my bowl of yogurt with fruit. She wanted me to lose weight, but I was not a fan of strawberries.

"Sure, Peter," my mom said. "It will be something different. A change of scenery."

Dad stood by her with his coffee. "The island is quiet and relaxing. And my mom could use the company. I'm sure since Grandpa passed it's been tough."

"Really? You want me to give someone emotional support during a difficult time?"

"I guess," Dad said, looking at Mom. "Just for the summer. Middle of August, tops."

Mom handed me the bowl without strawberries. "We thought that while you're away, we'll look for a different school. One that can handle your needs better."

"Will we have to move?"

"If we do, we do," my dad said. "We'll figure all that out while you're on vacation."

Vacation? That was a nice way to spin it. "What'd the A-Team say? They won't like it."

Chapter 7

In my house, the A-Team stood for two things. One was the group of professionals (minus Chad, in my opinion) who helped me cope with my issues. I have autism, technically called ASD—autism spectrum disorder. I was diagnosed when I was eight. Throw in the natural anxiety that came from being a kid with autism, and it was obvious that growing up in my home town hadn't been easy, even with my parents' support and my A-Team.

What was the second thing the A-Team stood for in the Mulligan home? It was obvious: the 80s TV show, The A-Team, movie remake, 2010! I owned the complete television series: all five seasons. I got it at Walmart. I loved that show's theme song about a commando unit falsely imprisoned who escape and operate in the L.A. underground as soldiers of fortune: "If you have a problem, if no one else can help and if you can find them... maybe you can hire the A-Team." Then the music started! It was great!

Each week, I repeated those lines and hummed that song as we visited my treatment team. I was sure they would talk my parents out of their plan. Me on an island? I couldn't even swim. I had a problem, and no one else could help. I was really counting on my A-Team.

We started with Mom's favorite: Chad, the personal trainer who turned her on to CrossFit after her PX90 craze. Mom used to be on the chubby side like me but not anymore. She was sure if I dropped a few pounds and became more active, my whole attitude would change.

"Mrs. M, I don't know," Chad said. "Peter's lost some weight. I think we're on a roll here. But not seeing him all summer, he could gain it back. Right, Movie-Dude?"

Great! Chad was on my side. If he only knew that weight loss was due to a bad taco. I couldn't eat for three days. He nicknamed me Movie-

Dude after we got into an argument. For a man of sports, Chad had never seen Rocky, 1976, which won the Academy Award for Best Picture! He still hadn't seen it. How could a man of sports not see a flick like that?

"But," Chad continued, "he's your kid." He shook my hand. "Good luck, Movie-Dude." That was a quick change. "No Butterfingers and keep up the planks. Never know when you're gonna need to plank."

What? When would I ever need to plank? Strike one.

On to Miss Nunzio, the school social worker. She was a lovely woman of Italian heritage and unmarried in her forties. I was hoping this would be the summer she would finally meet someone special and get married. We'd spent hours in her office talking. I couldn't tell you how often she had a first date that never became a second. I always listened. She liked me. She would be on my side. She would help save me from the island.

"I'm not sure, Mrs. Mulligan," she said. "Peter and I seemed to be making real progress until the incident." She wrote something down. "But you're his mom and you'll do what you want. Here's my cell. Call me if you need me. Take care of yourself, Peter."

Wow, did not see that coming. Strike two. On to my therapist. "Help me, Dr. Carlos. You're my only hope." Movie reference, Star Wars: Episode IV – A New Hope, 1977. Way too long of a title.

Dr. Carlos and I always met alone first, then with my parents. I expressed my fears of the island: a grandmother I had never met, kids picking on me, hurricanes. Then, we went over the incident. Eventually, the words "weirdo" and "hero" came up. He thought this was important.

He asked me how I defined each, how I saw myself, and finally if all humans had "hero potential" in the right situation. I thought about it. I ticked off a dozen movies where a reluctant character becomes a hero and saves the day. So, I answered yes. Dr. Carlos smiled.

"But only in the movies," I added. "In real life, Doc, especially my life, never. A weirdo cannot be the hero."

Dr. Carlos extended his hand. "Peter, my young friend, I will see you in September."

Strike three. I was out to sea. I tried my best to change my parents' minds. I argued. I promised to take any summer camp without any complaints. I'd do planks every day. I would even eat strawberries—maybe. I would lose weight. Nothing.

Then, I cried. But none of it mattered. My mom had made up her mind. Dad, too.

So, a few weeks later after finishing 5th grade on home instruction with tutors, I found myself in the middle of the Delaware Bay on the Joyce

Mary ferry going to Johnson Island. I sat on a bench with my parents facing the back of the boat. Water sprayed up and misted my glasses. For a ferry, the boat was awfully small. It had enough room for maybe twenty passengers on the back deck. That was it.

The pilot house sat so close to the boat's front, there was no place to stand and say, "I'm the king of the world!" Titanic, 1997. That was the one thing I had been looking forward to. But now, I didn't feel like doing it anyway. I sighed. Mom patted my knee. I wiped my glasses.

I decided in that moment that maybe my parents were right. Maybe I needed a change. Maybe this summer wouldn't be so bad. What was the worst that could happen? It wasn't like I could die or anything.

Chapter 8

During the walk from the ferry to my grandmother's house, I didn't notice much. I kinda felt like one of my favorite cool-guy actors, Steve McQueen, from The Great Escape, 1963. A bunch of times in this classic World War II, prisoner-of-war flick, Steve was captured by the Nazis and walked a long, lonely path to the cooler—solitary confinement. The only difference? I did not march with my head held high like Steve the 'Cooler King.' I dragged my suitcase and shuffled along with my eyes on the narrow road below. For me, there was no escape.

My dad talked. My grandmother listened. She was thin for her age, wearing jeans and a red plaid shirt, untucked and blowing in the breeze. She had gray hair and those glasses with the chain around your neck. She walked pretty fast for an old lady.

I followed everyone through the gate of a small picket fence, badly in need of paint. The yard looked green and overgrown with tall weeds. I trudged up the stairs onto the porch and through the screen door. There was a bright tiny living room—worn loveseat, beat-up recliner, old-fashioned TV. No flat screens. Dad told me to bring my suitcase upstairs. I did.

My bedroom was simple: bed, small nightstand with a lamp, and a dresser. Everything seemed like hand-me-down or yard sale stuff. The scuffed hardwood floors creaked under my weight. I flung my suitcase on the bed, made with white sheets and a white pillowcase. The pale green walls were bare except for a bad painting of a lighthouse. Flowing lacy curtains covered two open windows. A metal folding chair leaned sadly against the wall.

Jeez Louise! It was going to be impossible to fall asleep in here! Especially since, we realized on the ferry, I didn't bring one poster. I sat on the edge of the bed. It creaked, too. The tan blanket was army surplus and rough on my hand. I sighed.

I went back down, the stairs creaking all the way. Big surprise. I joined my family. I plopped in an old wooden chair around a small dining room table.

"Mm-hmm." That was what my grandmother muttered as my parents told her about the incident. That wasn't all. She also nodded and said, "Uh-huh."

They told her about looking for a new town with a school system that might be better equipped to deal with my issues. They'd take care of the whole thing—new school, new town, new house—before the end of the summer.

"Mm-hmm," she said.

They described my A-Team and what I might be like without therapy; they also gave her a few tips on how to deal with me when I get upset.

"Uh-huh," she said.

My dad handed her stapled papers. "Here's all of our information if you need it. You probably won't, but if you do, here it is. Numbers and email."

"If you can't reach us, and he's really upset, you can call Dr. Carlos," my mom said, flipping the page. "Or Miss Nunzio, she lets us call in the summer."

"And here," Dad said, pointing, "are schedules, behavior techniques, exercises."

"Don't worry," my grandmother said, finally using real words. "He'll get plenty of exercise. Plenty of fresh air, too. Heaps a yardwork to get done."

"That's not exactly what we meant," Mom said.

"Garden needs weeding every day."

What?! Weeding?

"Fence needs painting."

I knew it!

"Grass needs mowing."

Mow the lawn?

"Mom, Peter's never done yardwork," Dad said. "He's never mowed a lawn before."

"First time for everything," Grandmother said.

"I don't know about that," my mom said. "Couldn't he really hurt himself? I don't know if I'd trust him with a lawnmower."

"Humph," the old lady grunted. "He can't hurt himself. It's not a fancy electric or gas kind. It's an old push one. Soon as he stops pushing, the blade stops cutting."

"Roger, are you sure we're doing the right thing here?" my mom asked my dad.

"We've been through this, Sue. What other options do we have?"

"We have tried everything," my mom sighed.

"A change will be good," Dad reassured her.

"I hope so," she said.

"No wonder the kid's a wreck," my grandmother said.

Thanks, Grandmother. I was sitting right here.

"You two worrywarts must drive him nuts. He'll be fine. Nothing happens here. It's quiet. It's peaceful. It's kind of boring. You grew up here, Roger." She looked at my dad. "You turned out fine. Mostly fine." She glanced at my mom who didn't catch it. She turned to me.

"Right, Peter? You and your Gram for the summer. You'll be fine, right?"

"Mostly fine, I guess, Grandmother."

"Grandmother?" She snorted. "I go by Gram 'round here, Peter."

"I just, you know, I have this formal nickname thing," I explained. "And I see myself calling you Grandmother."

"Humph. You can call me that if you like, but I only answer to Gram."

Oh boy.

"Now, if you two ain't staying the night, which you're more than welcome to, you've got to catch the ferry."

"Right, Mom. Thanks," my dad said.

Everyone got up for hugs. And surprisingly, my mom hugged Grandmother, I mean Gram. Oh, this was gonna be hard.

"You'll take good care of him?" Mom asked.

"Don't worry, Sue. It's an island. He's as safe as an eagle's baby. The only thing that can hurt him is weeding or water."

My parents looked at each other.

"He can swim, right?"

"He took some classes," my dad said.

"Some," Mom said.

I cried my way out of Little Guppies Swim School after week three.

"I'm not what you call a really strong swimmer," I said.

"Oh," my grandmother, I mean Gram, said. "I reckon I should bring a rope."

We laughed uncomfortably, but before we left to walk back to the dock, she stopped at the run-down shed in her small backyard. She came out with a coil of rope over her shoulder.

"We better hurry now," she said. "You'll miss the Joyce Mary."

27

Chapter 9

As passengers climbed aboard the ferry with my parents, it seemed like half the island had come out to wave goodbye. Boys in bathing suits stood on pilings waiting as the Joyce Mary prepared to leave.

The sun was beginning to set, and it looked beautiful. The sky was huge. Orange light melted into pinks and reds. The clouds turned that blueish purple. Gram and I stood on the dock. (Ha, I got her name right!) I waved to my parents who leaned on the ferry's railing. They waved back.

The kids on the island gathered around me. I guess they wanted to check out the new guy.

Gram wandered away, chatting with someone. Two Asian girls about my age sidled up on either side of me. They both wore pink shirts and Bermuda denim shorts frayed in spots. They stared at me. It was getting weird.

"Hi," they said at the same time.

"Good evening," I said.

They edged closer to me. Nervously, I fiddled with my Oxford shirt, twisting the bottom hem around my index finger. I noticed their shirts sported faded Hello Kitty faces. They both inched even closer. "Um, do you want something?" I asked.

"Do you have anything in your pockets?" one said.

"Me?"

"Yes, you," the other said. "Who else are we talking to?"

"Um, let me check. No."

"All of them," one said.

"Your back pockets too, dum-dum," the second one added.

I looked toward Gram. She was listening to a fisherman. The ferry slowly pulled away. And did that one girl just call me dum-dum? I checked my other pockets. I tried to go along. "Let's see, ladies, I have... my wallet."

28

"Give it to me."

"Give it to her," the other girl ordered.

"Why?" I said.

"We won't steal your money."

"We just want to see it."

"Why, may I ask?" I said.

"Island tradition," they both said at the same time.

"Better do it, Pete," Gram called, turning away from the fisherman.

"But—"

"He doesn't believe us," the first girl said. "We're telling the truth."

"It's an island tradition. We're trying to help you," the second girl added.

"Right, Gram Mulligan?" the first one called.

"Right, girls," answered Gram... Mulligan?

"See," the first one said.

"We told you," the second one agreed.

They took my wallet. They talked in a fast-paced Ping-Pong way. It was hard to keep up and even harder to say no. They looked the same, they sounded the same. They must have been twins. They both had short black hair and brown eyes, sort of like the tiny magical twins in Mothra vs. Godzilla, 1964. Except these girls were normal-sized, and I imagined not magical and I was sure they didn't go on amazing adventures on faraway islands filled with monsters to sing songs to a giant prehistoric moth who fights Godzilla. Mothra vs. Godzilla, 1964, was one of my favorites!

"Can I see your glasses?" one asked.

"Okay." I didn't want to, but I gave the first girl my glasses.

"Hey, cute eyewinkers," she said.

"What?" I asked, confused.

"My sister likes your eyewinkers. They're long."

"You mean my eyelashes?" I said.

"Nice, right?" the first twin asked her sister.

"Yeah, for sure," said the other one, who reached in the pocket of my blue dress shirt. My stomach did a loop-de-loop. The only girl my age who ever touched me before wore boxing gloves. I looked for Gram. She had her back to me, still talking.

The twin fished around in my pocket then said, "Empty."

"Good. But he should take off that shirt anyway," her sister decided.

"Take off my shirt?" I gulped.

"Yeah, it's too nice. Take it off."

Oh boy. "I assume this is part of your island tradition," I asked.

29

"Of course," the first one said.

"You're learning, dum-dum," twin number two added.

I sighed. I hadn't even been here for twenty-four hours and the name-calling started already. I hoped things would be different this summer. Oh well, at least I was used to it. I took off the Oxford and revealed my T-shirt. Now, they'd let me have it.

"Cool. Frankenstein."

"Ooh, where'd you get it?"

"Very cool."

"Old school. I like it."

My head swiveled back-and-forth as I took in their lightning quick... compliments? They liked my monster T-shirt? It must have been sarcasm that I missed. I handed them my dress shirt.

"Actually, it's not Frankenstein," I said. "It's Frankenstein's mon—"

"Take off your sneakers," twin number one interrupted.

"My sneakers?" I asked.

"It's for the best. Trust me," she nodded.

"Okay." I took off my Converse.

"The socks, too, dum-dum," the meaner twin said. "He knows nothing, Gram Mulligan."

Gram turned toward us. "He's new, girls, that's all. Here." Gram handed the girls the rope from the shed, which had a loop on one end. They put the loop on the dock.

"Stand there," the first girl said.

"What?"

"Go ahead," the second one said. "Inside the circle."

I did. "Now, what do I do?"

"Easy. Wave to your parents."

"Wave bye-bye to your momma and dada," one twin joked in a baby voice.

I waved. Mom and Dad waved back.

Then, for a split second I saw a strange look of panic on Mom's face, her waving hand stopped and shot to her mouth, and Dad's hands, which were both waving high in the air, stopped on the sides of his head, like something bad was going to happen.

Then, it hit me. Something bad was going to happen!

Chapter 10

One of the girls pulled the rope up around my chest and tightened it. The other girl, who called me dum-dum, pushed me off the dock! Splash! I hit the water and was under in a second, desperately flailing my arms, then back up, gasping for air. I felt the rope tighten under my armpits. It kept my head above the water.

Gram and twins held the rope and heaved. Everyone was laughing and cheering. Other boys waved to the ferry and jumped off the pilings. Some did cannonballs. They landed near me. The bay water bubbled as I tried to keep my head up. They swam to me, laughing.

"Are you okay?" one boy asked.

I spit out water and nodded. I was struggling to tread water. Was I okay? Mostly, I was stunned. Too stunned to be upset, too stunned to be angry, too stunned to even cry. My clothes were wet and heavy and stuck to me.

"Hey-o, pull 'em out!" the boy yelled.

Gram and the twins laughed as they hauled me to the dock.

"Island tradition, Pete!" said one twin.

"Oh, he's heavy," said the other.

"Swim as best you can," Gram said. "Come on now. To the ladder. Help him, Billy. Come on, boys. Give him a hand. Swim, Peter, swim!"

"I'm trying," I whined.

"He's like that Goonie," one twin said.

"Yeah, Pete, you're heavier than the Truffle Shuffle kid!" the other said.

"There," Gram suggested. "Grab the rung. All over. Come on out."

I climbed the ladder, out of breath. "Actually, his name is Chunk... and the movie is called... The Goonies, 1985... directed by—"

31

"Later, Pete!" Gram cut me off. "Wave to your mom and dad before they dive off the boat and swim back. Let 'em know you're okay."

"See what we did?" the first twin giggled as she helped me climb up the dock.

"Yes, you pushed me in!" I said.

"Yeah, it's tradition. Now you're an islander," she said.

"For the summer," the other explained, "you're a Bay Boy. Like them." She gestured to the other boys who were climbing up the ladder. The whole wet group of kids patted me on the back. We all waved to my parents. People shouted, "Come back soon!"

"I'm okay!" I yelled to my parents.

They waved back.

"You should have seen your face," one twin said. "It was so funny."

"Were you scared?" the other said.

"Very much."

"Take your stuff," the first one said, giving me back my glasses and things. "Here. You need to learn to swim better. We'll teach you tomorrow."

"Is it hard because you're so chubby?" twin two asked. "Is that it?"

"I never really thought about it," I said. Time for the weight jokes.

"I bet that's it," one said.

"We're not chubby and swimming is easy for us," two added.

The boat turned out of the marina now, and my parents were out of sight.

"All right, kids, that's it, show's over," Gram said. "Cookie's Place!"

The half-dozen kids cheered.

"We're eating cookies?" I asked the twins.

"No, dum-dum, we are eating at Cookie's. You'll see."

"Two-stickers for everyone," Gram announced.

"What about cones, Gram Mulligan?" said a boy with a SpongeBob towel.

"Two-stickers is all, Billy. I ain't no Rockefella."

Our party walked a block, and we were at a small restaurant called Cookie's. It was decorated 50s style with a checkered floor and records on the wall. Gram told me to wait outside. The twins and I sat on a bench. The other kids hung around, too, some sat on another bench, some stood in the street. I guess it was a street. I wasn't sure.

It was paved like one, but I don't think it was the size of a real street. It wasn't wide enough. It didn't have a yellow line down the center, either. Come to think of it, I hadn't seen any cars yet. When I first got off the ferry, we walked to Gram's house. Then, we walked back.

I was dripping wet. A boy gave me his towel. He said that he was dry.

One of the twins commanded another boy—Billy, I think—to give me his SpongeBob towel, and he did.

"He likes my sister, that's why," whispered the second twin. "She doesn't like him much, but he likes her. Funny, right?"

"I suppose," I said. We sat for a minute or two. I raised my hand. The twins look puzzled.

"What is he doing?"

"What are you doing?"

"I have a question," I explained.

"Oh, like school, you're raising your hand. I get it."

"Ask it then."

"Okay. Question," I said. "Where are the cars?"

"What cars? No cars here," the first twin said. "Only a few trucks for moving stuff. Only bikes, scooters, skateboards, and—"

A golf cart buzzed down the road. It beeped. Everybody waved. The driver saluted back.

"Golf carts?" I said.

"Right. Now you're getting it, dum-dum," the sassier one said.

Wow, that one sure liked to call me dum-dum. It got quiet then. No one talked. We looked at the sunset. I started to get upset: homesick, being tricked, here for the whole summer alone. Gram came out with double ice pops for everyone. Oh, so that was a two-sticker: one of those double popsicles with two sticks.

"Here you go," she said, passing them out. "One for you, and one for you. Don't crowd me. You'll all get one."

The kids said, "Thanks, Gram Mulligan."

Gram Mulligan, again? I guess that's what everyone called her.

"And for my new roommate, the last two-sticker. Hope you like orange."

I frowned. I did not. "Actually, I prefer cherry."

"Oh."

"Or grape."

"I see."

"I have been known to eat lime, too."

"Humph," she mumbled. "So… you don't want it?"

"I didn't say that." I took the popsicle.

She smiled. "Good." Then, she strolled back inside Cookie's.

I had to admit, even though mine was orange, the frozen fruit sugar tasted delicious—no sugar-free stuff like my mom always gave me. We all sat and licked our two-stickers. I forgot about being homesick for a little while.

Chapter 11

Back at Gram's house, after showering and unpacking, it was late, like eight-thirty. I was in bed. My first day on the island was about to end. Gram was not much of a talker. Also, she was not much of a tucker-inner.

"Good night," she said. "See you in the morning."

She turned out the light. She shut the door all the way. She didn't leave it half-open like my parents did. Not even a little crack so I'd feel safe. She closed it, and I was alone in the room. I sighed. The door opened. She popped her head in. "I forgot something."

"Yes?" I said, sitting straight up.

"The twins are coming over tomorrow. They'll teach you how to swim."

The door shut again with a definitive clunk.

"Good night," she yelled from the other side.

"Good night," I said weakly. I fell back in the bed.

What? The twins? Great. After everything they did: name-calling, deception, pushing me in, laughing at me. And now they were going to teach me how to swim? They might drown me. Or maybe have me swim where the water is infested with sharks or piranhas or extra-deadly electric eels. I didn't know which way of dying would hurt more: big chomping teeth, tiny razor-sharp teeth, or electrical stings searing my flesh?

As I lay there alone in the half-darkness, in a strange new house, in a strange new room, on a strange new island, I got scared. No movie posters to count, either, just lacy white curtains, the pale green wall, and that dumb lighthouse painting. The feeling that I might have a good long cry started to rise for the first time since I'd been on the island. I knew it hadn't been long—I'd only been here about six or seven hours—but I thought it was a pretty good 'No Waterworks' record so far.

I'd better find a way to get out of that lesson tomorrow or I'd never get to sleep. I decided I would simply tell Gram I didn't want to go. Easy. I was sure she'd understand. Maybe.

I crept out of bed and found Gram in her old-fashioned living room watching a movie. Hmm, a black-and-white movie, too. And it looked like she was watching it on a VCR. I hadn't noticed that before. Focus, Peter. The swim lesson. Get out of the swim lesson.

"Gram?" I said. I was nailing her name now.

She paused the movie. Thank goodness. I could never concentrate with it playing. My eyes drifted to the freeze-frame. Was that a tank? Focus, Peter!

"What?" Gram asked.

"I was thinking, um, I don't know if I want to go swimming tomorrow with the girls."

"Why not?"

"Because of what they did tonight," I said, crossing my arms.

"Pushing you off the dock?"

"Yes."

"Sit down, Peter."

I sat down on the loveseat next to her.

"If they hadn't pushed you in, I would have done it."

"You would've pushed me in?" Even Gram was out to get me. "Why?"

"Because it really is an island tradition. All the boys your age jump off the dock or the pilings as the ferry leaves. They do it every day when the weather's nice."

"How come?"

"I guess, there isn't much to do here. And that's what the boys like to do. Your dad did it when he lived here."

"He did?" This was news to me.

"And your grandfather. And his father and so on... blah-blah-blah," she said, waving her hand in a spinning gesture. "No big deal."

She reached for the remote to restart the movie when I said, "I still don't want to go."

Gram sighed. "Don't you understand the girls were helping you? They took your things, important things like your wallet and glasses and shoes and such, before they got lost in the bay. I asked them to do it. I asked them to put the rope around you. And I'm glad I did. You can't swim, which is why you are going tomorrow." She picked up the remote.

"But one called me a dum-dum over and over," I explained. "That's not very nice."

"That's Kat Jin. She's the sassy one. That girl's one of the blue hen's chickens."

Blue hen's chickens? What did that mean?

"Sofia's the other," Gram continued. "I wouldn't worry though, from what I hear, Kat calls lots of folks around here dum-dum and worse."

I sat there, unconvinced.

"Well, so what?" Gram said. "She called you dum-dum. Ain't you ever heard of sticks and stones will break my bones... blah-blah-blah? She still helped you. They both did."

"I don't know," I said, shaking my head.

"Humph, you don't know, huh? When you think about it, weren't you a dum-dum?"

"Me?" This made no sense.

"You didn't know about the tradition yet, right?"

"I suppose."

"You were too dumb to figure out what they were planning, right?"

"I was, yes."

"There was no way you could've known, right? You don't know our ways. Your dad never brought you here."

"That's true."

"So, you were a dum-dum. We're all dum-dums sometimes, if we're honest with ourselves. And if people are honest with us, I think it's okay for them to let us know when we're being dumb. No sense getting upset, if it's the truth; and I think in your case, it was the truth."

"But they laughed at me, they all did, when I fell in," I complained.

Gram smiled. "Sure, Peter, we all did. It was funny. You should've seen your face. The other boys jumped in, too. We laughed and cheered at all the boys in the water, you included."

"Cheered?"

"Sure. Everyone on the dock laughed and cheered because you got pushed in and you were a good sport about it. And now you're someone who lives on the island—a Bay Boy. Everyone knows you're here for the summer. I told them."

Hmm... she made some good points. But just the same, I didn't know how long I could be alone with those twins. I thought it would be trouble. "Still, Gram, I think I'd rather just stay here with you tomorrow."

"Nonsense," her voice became as serious as her face. "You'll go with them. To live on Johnson Island, you need to swim. And I'm too old to teach you, and that's that."

That's that?

"Now go to bed."

Chapter 12

She turned back to her movie and hit the play button.

Wow, I guess that was that. No way out of it. I was getting swim lessons from the twins. I lowered my head. I creaked halfway up the narrow stairs feeling defeated and lonely when I heard Humphrey Bogart's voice. He was a cool, old school actor, famous for playing tough guys. I could do a really good impression of him, even though my acting teacher didn't think so.

I slowly walked back to the living room. I poked my head in from the hall.

"What are you watching?" I said.

"An old movie. You probably wouldn't like it. Go to bed."

"I see it stars Humphrey Bogart."

"You know who Humphrey Bogart is?" Gram said, surprised.

"Sure. I know Bogie. I think he's best in Casablanca, 1942. 'Here's looking at you, kid.'" That was a famous line from the movie delivered in a perfect Humphrey Bogart voice. "Though what a performance in Treasure of the Sierra Madre, 1948. Remember the part when the bandits say 'Badges? We ain't got no badges! We don't need no badges! I don't have to show you any...'"

"...stinking badges!" we both said at the same time.

Gram paused the movie. "I heard you only liked monster stuff, like Dracula and Wolf Man or Godzilla."

"Not just monster movies, though they're still my favorite. I've been going through phases. First it was Bruce Lee and 70s action flicks, then kung fu and samurai movies, the 80s—they were fun—then, top 100 movies-of-all-time. That list got me into classics, like this movie here."

I looked at the freeze frame. I rubbed my chin. "Looks like something from the 40s, I'd say early 40s, Humphrey Bogart, probably Golden Age Hollywood."

She put her reading glasses on and checked the VHS tape box. "Well, well, 1943, you're right. That's the champ. This movie was one of your grandpa's favorites. It's called Sahara."

"1943," I added quickly.

"Right," Gram nodded. "I said that."

"I know."

"Anyway, Sahara—"

"1943," I interrupted.

"—is about…" Gram narrowed her eyes. "What's going on, Peter?"

"Um, it's just this thing I do, after a movie. I sort of can't help it. If I know the release date, I have to say it."

"So if I say Sahara—"

"1943," I cut in. "Sorry."

"You have to say 1943. Really?" She paused a moment. "Hmm… Gone with the Wind."

"1939."

"Well, I'll be. Let me see… Singing in the Rain?"

"1952."

"Okay, I get you," she smiled. "I suppose dates are important."

"I think so."

"Anyway, in Sah— this movie, Bogie is a tank commander who gets separated from his division in the desert after a battle. As he tries to find water, he keeps picking up stragglers. Because you don't want to leave anyone behind in the desert."

"That makes sense."

"So right now he's got a French soldier, some British, and a South African, but he picks up more. They're all different, but this ragtag group has to help each other to survive. They're heading to a well for water, but a whole Nazi division is in the desert, too."

"Movies with Nazis are so interesting, the ultimate bad guys."

"True, I guess," Gram said as she got up and walked by me to the kitchen.

"Do you own a lot of movies?" I called to her.

"Sure. Your grandpa loved movies. He collected as many as he could find."

"Really?"

"Passes the time here on the island. Got himself a whole cabinet full," she said, coming back with a napkin holding four Fig Newtons. She sat down again.

I noticed a half-open cabinet in the corner. I opened it fully. She was right. It was stuffed with VHS tapes. Some tapes had their original box with the movie poster picture. Other tapes, without boxes, had the movie title written on a sticker.

"Pretty impressive," I said. "Is this Grandfather's handwriting?"

"Mm-hmm," Gram nodded.

It looked sort of like mine. We made our H's exactly the same way. I shut the door and headed for the stairs. It was already past my bedtime. I stopped in front of Gram.

"Do you want to watch the movie with me?" Gram asked.

"I do. But... I shouldn't. I mean, it's a very tempting offer, very tempting."

"So why don't you watch it?" she asked.

"It's going to get over way past my bedtime, and my therapist says when I don't get enough sleep, I get overly emotional. So my parents are very strict with my bedtime."

"How many hours do you need?"

"Between ten and twelve."

"Ten and twelve! Your parents make sure you get that every night?"

"Ten during the week. Twelve on weekends. Eight o'clock bedtime."

"Even if you're not tired?" Gram asked.

"Yes, ma'am."

"Did you get ten hours before you got all woolgethered at school?"

"Woolgethered?"

"When you cried and wouldn't let go of the desk? You get ten hours that night?"

"I did."

"Uh-huh." She took a bite out of the Fig Newton. She chewed it slowly. Very slowly. I heard a clock ticking somewhere in the house.

"Well, good night then. I'm going to watch it." She clicked the remote.

Jeez Louise! This was a pickle. How would I ever fall asleep knowing a classic, Hollywood war movie was playing right underneath me? But my parents would be so mad if they found out I stayed up late. It was a big rule to help me not cry in school! Come to think of it, I wasn't in school right now. I wasn't really that tired either. And, to be honest, if I went to bed now, I'd only worry about that swim lesson. Oh, what to do? Sleep or Sahara, 1943? Sleep or Sahara, 1943? Sleep or—

"Peter, you're standing in front of the TV," Gram said, snapping me out of it.

"Oh, sorry," I said, but I didn't move. "Um, Gram, I was thinking, how about I won't tell my parents, if you won't tell my parents?"

"I have a feeling, Peter, that this is the first of many things we won't tell your parents."

She smiled at me. "Sit, young man. Bite a bit of fig cake."

I sat. I ate a Fig Newton. We watched the movie. It was great. It was great watching it with Gram, too. When it was over around eleven, I fell right to sleep, dreaming of sand and tanks and defeating Nazis. I'd forgotten all about the swim lesson. And that was how my first day on the island ended.

Chapter 13

The next day, I woke up early. Gram's lacy white curtains poured sunlight in my room like a naked lightbulb shined in a crook's face during an interrogation. Sleep was impossible.

"Morning, sunshine," Gram said.

That was the truth.

"Breakfast in five minutes."

I rolled out of bed. I opted for my Dracula T-shirt today. In the kitchen, Gram stood fresh as a daisy in jeans and a pale yellow, cotton shirt. She handed me a plate of scrambled eggs, toast, and orange juice. I told her I wasn't the biggest fan of eggs.

She said, "So what?"

I stared at the food.

"You think eggs are a big fan of you?"

She didn't offer an alternative.

"You got a busy day. Eat up. You'll need the energy. Chores first. Swim lesson later."

Oh yeah, the lesson. I forgot. Gram was right. I would need energy to deal with those fast-talking twins. I wondered if there was a way I could still get out of it. I forced myself to eat a small forkful of egg. "May I ask what the first chore is?"

"Yardwork. Weeding."

Ugh. Of all the chores, in all the world, weeding had to be mine. As much as Indiana Jones hated snakes, I hated weeding. So boring and tedious. My parents tried to make me weed once. I took so long that my dad did it. They never asked again.

"Got a lot of it, too," Gram said as she sat down with me sipping coffee in a mug that read BAY DAY 2001 in faded lettering. "I'll be honest, it ain't gonna be pretty. I'd a done it myself if my back hadn't been acting up this month. It's a jag of work, can't take no holidays, this being Johnson Island and all."

"What's the island have to do with it?" You know, the egg wasn't that bad.

"Ha! We got the biggest concentration of johnsongrass in the world, kid. Fastest growing, too. It's on the top-ten list of the world's deadliest weeds."

"Don't you use Trimcut?" I recited the famous weed killer jingle. "When your lawn is in a rut! Win the war and buy Trimcut! Trimcut. Kills weeds dead!" Perfect impression.

"That's funny, Peter," she said with a straight face. "I've seen the commercials."

"You know, most people smile when they think something is funny."

"I'm smiling inside," Gram said dryly. "You think I'm stupid? I tried Trimcut. Didn't do a lick of good. Don't work. Nothing does. Bought internet stuff from China where there ain't no chemical restrictions. Stuff that saved the Amazonian rainforests from kudzu. Zippo. I even wrote the Trimcut company—Botanica. They sent some scientists to check it out years ago."

"No way." I bit the toast. Oh, Heaven! Real butter.

"Yes, indeed. Letter's right behind you, hanging on the wall."

I turned to see a framed letter dated August 26, 1997 in impressive letterhead. I read it out loud:

Dear Mrs. Mulligan,

On behalf of the W.S.S.A. and the weed community, we hereby commend you and Johnson Island for your contribution in the fight against invasive plant species.
So much as it needs, to dew the sovereign flower and drown the weeds.

With the Deepest Respect and Appreciation,

The Weed Science Society of America & Botanica, Incorporated

Gram beamed proudly. "That fancy talk at the end is Shakespeare. I had to look it up. Didn't matter, though. Not one weed killing concoction they cooked up worked. Weeds still kept coming back. Got pretty controversial with the historical society, too."

42

"Why?" I finished the eggs. Pretty good.

"Well, the society always figured the island was named after Captain Reginald Johnson, some Revolutionary War hero, who harassed the British navy from here. Ain't no proof, though. No documents. Now, it might be the early mud-footers named this place for the weed they hated the most—johnsongrass. Ha! Funny, right?"

"Sure," I said, smiling along with her. I sipped my orange juice.

"Enough gabbin. Point is—only one thing kills those green little devils. Yanking 'em out! Let's get you to work. 'Have your fun, when chores is done.' That's what we say in this house."

Before I knew it, I was outside weeding the overgrown flower beds along the fence in the front yard. She had flower beds everywhere. It was hot, and pulling weeds was pretty messy work. I wore gardening gloves, but half the time I couldn't grab the weed, and so I ended up taking them off. Whenever I wiped my forehead to get the sweat off my face, I put dirt and grime all over it. My back ached quickly. So I'd go to a spot, sit on the grass, and pull.

After a while, Gram came out on the porch and shook her head. "Humph. I have never seen a body move so slow."

"I'm going as fast as I can."

"You go any faster, you'll go in reverse."

"What does that even mean?"

"It was sarcasm."

I raised my hand. "Question."

"Go ahead," she said, rolling her eyes.

"How can you go so fast, you're in reverse? Is it a time space physics thing, like in the first Superman, 1978—"

"1978, I'll be," she mumbled. "He knows that, too."

"—when Superman flies so fast he makes earth's orbit reverse, so he can go back in time to save his true love, Lois Lane?"

"Superman? If you're Superman, I'd say working is your kryptonite."

"What?"

"Humph." And she went back in.

I went back to pulling, flipping dirt in my face, and throwing weeds in a bucket. The sun beat down as it rose higher. After what seemed like forever, I heard the screen door open and Gram's footsteps on the porch. She inspected my progress and shook her head. She went back in. I went back to work. She came back out and handed me a glass of lemonade.

"Drink it."

I hesitated.

43

"Unless you're not a fan of lemons."

The way this morning had gone so far, I decided to not reveal my deep disapproval of lemons and just drink it. Surprisingly, it was good.

"You like it?"

"Indeed," I said.

"Freshly squeezed. Makes a difference. Imagine your mom buys the powdered junk."

I guzzled it down. "Delicious. My only regret is that it's satisfying taste will be associated with these weeds, which no doubt arise from the darkest depths of Hades."

"Humph."

"Do you think—now I'm just throwing this idea out there—do you think I could do half today and half tomorrow, a sort of divide and conquer, if you will, boss-ma'am?"

"Boss-ma'am?" She thought for a minute. "Back to work."

"Humph," I grunted.

She turned back to the house. "Nice try, Pete."

"My name is—" She shut the door. "My name is Peter, not Pete," I said under my breath. I yanked another weed and angrily tossed it at the bucket. I missed.

Chapter 14

Soon, I found myself not pulling weeds but daydreaming about which movie I could pretend to be in to make this job less horrible. This was tough. What movie had a hero sitting on wet grass pulling stuff out of the ground? Jeez Louise!

"There isn't one," I grumbled to myself.

"One what?"

I guess I was talking out loud. I raised my head. A kid, about my age, sat on a bike looking down at me. He had messy blond hair and blue eyes with a cleft in his chin.

"Hi," he said.

"Hello, sir," I said.

"I'm Billy. Billy Pruitt."

"Most folks call me Peter."

"I gave you my towel last night. The SpongeBob one."

"I am most appreciative for that gesture, sir." Billy gave me that look, and I knew what was coming. Oh well.

"You talk funny," he said.

"I have been told that."

"It's different."

"I have been told that too, sir."

He stepped off his bike and squatted down near me. The picket fence between us. "What did you mean before?" he asked. "You couldn't think of one what?"

"Um, I believe, one movie that would make weeding less awful."

"Yeah, weeding sucks."

"I concur."

"What?"

45

"I said 'I concur.' I agree. 'Concur' means 'agree'."

"I knew that. I forgot, ya know. I guess you're smart."

"Well, I think in that department you might be mistaken," I said.

"I live over there." He waved down the block.

"I live here." I gestured behind me, accidentally tossing dirt in my face. "Yech."

"For the summer, right? You're Gram Mulligan's grandson, right? She told me."

"You are correct, sir."

"Why do you keep calling me sir?" Billy asked.

"Um, that's a good question. I can't help it. It sort of pops out. I don't know, it just sounds good to me, I guess. It fits you in my head. It's a sign of respect."

"Humph," Billy said.

What was it with the 'humph' around here? I did it earlier. Was I picking up their weird lingo? "If you don't want me to call you 'sir,' I can try to stop."

"No, it's fine. We can hang out when you're done. I'm going to the rec center up there. Just at the end of the road. You can't miss it."

"Thank you for the invitation, sir."

"How much more you gotta do?"

"All that." I pointed to a large green area.

"Well, hurry up, Pete," Billy climbed on his bike. "You could be here all day."

"I will hurry, Billy. I most certainly will. But my name is actually—"

"See you."

He pedaled away. I surveyed the blanket of weeds that still needed to be pulled. "Humph," I mumbled to myself. Dang it! There it was again! The sun glared down and I got back to work. Soon, more folks came down the road.

"Hey-o, Pete," a man said as he beeped his golf cart.

"Um, good morning," I blurted out, unprepared for the salutation, the golf cart already passed. Strange that he knew my name. Oh well. I grabbed another weed.

"Morning," said an older woman, who stopped her golf cart. "Gram Mulligan putting you to work, I see. Good for you, Pete Mulligan, good for you. Have a nice day."

"You, too." She drove away. I grabbed the same weed as before.

Ding-ding! A bicycle bell sounded, and four scraggly men on bikes with fishing poles pedaled by. They didn't say good morning, but each gave me a nod and wave.

"Good morning," I said.

"Sure is, Pete Mulligan," the last one said.

This went on for the next hour. I bent down to pull a weed, and an islander driving by shouted out a greeting. Jeez Louise! Gram wasn't kidding. She must've stood up at church and announced to the whole congregation or personally dialed every citizens' number to inform them that Peter J. Mulligan, her grandson, was staying on the island.

Folks kept coming down the street waving and beeping and good morning-ing me. Not everyone just greeted me, too. Many of the kids stopped by for a chat. I learned a lot.

Turns out red-headed Steven Fitzpatrick, nine-and-a-half, known as Fitzie, placed first in last year's fluke contest, which he attributed to his new Saint Croix fishing pole. "I know how it is," Fitzie said. "I weeded and mowed lawns all last summer to buy that pole." Fitzie wanted to be a waterman like his dad. He crabbed every day and owned a rowboat he named Titanic II, because his rowboat sunk in a storm the day after his dad bought it for him. But they fixed it. I didn't tell him sequels were never as good.

"Cool shirt. Bye," Fitzie said as he left.

Pony-tailed Amelia North, nine, was recently on her boogie board when a shark fin glided by her. "Everyone said it was a basking shark, which wouldn't hurt me, but it looked like a great white shark to me. You know like in that movie."

"Jaws, 1975?"

"No, Sharknado."

"Oh," I said. "2013, I believe." The made-for-television flick. Hilarious B-movie crap.

"Did you see Sharknado?"

"Released 2013, I believe. I did see it, young lady."

"I saw them all. Don't you think that could really happen? Maybe, right? If the conditions were just right. Your shirt is scary. That's Dracula, right? Do you like mine?"

It was a collection of Disney princesses. "I do."

"This shirt has power, Pete."

"Actually, I go by Peter."

"That's why the great white shark swam by. My princess boogie board was upside down, so the shark was staring at the princesses, who must've scared him. There's power in these ladies, Pete. There's power."

"That's Pete-ter," I said slowly.

Amelia climbed on her bike. "I'm going to the rec center. Come later when you're done."

Next was Frankie 'Dimsy' Dimsmore, glasses and crew cut. He was the island's best chess player. Victoria 'Vicky' Whitman, brown bob haircut, told me that she has the best singing voice in the church choir since local Johnson Island star, Leona Dartmouth, left the choir and island in 1952 to pursue a semi-successful career as a gospel Christian singer.

Then it was over. No one stopped for a long time. I assume that was the island's rush hour. Everyone had gotten to the rec center or church or boat or job or wherever they were going. I got back to work, finally.

I was alone again, dirtier than ever: pulling a weed, plopping it in the bucket, dumping the bucket in the backyard composter. Over and over again. It was boring and repetitive, and now without people passing by on the road, a little lonely. A lot lonely.

I grabbed this one long weed that just wouldn't come out. Before I knew it, the thing was tangled around my wrist. I yanked it about an inch. It snapped back and pulled me down until my hand hit the ground, like a rubber band. This was weird. Had I been in the sun too long? I pulled it up. It seemed to pull me back down. It wrapped itself around my wrist so tightly it really hurt.

"Hey, let go, you stupid—"

Then, my hand came free. I noticed two shadows. I looked up.

Chapter 15

The twins stood over me. They wore large white T-shirts that covered their red bathing suits. Bathing suits?! After weeding all morning, I forgot about the swim lesson! I had to think of something to get out of it. Come on, Peter, think! Before I could come up with an excuse or even an idea for an excuse, their Ping-Pong style of conversation fired away. I could barely keep up.

"We said we were swimming today, Pete," said Sofia, I think.

"Actually, my name isn't Pete, it is—"

"Ten o'clock. Remember, we told you last night at Cookie's?" added Kat.

"I know but—"

"Cool. It's a Dracula shirt today, Kat," Sofia noticed.

"I vant to suck your blood," Kat said in a vampire voice.

Hey, that was funny. Kat could do a pretty good Dracula. I wondered if they really liked my T-shirt. It was probably sarcasm again, and I missed it. Things sure were weird on this island.

Island? I got it! I'd tell them that I forgot to pack my bathing suit. I didn't, of course. My mom would never forget to pack my King Kong swim trunks. But it was the perfect lie! Couldn't swim without a swimsuit, and it'd be a week before my parents could bring new ones or mail some here. By then, I'd convince Gram to let me skip it. Did I really need to know how to swim? I'd wear a life jacket. Now, I had to figure out when to tell them, if they'd stop talking for a second.

"How'd you get so dirty?" Sofia asked.

"Yeah," Kat chimed in. "What are you doing?"

"His chores," Gram called from the porch. We faced her. "Don't worry. He's still swimming. After he's done his weeding."

49

"Actually, ladies," I began, thinking this was the perfect time to drop my swimsuit lie. "I've been meaning to mention that I forgot—"

"What's left to weed?" Sofia asked Gram, ignoring me.

"That big patch over there." Gram showed them. "He's been at it since eight."

"Eight?" Kat said. "You're so slow!"

"Come on," Sofia said to her sister. Kat followed.

I planned on telling that bathing suit lie right then, but they walked away from me. They quickly dropped their backpacks on the porch. They went to the big patch and got to work pulling weeds. They were helping me. That was unexpected. I was thrown off.

"There's lemonade and oatmeal cookies when you're done," Gram called to us.

"Thanks, Gram Mulligan," the twins said.

Cookies? This was news to me. "I didn't know cookies were involved!" I said to Gram. "That would have motivated me."

"I don't think anything would've motivated you," Gram called back.

"Humph," I grumbled.

The twins worked much faster than me, yanking weeds and tossing them in the bucket like a well-oiled, weed-whacking machine. Instead of sitting down in a section and pulling like I had, the girls bent over and ripped out three or four at a time.

"Don't sit and do it," Sofia said.

"We used to do that," Kat added. "Takes too long. You have to get it over with."

"These weeds are your enemies, Pete!" Sofia said like a drill sergeant.

"They must be killed and destroyed!" Kat ordered.

"You ladies weed your yard, too?" I asked.

"Ladies? You hear that, Kat? He called us ladies," Sofia chuckled.

"We weed every day, dum-dum. Every kid has that chore on the island. We all hate it."

Hmm. Again with the dum-dum stuff. Not very nice. Maybe they were only helping me to gain my confidence and drown me later. Diabolical. I had to get out of that swim lesson.

"Do it fast and quick," Sofia said. "Weed one section at a time. Gram Mulligan hasn't done it for a while. That's the problem with this yard."

"She's old, Sofia, and her back is bothering her."

"I know, Kat, I know," said Sofia.

For evil twins, they sure were nice to Gram. I wasn't sure what to make of them. On one hand, Kat kept calling me dum-dum. On the other hand, they were helping me. I did take their advice and knelt on one knee instead of sitting. I noticed that long weed that wrapped around my wrist was gone. I guess the girls got it. They must be strong.

"This yard is simple," said Sofia.

"Yeah," said Kat. "Listen to her. She came up with our system."

"Oh, so you are Sofia, and you are Kat," I said pointing to each twin, just to be sure.

"Very good," Kat said. "Sofia Jin and Kat Jin. Everyone confuses us. I don't know why? I'm so much prettier."

"You look the same to me," I said.

"No duh, Pete," Kat rolled her eyes. "That's the joke."

Sofia ignored her. "The weeds come back really fast, but they'll be small and weak. Easy to pull. So tomorrow, do by the porch. Next day, by the fence here. Next day, the spot near the mailbox and the front gate. Next day, the garden. Do it in that order, a little bit at a time, a little each day, that's what we figured out, in rotation. It'll take you about half an hour each day."

"If you work faster, slowpoke," Kat said.

"I'll try," I shrugged.

"Don't try," Sofia said, in a voice trying to sound like Yoda. "Do... or do not."

"There is no try," Kat added in her Yoda-voice. "Pretty good, right?"

"Who was that supposed to be?" I laughed. "Cookie Monster?"

"Cookie Monster?" Kat said. "It was Yoda!"

"They were the worst Yoda impressions I ever heard," I blurted out.

"What?" Sofia said. "We sound just like Yoda!"

"Ladies, to be honest, they're terrible," I said.

"Oh, you're so good? You can do better?" Sofia asked.

"Let's hear it. Let's hear you do better!" Kat challenged me.

I hated to brag, but if there was one thing I could do, it was impressions. I'd show these girls a thing or two. I hoped.

"Okay, let me think," I mumbled to myself. "The Empire Strikes Back, Episode V, 1980, Yoda... um... okay. This is when Luke tries to use the Force to lift his X-Wing out of the swamp on Dagobah and he can't and he says, 'It's too big'."

I cleared my throat. "Here we go." I tightened my cheeks and scrunched my face. "'Size matters not. Look at me. Judge me by my size, do you? Hmm? Hmm. And well you should not. For my ally is the Force, and a powerful ally it is.' How was that?"

The twins applauded. "Wow," Sofia said. "He's good."

"Very good," Kat added.

"Thank you," I said, bowing. Jeez Louise! They liked my impression. Nice change from home. Usually after I did an impression at Stone Hill Elementary, kids would say, 'Shut up, weirdo!'

"Now," ordered Sofia, "say, 'these weeds, I do hate'."

"These weeds, I do hate."

"No, dum-dum, say it like Yoda," Kat corrected.

"Oh, sorry." I cleared my throat. "These weeds, I do hate."

They laughed. "Now say..." said Sofia, "Um, say..."

"I know," interrupted Kat, "say, 'diarrhea, I must do'."

Sofia giggled, "Oh, that's disgusting."

"I don't think Yoda would say something like that," I said.

"I know, that's why it's funny! Say it!"

I cleared my throat and in my best Yoda said, "Diarrhea, I must do. Messy, it will be."

They laughed. Kat was right. It was funny to hear the Jedi master say that. It went on like that as we worked together. They thought of silly lines Yoda would never say, and I would say them. They would laugh. Kat had more silly lines than Sofia, but who was counting?

Quickly, the weeding was finished. The twins had actually made the yard work fun. But with all the laughs, I had this nagging feeling that I was forgetting something.

Oh, the bathing suit!

Chapter 16

We sat on the porch eating delicious, right out of the oven oatmeal cookies and sipping more of Gram's freshly squeezed lemonade. It was there that the ladies told me that we were going to Fish Hook Beach, which was named after the south corner of the island that stretched out like a fishing hook into a natural sandy beach.

Just the thought of swimming made my throat tighten. I pushed hard to swallow Gram's cookie. I racked my brain with the right way to mention not having my bathing suit and the right time to do it. I kept thinking of The Sting, 1973, the greatest con artist movie of all time. It won seven Academy Awards! A con game or 'confidence game' was when you tricked someone into giving you stuff, usually their money. The con men in The Sting, 1973, tricked an Irish mobster out of half a million dollars. They played it perfectly, but those con artists had time to plan!

"Hey-o, Gram Mulligan," Sofia said. "We need a bike to get to Fish Hook."

Which I didn't have. Guess we couldn't go. Thank you, Sofia!

"Got a bike in the shed," Gram said.

Great. So much for getting out of it. Jeez Louise!

In the backyard, Gram rummaged through her shed. It was packed with stuff. It seemed like she never threw anything away. As Gram moved things around, the twins argued about how old they were when they learned to ride a bike.

"We were eight," Sofia said.

"We were seven," Kat disagreed.

"Eight."

"Seven."

"Whatever, Kat," Sofia said, tired of arguing. "How old were you, Pete?"

"Four," I answered, half-listening.

"Four?" they both said, shocked.

"That's so young," Sofia said.

"No way," Kat scoffed.

"It's true," I said, forgetting about my scheming. "I was obsessed with E.T. the Extra-Terrestrial, 1982, and I wanted to dress as Elliott for Halloween. I had the red hoodie, a cute, stuffed animal E.T., and a little bike with a milk crate on the handle bars. The only thing I needed to make the costume authentic—learn to ride the bike. My mom and dad said it would be fine if I just kept the training wheels on. It would still be a good costume. But it had to look real! There weren't any training wheels in the movie."

"Cute as a button he was," Gram called from the shed. "Your dad sent a picture."

"He did?"

"Still got it."

Interesting. I didn't know my dad sent her pictures, and she kept them. That was… nice.

"You really learned at four?" Kat shook her head. "I don't know think so."

"I did. I practiced in my basement every day for weeks. My dad would come down and help. Then one day in October, right before the 31st, I learned how to ride. Just like Elliott, I pedaled my E.T. up to each door and said 'Trick-or-treat' and had a great time."

The twins smiled at each other.

"Don't you ladies just love E.T., 1982? A young Drew Barrymore, Henry Thomas could make you cry, nominated for nine Academy Awards, the heartwarming tale of a kid who saves a lovable alien who becomes the best friend he never had?"

"We never saw that movie," Kat said.

"What?!" I asked.

"Nope," Sofia added.

"Really?" I was shocked. "Well… that's… outrageous! You have to see it! As soon as possible! Gram, do you have it in your collection?"

"I think so."

"We have to see it! All of us, tonight! This is unacceptable!" Without thinking, I twisted my dress shirt hem around my finger, really tight.

"Okay, no problem," Sofia said. "We'll watch it someday, right, Kat?"

"Yeah, that movie sounds decent. I like aliens."

"Decent! What? E.T., 1982, is not 'decent,' ladies! It's amazing!"

"Sure, if you say so," Sofia said.

"We'll watch it," Kat added.

"When?" I demanded.

"Whenever, they want, Pete," Gram said, coming out of the shed with the bike.

"But, it's such an amazing movie!"

"I know, Pete, they said they would watch it," Gram repeated.

"We have to!" I whined.

I could tell by the way Gram was looking at me that I was making too big a deal of this. The twins stared at me. It was just, I wanted them to see it so badly. That feeling was rising up inside of me—like I might cry. I needed to know they would see it. How could they not? Gram must have caught my eyes welling. She gently touched my shoulder.

"Take it easy. We'll watch it one night soon," Gram said. "We'll all get together. I'll make popcorn and you girls can come over and watch E.T.—"

"1982," I added compulsively.

"—with us, okay?" Gram finished. "How's that sound, Pete? Maybe later this week."

"Sure," Sofia said.

"I like popcorn," Kat added.

My eyes bulged at Kat. Popcorn?! This wasn't about E.T., 1982, but about popcorn?

"That sound good?" Gram asked me.

I wanted to know the exact date. But as long as it was this week, I could live with it, I guess. That crying feeling went away. "Sounds good enough."

"Great," Gram said. It was quiet for a moment. Awkward quiet.

"Nice bike," Kat said, looking at the dirty bike. It was rusty and covered in cobwebs.

Gram chuckled. "This old thing was Pete's dad's. We might have to lower the seat a bit. And it needs some cleaning up."

After more digging, we found the tools. We lowered the seat. The twins pumped up the tires. Gram wiped off the cobwebs with a whisk broom. I squirted oil on the chain.

"Good as new," Gram said.

The twins and I eyed each other skeptically. The bike had a front basket and two small side baskets over the back tire.

"Sure are a lot of baskets," Sofia said.

"Sure. No one had golf carts then. Peter's dad used these to pick up groceries for me, for his school books and fishing poles and what have you." Gram clapped her hands at me. "Well, time's a wastin', kiddo. Skedaddle!"

"Ske-what-le?"

"Skedaddle! Go change into your bathing suit."

"Oh. My bathing suit, you say." This was it. I had to make my move. I turned to the twins. "Um, you know what? Funny thing…" I stopped talking. Wrong start! Try again, Peter. It had to be perfect. Look disappointed. "Oh no, I am so sorry, I just realized that I forgot to pack my trunk… my swimsuit trunks. I mean my bathing suit. I forgot to pack my bathing suit." Very casual. Just like in the movies.

"No, you didn't," Gram said.

"Yes, I did." I swallowed uncomfortably.

"No," Gram said. "They're on your bed upstairs."

"They are?"

"I unpacked your suitcase this morning. King Kong ones, right?"

Jeez Louise, she's good. "Yeah," I sighed. "1933."

"Well, go on," she said, clapping her hands. "Skedaddle!"

"Okay." I trudged into the house.

As I hit the back door, I overheard Gram talking with the twins. "That boy is slower than a snail on Sunday. Now, girls, promise me you won't let him drown. Learn him good."

"We won't," Sofia said.

"We'll take care of that dum-dum."

Oh boy. Those twins were diabolical.

"And stay away from you-know-where," Gram said seriously.

You-know-where? Where was that? Part of the beach? What were they talking about?

"We will," the twins answered at the same time.

"I mean it, girls. I don't like that place. Not one bit."

Chapter 17

We pedaled our way to Fish Hook Beach.

Inside, I was a nervous wreck. I could picture the island's newspaper headline: Visiting Grandson Drowns During Swim Lesson! First Full Day on Vacation! Oh, the irony.

Outside, I played it cool. We turned right outside of Gram's house, the opposite direction than the islanders did that morning. This main street ran the island's entire length from the north, where the ferry dropped me off, to the south. The girls explained that the north end at the top of the island was called the Up'ards. They had weird names for everything. The Up'ards had the rec center, the marina, the grocery store, the church, post office, and restaurants. The bottom end of the island was nicknamed the Low'ards. Here, you had homes and Fish Hook Beach at the southern tip. Gram lived in the middle of this main road called, believe it or not, Broadway.

As we biked down Broadway, we passed simple white homes very close to each other. Every house had a tiny front yard with a fence, mostly chain link but some little white picket kinds. I guess folks liked to fence off their land, since the island was so small. The twins showed me who lived where and who they liked or didn't like. Case in point being this one boy.

"Tim Meeks." Sofia pointed to a house badly in need of paint. "I'd watch him. He's an older kid. Not so nice."

"Cheats, too," Kat said. "Any game at the rec center."

"He thinks he's funny," Sofia said. "Always calls me Tweedledee."

"And me Tweedledum," Kat added.

"Alice in Wonderland, 1951 animated, or Johnny Depp's version in 2010," I mumbled, but they ignored me.

Then, as an afterthought, Sofia said, "But really, he's all right."

Kat agreed. "Yeah, he's all right, I guess."

That was the strange thing about the girls, as much as they complained about Tim Meeks or the half-dozen other kids, they'd end with that phrase: 'But really, he or she's all right.'

"That's not how it is where I live," I explained. "Mean kids are always mean."

"How?" Kat wondered.

"For one, they make fun of my monster T-shirts. They say they're stupid or lame or weird or dumb or— "

"Your T-shirts?" Sofia asked, surprised.

"I love your T-shirts," Kat chimed in.

"Too scary for them probably," Sofia said. "Mainlanders are babies."

"Chickens and scaredy-cats," Kat added. "But, they're probably all right."

"Yeah," Sofia agreed. "Deep down, all right."

I don't know why, but in the end, they considered everyone 'all right' no matter what. I thought it must be an island thing. I hoped they would be all right with me, like they promised.

We turned toward the west side of the island. We bumped along over a wooden bridge with a thump, thump, thump on our tires. Then another small bridge. We turned left onto a street called, believe it or not, Westway. Further on, we thump, thump, thumped over another little wooden bridge. In my chest, my heart made the same noise. We were close now.

I could hear the waves. Maybe I could ride away. Impossible. Gram had laid down the law. I had to learn to swim. It'd be so much easier if my parents or the A-Team were here. A couple of tears, mention I feel a little anxiety, and easy-peasey I'd be reading comic books and sipping lemonade on Gram's porch.

"Get ready," Sofia said.

"Almost there," Kat added.

Green marshlands surrounded us, and cotton ball clouds dotted the bright sky. A breeze blew in off the bay that cooled me. The road ended, and we started down a sandy, dirt path. Now, the marshland grasses stood tall as a person, like we were in a green tunnel.

We pedaled to the end of the path and wow! We made it to the most beautiful beach I'd ever seen. It would have made a great shot in a movie, but I didn't know if a camera could even capture it. We stopped our bikes and appreciated the beauty. The twins exhaled dramatically.

"Well?" asked Sofia. "Pretty good, right?"

"Spectacular, ladies," I said.

"Ladies, still?" Kat laughed. "He's a crackup."

The beach was empty and natural—nothing like the beaches from my family's visits to the Jersey shore—no boardwalk, no tourists, no lifeguards, no umbrellas, no people crammed next to each other, no beach badges.

Beach badges? Ah-ha! One last chance to escape! I turned to the girls and said in my best 'fake' disappointed voice: "Oh no, I never asked Gram for a beach badge. Guess we can't swim today. Want to get some lunch?"

"Beach badge?" Sofia laughed.

"We don't need beach badges, here," Kat said.

"Really?" I mumbled in my best 'real' disappointed voice. "We don't need no stinking badges?"

"Right!" said Sofia mimicking me. "We don't need no stinking badges!"

Ha! At least if I was going to drown, I had the consolation of knowing that Treasure of the Sierra Madre, 1948, got quoted twice within one twenty-four-hour period. I followed the girls to a quiet spot where the fish hook made the water smooth and deep enough to swim.

I had to admit, the sandy bottom did feel good on my feet. Then, gulp, the lesson commenced. In the shallow part, the twins ordered me to do this and to do that.

Don't forget to cup my hands. Don't forget to kick.

Don't forget to turn my head. Don't forget smooth strokes.

Don't splash so much. Don't forget to breathe.

I tried to do everything they said, huffing and puffing. At one point when I was practicing holding my breath underwater, I knew I heard Kat say, "We should make a death!" But both twins swore up and down Kat really said, "He should take a breath." I wasn't sure, though.

For most of the time, I did all their 'Don't Forget to Do This' stuff in the shallow part of the beach. I could easily stand up whenever I panicked. I panicked a lot.

"Pete, you gotta go deeper," Sofia suggested. "You know, at least a little bit." Each girl took a hand, which was kind of nice, and pulled me out more.

"What about sharks?" I said.

"Don't be a dum-dum," Kat snapped. "The sharks are on the other side of the island. They usually don't swim over here."

"What?!"

"She's kidding with you, Pete! There are no sharks on either side!" Sofia laughed. "A little further, that's good, now...Swim!"

They yanked me forward and let go. A small wave hit me, and my head dipped under the water. I couldn't feel the bottom. Oh boy, I guess it was time to swim! I cupped and kicked and stroked and head-turned and splashed and forgot to breathe and remembered to breathe and swallowed a huge gulp of water and sunk.

"Pete!" the twins screamed.

At least I'd be in the island newspaper.

Chapter 18

The most important lesson I learned that day at Fish Hook Beach was not a swim lesson. It was this: the twins were not trying to kill me. Actually, they saved me. And let me tell you, it wasn't easy. They heave-ed and ho-ed and dealt with me thrashing about like a lunatic. Eventually, they dragged me to the shallow water, where we sat out of breath.

"That's... enough... for... today," Sofia gasped.

Kat panted. "We... have... all... summer."

"Sounds... good... to... me," I wheezed.

Later, we sat on our towels. They peppered me with questions. I wanted them to like me, so I tried not to sound like 'weirdo' Peter and reveal too much about Stone Hill Elementary and my crying. I wanted to be cool—Cooler King cool—like Steve McQueen.

Sofia started. "Do you like school?"

"Not much," I answered.

Kat asked next. "Do you like sports?"

"Not really." They started that back-and-forth thing.

"Are you smart?" Sofia asked. "You talk like you're smart."

I hesitated. I couldn't tell them about my real issues. "Well, it's more like—"

Kat interrupted. "Do you play video games?"

Every kid loved video games. I knew I should say sure. But I didn't play a lot of video games. They gave me headaches. What to do? Finally, I said, "Um, a little, not a lot."

"Same with us. Too much money," Sofia nodded. "Why did you come for the summer?"

I couldn't tell the full story. "My parents thought it would be a good idea."

"How come you never came before?" Kat followed up.

Oh boy. Be cool. I went with logic. "I imagine my parents thought it was a bad idea?"

The girls nodded. Whew. So far so good. I hadn't seen that look of disgust or disappointment come over either girl's face yet. "What did you do last summer?" Kat asked.

"Let's see, oh, karate camp," slipped right out of my mouth. Why'd I bring that up?!

"Ooh, karate! You know karate?" Sofia exclaimed. "So cool."

Backtrack, Peter. Backtrack. "I wouldn't exactly say I know karate."

"And so modest. Do you have a black belt?" Sofia asked.

"Not exactly."

"What kind of belt do you have?" questioned Kat.

"A white belt with a yellow stripe, but—"

"I never heard of that," Sofia said. "Very rare, I'll bet. He must be good, Kat. Show us some moves."

Moves? What moves? My only moves were karate stance or accidentally punching the girl I liked in the face. I needed a good excuse, fast. Then it hit me—pun intended! "Sorry, I can't. Master Jeffrey said I can only use the martial arts for self-defense." That would change the subject.

"Ooh, Master Jeffrey," Sofia repeated.

"You have a master," Kat said, in an impressed voice. "Interesting."

"Ever have to defend your master's honor, like in a Bruce Lee movie?" Sofia asked.

"You ladies like Bruce Lee?" I said, surprised.

"Duh, of course, Pete. We're half-Chinese," Kat said. "Every Chinese kid likes Bruce Lee."

"Really?"

"No! She's kidding, Pete!" Sofia said.

"Don't be such a racist, Pete!" Kat added. "Our dad showed us the movies. He loves Bruce Lee. Too much. But Sofia and I like him." Kat jumped up into a Bruce Lee fighting stance. "Remember when he said, 'Boards... don't hit back'."

Ah-ha, something I knew about. "Enter the Dragon, 1973. Did you ever see Fist of—"

"Do you have a girlfriend?" Sofia interrupted.

"No, not really, but did you see Fist of—"

"Ooh, not really," Sofia repeated.

"What's that mean?" Kat said quickly.

"Probably means that he did have a girlfriend. Right, Pete?" Sofia said. "What happened to your girlfriend, Pete?"

"I broke her nose," I blurted. I couldn't believe I told them that! Bernadette wasn't even my girlfriend! Both girls gasped.

Kat slapped my shoulder. "Pete! Domestic violence!"

"Not you?!" Sofia said, shocked.

"No, no, no, by accident. She was in my karate class. Master Jeffrey made us spar."

"Ooh, how romantic," Kat said.

"It wasn't."

"She's joking," Sofia said. "What was your girlfriend's name?"

"Bernadette, but she wasn't really my—"

"So let me get this straight," Sofia cut me off. "You broke Bernadette's nose by accident in karate class. Hmm, you must be good. A white belt with a yellow stripe must be good, Kat."

"Close to black belt, right?"

"Ladies, it was a lucky punch, an unlucky punch if you think about it, an accident. I—"

"He's so modest," Sofia smiled.

"I like that," Kat agreed.

Wait. She liked that? She liked something about me? Did they actually not mind being around me? This was such a strange conversation. And even more strange, we had talked about Bernadette. I said her name. Out loud. For some reason, I didn't feel upset. Before I could even think, they started up again.

"We don't have any boyfriends," Sofia said. "Not allowed! Too young, our dad says."

"But boys like us, Pete. All the boys our age!" Kat said proudly.

"Don't lie, Kat!"

"One boy likes Sofia," Kat teased.

"That's not true! We're friends!"

"Uh-huh. Sure you are." Kat winked at me. "Billy Pruitt. He has a big crush on Sofia."

"Billy Pruitt? We met this morning," I said.

"Did he talk about Sofia?" Kat asked.

"Not that I recall."

"Let's get going, Pete," interrupted Sofia. "She's so immature."

We gathered our things and biked back to Gram's house. As we did, the twins talked, but I had two thoughts running through my head that distracted me. One was this: Could it be that I was over the whole Bernadette thing? I kept waiting to feel upset or funny, but nothing happened. The other thought? I kept wondering why they told me that boyfriend stuff.

63

Chapter 19

After a dinner of fried crabs on white bread—I never knew how delicious crabs tasted—Gram and I went for a walk. As we strolled down Broadway, we met lots of other people out walking, too. This was a Johnson Island thing.

"Sure enough, Pete," Gram said, "most folks go cruisin' after dinner."

"Cruisin'?"

"That's what we call it. Island's cool. Sunset's a comin'. It's a nice time for a chit-chat. Some folks walk. Some ride bikes or scooters. Others love their golf carts."

Beep. Beep.

"Hey-o, Gram Mulligan!" The golf carters called to us as they zipped by.

"Evening," Gram said.

We cruised further down Broadway. I gazed up at the tall Johnson Island water tower. It had a big red crab painted on it. When my eyes came down, I noticed an old abandoned building with a small marquee. Could it be? "Is that a movie theater?"

"Uh-huh, it was."

"Wow. Did you see movies there?"

"Sure, all the time. Your grandfather and I had our first date at The Palace."

"The Palace?"

"Mm-hmm, that's the name. Looked like one, too. Small little thing. About sixty or so seats, I think, but boy, oh boy, was it a beauty. Comfy chairs, red curtains, this here marquee lit up with light bulbs on movie nights. Some rich fella built it. Long time ago, just when movies began. Rumor was he partnered up with Thomas Edison. Fella was from

Princeton, New Jersey. Came here every summer with his family. He liked to watch movies, so he made himself a theater. It was wonderful."

"What happened?" As we stood under the sad marquee, where water-stained plywood blocked the doors, I peered through a dirty window. I couldn't make out much, other than the building was a wreck.

"Oh, what usually happens on Johnson Island," Gram sighed. "There's a storm. Repairs cost too much. Once Spanky Woodson—he ran the theater last—was too old to keep it up, his family wanted nothing to do with it. They moved off the island years ago. Don't care a lick. Heard they plan to knock it down soon. I'm glad your grandfather isn't alive to see it. It'd break his heart."

"It's breaking my heart," I said.

We kept walking down Broadway together as folks passed us on golf carts and waved.

"You know," Gram said, "National Geographic magazine did an article on it once. Places in the world that were like going back in time. Watching a movie at The Palace on Johnson Island, they said, was like taking a trip back to the 1930s. Even quoted your grandfather in the article."

"Really, what'd he say?" I asked.

"He said if it wasn't for The Palace, he'd never have fallen in love."

I could sense Gram's emotion when she said this. I figured I should do something. I gently slid my hand into hers. She squeezed mine back. I guess that was the right thing to do.

"Times do change," she sighed. "They change slow on the island, but they do change."

"Hey, Gram? What was the movie?" I asked.

"Hmm?"

"What was the movie you and Grandfather saw on your first date?"

"Casablanca."

"Oh, yes, 1942, very romantic. Perfect picture for a first date, I would think."

"Mm-hmm."

"Hey, wasn't Grandfather in the war?"

"He was."

"Then how did you see that movie together?"

"It was after the war."

"That's when they showed Casablanca, 1942?"

"Mm-hmm. Everything moves slow on Johnson Island, Pete."

We walked on quietly, and I felt compelled to say a line from that movie. So I linked my arm around Gram and said in my best Humphrey Bogart voice, "Louis, I think this is the beginning of a beautiful friendship."

Gram patted my arm and came right back at me with another famous line from Casablanca, 1942: "Here's looking at you, kid." She even changed her voice to sound like Bogart a little. I was starting to think, as far as old ladies went, I really liked this one.

Out of nowhere, Sofia and Kat burst through a fence gate and almost knocked us over. Billy Pruitt was right behind them. Wet blotches stained their clothes. They held super-soakers.

"Whoa, girls, slow down," Gram said.

"Sorry," Sofia apologized, out of breath. "We're in trouble! Tim Meeks is after us!"

"We blasted him good!" Billy laughed.

"Now he's so mad, he could tear up a crab cooker, dum-dum!" Kat said, punching Billy's shoulder.

Kat just called Billy dum-dum! Gram was right. She sassed everyone, not just me.

Sofia touched Gram's arm. "Gram Mulligan, we need Pete's help," she said.

"Yeah, he's a big target," Kat said, ducking behind me.

"Was that a fat joke?" I asked, turning to see her.

She poked her head out from behind me from side-to-side laughing. "No. Maybe. Yes! Now, make a hurry, Pete. We need you."

I gave Gram a look. "Make a hurry?"

"They want you to hurry up," Gram explained. "You want to play with them, Pete?"

"I don't know." They'd warned me about Tim Meeks. Now they were playing with him? Who knew what he'd do? I needed an excuse. "I don't have a water pistol."

"Sure you do." Billy Pruitt reached in a knapsack and pulled out a super soaker... that looked amazing! More like a super-duper soaker!

"Wow... I've never seen one like this," I said, impressed.

"It's my own design," Billy bragged. "I like to soup 'em up. I fix 'em, too, if you have one that breaks. I won't charge you much."

"Enough with the commercial!" Sofia said. "You coming?"

"Um... I don't know... we were going to watch a movie, but... I guess. Okay."

"Good! Make a hurry, he's coming!" Sofia grabbed my arm and we took off.

"Have him home by nine-thirty, girls!"

"Sure thing, Gram Mulligan!" Sofia called back.

"No playing near Meta-Gro, too!" Gram called like she meant business.

"We won't!" the twins yelled together.

66

"What's Meta-Gro?" I asked.

"Never mind, it's out of bounds!" Billy said running ahead of me. "Come on!"

I tried to keep up with them, and what happened after that was one of the scariest but most exciting evenings of my life. Tim Meeks was truly a jerk. His stringy red hair dangled under his red baseball cap he wore backward. He was fifteen or so and everything he wore, where he wasn't wet, sported stains. Right away, he found our hiding spot behind the broken picnic benches in the back of Cookie's. I panic-fired that super-duper soaker so fast I ran out of water. "Gotcha, babies!" Tim Meeks shouted as he blasted us—me mostly, because I was the slowest and lagged behind.

Right on cue, he teased the girls with Tweedledee and Tweedledum.

"I hate being called Tweedledum," Kat said as we ran. Was it the 'dum' part?

Meeks nicknamed Billy 'butt-chin,' because Billy had a cleft in his chin that sort of looked like a butt. Meeks didn't leave me out.

"Who's this piggly-wiggly?" Meeks said, cackling meanly. "He's so slow!"

Typical fat joke! The girls were right. He was mean. But for some reason, I was smiling. I wasn't mad or sad. For the first time, I wasn't the only one being made fun of. Eventually, Tim had to refill his water gun, and the four of us escaped.

"This way, Pete!" Sofia called.

We hid behind an upside-down rowboat, the four of us wet and out of breath.

"What's so funny?" Kat asked. "You're grinning like a goofball."

"I don't know," I answered.

"Because it's fun, right?" Sofia said. "Told you."

I nodded. She was right. It was fun. But mostly, it was because I wasn't alone. This was what it was like to have friends.

"Ah-ha!" Tim Meeks shouted. He leapt on the boat and fired away. We screamed and ran. It was so exciting, the whole darn night.

When I made it back to Gram's house at nine-thirty, I took a shower. We watched the first half hour of The Wizard of Oz, 1939, but I was so tired, I couldn't keep my eyes open. As I lay in bed, I didn't need to count movie posters or anything like that. I said out loud, "Toto, I've a feeling we're not in Kansas anymore." And then I passed out. I vaguely remembered a dream where Sofia, Kat, Billy, and I walked on the yellow brick road in Oz. They looked normal, but I had a tail like the Lion. When Sofia noticed, she pulled it off and we all laughed. Weird, huh?

Chapter 20

At the end of that week, the E.T., 1982, movie date was on. Not that it was a date. I mean, one gentleman could not date two ladies anyway. It was a viewing, a showing. It was something special: movie night at Gram Mulligan's. I was so excited, I caught myself fluffing the pillows on her couch and loveseat every time I passed them. I wanted it to go perfectly.

It would be such a good break from my daily dose of early morning yard work and late morning swim lessons. I thought my swimming had slowly improved. I was almost up to doggie paddle. Total honesty—I did a pretty solid puppy paddle. Kat said I swam like a rock.

On the afternoon of movie night, Gram sent the twins and me to buy popcorn at Bailey's—the Johnson Island grocery store. "Get the cheapest Bailey's got," Gram ordered. "I don't like the fancy stuff, just microwave."

We took the long way back, and I got the official tour of the Up'ards, near the marina where the ferry had dropped me off. We were coming back down Westway when I finally saw it.

It was the most overgrown, unkempt yard ever. Not even the movies could make a place look like that. You couldn't see the house because everywhere, and I mean everywhere wild bamboo shot high into the air, and bushes and weeds and vines covered everything. The green growing mess stopped at the fence like walls guarding a fortress. As bright and hot as the island was everywhere else, this yard looked dark and cold through the foliage.

"That is the creepiest yard I've ever seen in my life," I said.

"Yup," Sofia agreed. "Uglier than a mud fence."

"It is worthy of Psycho, 1960, or Monster House, 2006!" I said.

"I don't know what you're saying, but if you mean scary, you're right," Kat said.

"Who lives there?" I asked.

"That's the Meta-Gro facility. Can you believe it hasn't even been closed a year? Last September," Sofia said.

"And it grew that much?" I asked.

"Crazy, right? Our dad worked there," Kat said. "Your grandfather, too, Pete. Come on. It's easier to see from the dock."

"Whoa, Kat," said Sofia. "We promised Gram Mulligan to keep him away from here."

"Not inside. Peeking through the fence," Kat explained. "I'm not that crazy."

"Okay, then," Sofia agreed. "Come on, Pete."

Oh no, no. This was a bad idea. And if I did go back there and Gram found out—I don't know what would happen. "We shouldn't," I said.

"Don't be a mainlander scaredy-cat," Kat said.

"I'm not scared," I lied. I was scared. "I don't want Gram Mulligan mad at me."

"Just a peek is okay," Sofia said. "It's crazy. You'll see."

The twins climbed off their bikes and walked them down a side path along the Meta-Gro fence. I stood on Westway, alone. I decided to stay there and wait. That was what Gram wanted. That was the right thing to do.

"Come on," Sofia called. I didn't move. "Suit yourself."

I would suit myself, thank you very much. I stood in front of the yard alone. Then, I started thinking, if we weren't going in, just looking through the fence, was I really doing anything wrong? I didn't think so. I looked up and down Westway. So quiet. Not a golf cart or person in sight. Just me and this creepy place. I was tired of being alone, like at home in Stone Hill. I liked being friends with the twins. It was just a peek anyway.

"Wait up!" I hurried down the path to meet them.

We walked on a dirt road next to the fence. Every once in a while, through the wall of green, I would get a glimpse of something like a bucket or a rake or the edge of a building, but not many signs of anyone having ever worked there. I thought that I spotted a bicycle, but I was probably wrong. "What did they do here?" I said.

"Don't know," Sofia said. "Some kind of research. They were growing things."

"Yeah," Kat said, "like making tomatoes bigger or making corn grow better, I think."

We turned the corner and came to the dock. We left our bikes and scrambled between the fence and the edge of the water. We held onto the fence, and at one point, I got stuck in a vine. To be more accurate, the vine got stuck on me, wrapping itself around my wrist somehow, like that weird weed at Gram's house. I really pulled to yank myself free. Well, like Gram said, Johnson Island was famous for their weeds. Finally, we climbed up to the dock. A gate guarded access from there, and several thick chains secured it.

Back there, I could see a little more of the main house but not much. It must've been two or three floors, but the bamboo, and I guess you could call them trees, grew right up and over the top of the house. As my eyes strained against the green shadows, I could just about see the main building covered with more briars and weeds. There were, I think, large barrels full of rainwater, and I could barely make out the overgrown paths that led to smaller buildings covered with creepers and vines.

"I can see why everyone worked here. It's huge." Then I noticed the faded red back door. It was cracked open a bit. "Look, the door is open."

"No way," Sofia scoffed.

"See it?" I pointed.

"Nah, that's a shadow."

"You think?" Kat said. "Maybe a tiny bit. There."

"You see, Sofia?" I said.

Sofia squinted. "Sort of."

"Look through here," I showed them again.

Then, there was a howl, a whoosh! All the plants shook and BANG! The door slammed shut! We jumped! And screamed!

My eyes bugged out. "Did you see that?" I asked.

"Hey! What are you kids doing here?" called a gruff voice directly behind us.

We jumped again! And screamed! We turned. A tall man stepped out of a Meta-Gro boat. His eyes glowed evilly. I realized it was just his mirrored sunglasses. He wore a beat-up frayed baseball hat and had a devilish mustache.

I was ready to run when the twins yelled "Ooger!" at the same time. Everyone relaxed. The man marched up to us holding a cardboard box.

"Girls, you know you shouldn't be here," he said. "What are you up to?"

"Just snooping around with Gram Mulligan's grandson Pete," said Sofia.

The man shifted the cardboard box in his arms so he could shake my hand. He had a big, rough grip. My hand disappeared in his.

"Pleased to meet you, Pete," he said. "I'm Ooger. I'm mayor of Johnson Island."

"Pleased to meet you, sir."

Ooger nodded. "Anyone in the Mulligan family is okay in my book. I spent many evenings talking with your grandfather on his porch. Sorry he passed and all, son."

"Thank you, sir."

"Now, what are you twins doing back here with Pete Mulligan?" Ooger asked sternly. "You want to get in trouble? You know this is private property and all."

"What are you doing here?" Sofia snapped back.

"What's in the box, Ooger?" Kat said peering in. "Aren't those boat parts?"

Ooger sighed, looking embarrassed. "I reckon they are. How'd you girls get so smart?"

"You're the mayor and you're stealing from Meta-Gro's boat?" I asked.

"I wouldn't say stealing. I'm pirating this stuff," Ooger said. "No one knows better than me what these busters from Meta-Gro did to us. I talked the town council into bringing them here. They promised us all sorts of economic growth: jobs, which we need, and job security. Then, they pulled up and left last year. Didn't even clean up this mess. We've tried every legal means to get 'em to square up, but no dice. So I figure a little pirating might be in order, you know?"

The girls nodded, but I didn't know what he was talking about. Pirating?

Mayor Ooger winked. "The way I figure it, Meta-Gro stuck us, so I reckon, I can stick 'em back a bit. Meaning every once in a while, I come by and take a few parts off this fine Dauntless they left. I bring 'em to the marina—"

"And use 'em on the Angel Fish?" Kat interrupted.

"Ooger's got the fastest crabber on the island, Pete," Sofia chimed in.

"Well, I ain't disagreeing about the Angel Fish being fastest. She is. But the parts go to baymen in trouble. They get free ones courtesy of Meta-Gro, you see. Like robbing from the rich, to give to the poor."

"Like The Adventures of Robin Hood, 1938," I said. That I understood.

"Exactly! Errol Flynn, one of my favorites. I like this kid, girls. He's got good taste in movies. Nice head for dates, I reckon, too. I assume we can keep a little pirating to ourselves?"

"Aye-aye, Captain," Sofia said. "Guys?" We saluted with an aye-aye, as well.

71

"Come by my shanty tomorrow. I got crabs for your parents, girls," the mayor said.

"Mmm," Kat licked her lips. "Thanks."

"And you, Pete," he said. "Gram Mulligan will want some, too."

"Speaking of her," Sofia said. "Don't tell her you saw us here. Pete's not allowed."

"Well," Ooger said, taking off his hat and wiping his forehead. "I can't lie to her. But if she don't ask me nothing, I got nothing to say."

As we rode to Gram's house, I felt the same way as Ooger. I didn't want to say anything about Meta-Gro, but if Gram asked me... Would I be able to lie to her? The bathing suit stuff was one thing, but this. I didn't know. I didn't think so. If she caught us, would she still let us watch E.T., 1982? Would I still be able to hang out with the girls? I hoped like heck she wouldn't ask!

Back home, we found Gram in the kitchen chopping veggies with a big knife. "About time," she said. "What took you so long?"

Oh, no! She asked! Sofia opened her mouth. Before she could pronounce one untrue syllable, I blurted out: "We took the long way back and looked at Meta-Gro, just along the fence, we didn't go inside, and we saw Mayor Ooger and I know we weren't supposed to, but we did, don't be mad! Can we still watch E.T., 1982, after dinner with the girls? Forgive me, milady!" Don't know where 'milady' popped out from, but it did, and I was down on one knee like a knight or something.

The room was silent. The girls, stunned.

Gram smirked while she chopped a carrot. "Humph, if there's one thing I hate," Gram said, "it's liars! Which apparently, you ain't, Pete. Meta-Gro curiosity satisfied now?" She pointed the knife at me. "Gonna keep away from there, right?"

I nodded. I turned to the twins. They nodded, too.

"Movie starts at eight, girls. See you then." And Gram went back to chopping. Whew.

She was quiet at dinner, but I usually did most of the talking anyway. She didn't seem angry. I wasn't in trouble.

Movie night went great! E.T., 1982, did not disappoint! Both girls cried. I did, too. I always did at the end of E.T., 1982—I mean, how could you not? It was such an emotional movie. If you didn't get a little choked up, you might have been born without a soul, or you might be a zombie. It was that magical. I even caught Gram bringing a tissue to her eye. Not being the only one blubbering for a change was nice.

"I gotta give it to you," Kat said. "Darn good movie, Pete."

I wanted to correct Kat and let everyone else on the island know that my name was 'Peter' not 'Pete.' But 'Pete,' which had a pretty good ring to it, was a better nickname than 'weirdo,' which had no ring at all. So I let it go.

Instead, I said, "I'm so glad you liked it."

Chapter 21

For a while, my Johnson Island summer rolled along smoothly. My mornings began with an early rise. The sun beamed in my room so brightly, except for overcast days, but there was no sleeping in then, anyway. After a hearty Gram breakfast, I was off to chores. Now that I was island savvy, I realized I wasn't the only one doing yard work. I saw and heard kids all around: weed whackers buzzing, leaf blowers whirring, loud engines of lawnmowers cutting down the Johnson Island weeds. Except for my lawnmower; I pushed an old-fashioned one, just like Gram had said.

At least I wasn't alone, and I wasn't even that slow any more. Most days, the twins helped me finish. One week, we painted Gram's little picket fence together. But no matter the chore, by mid-morning it was time for my swim lesson. That was when the fight happened.

I definitely passed doggie paddle by now. I stroked pretty well, too, but I still couldn't put it all together. Whenever I focused on my arms, I forgot to kick my legs. Whenever I kicked my legs, I forgot about my arms. By noon on that day, I was feeling peckish, which is a fancy way of saying "hungry" I heard in a movie once. I shared this with the girls.

"Peckish?" Sofia repeated. "What's that mean?"

"Oh, pardon me, ladies, it means I'm hungry."

"You mean you got a gnawing?" Kat said.

"What's that mean?"

"That you're hungry," Sofia answered.

"No offense, but you ladies talk funny."

"We talk funny?" Sofia said. "Peckish? Who in the world says peckish?"

"Peckish does sound pretty weird," Kat said.

"Well, call it whatever you want, do you ladies fancy lunch? I do."

"Fancy lunch? Nah, I have water," Sofia took a swig from her Hello Kitty water bottle.

"We ate a big breakfast," Kat said, patting her very flat belly.

"I ate a big breakfast, too, but—"

"So you're okay, then," Sofia said. "Good, back to work!"

"No, no, no. I am not okay. Peckish was the wrong word. I am starving, ladies, I'm much bigger than you two. I need lunch."

"Lunch, eh?" Sofia said. "You got any money?"

"I might."

The girls smiled at me. I rooted through my backpack.

"Why didn't you say you had money?" Sofia said rubbing her hands together. "We could go to Claudine's for a soft-shell crab sandwich. Or Cookie's for burgers."

"Delicious idea," Kat said as she watched me digging. "Depends how much money he has. How much money do you have, Pete?"

"I'm afraid, I don't have any money at all," I said.

"What?" Sofia said angrily. "Mainland kids are rich! I can't believe you got us excited to eat out and didn't bring any money."

"Didn't mommy and daddy leave you a wudget for the summer?" Kat said sarcastically.

"A what-it?"

"A wudget? A big wad of cash, dum-dum. Moolah! Money. Bills. Bones."

"I have some, yes. Not a lot. I didn't know you wanted me to bring it. If you had told me, I would've asked Gram for money."

"No, she doesn't have any," Sofia said.

"Well, we could go back to her house for lunch. I'm sure she'd make us something—"

"No, don't bother her," Kat said. "She's poor, too."

"Poor, too?" I repeated. "What do you mean poor?"

"The whole island is," Kat said. "Especially since Meta-Gro closed. We don't have money to waste. Only for important stuff."

"Jeez Louise!" I exclaimed. "Lunch is important!"

"Not every day!" Sofia yelled.

"You don't eat lunch every day?" I asked, astonished. I couldn't believe it. I hardly made it to each meal, let alone all the snacking I did.

"No, dum-dum, we don't," Kat answered. "We skip days. That okay with you? Besides, it's good for you not to eat too much."

"But you're supposed to eat lunch," I reminded them. "Every day. This is stupid."

"You're stupid, Pete!" Kat snapped back.

"You eat lunch every day and look how fat you are!" Sofia chimed in. "Like a blimp."

"Yeah, dum-dum, who wants to be a fatty who can't swim?" Kat poked my belly.

"Why should we eat a big fat lunch every day?" yelled Sofia. "And become a big fat, blubber-butt like you?!"

I was stunned.

Did they really just say those things? Over lunch?

I turned away and felt the tears bubbling hot behind my eyes. I slowly shrunk into my curly-cue position—I curled up and covered my face with my arms. It looked odd, but sometimes it stopped me from crying. My face burned red. I was on the edge. The very last inch of my emotional cliff. The twins noticed.

"Hey, Pete, what are you doing?" Sofia said quietly. "Are you okay?"

I nodded my head.

"You sure? You don't look okay," Kat said. "Why're you covering your face like that?"

I shrugged.

"Don't you want to call us a name?" Sofia asked. "You can be mean, now, and call us names. Don't you want to fight back?"

I shook my head.

"Come on," Kat said. "Don't be a crybaby. You can call us jerkwads, losers, weirdos..."

That was it. I started to cry. It was the word 'weirdo.' I thought these girls were different. I thought the island was different. I thought my waterworks finally turned off. But they didn't. They were on full blast, a gusher: tears and snot, tears and snot. The girls stepped back. They were shocked. They didn't know what to do. I stood up and trudged down the beach.

"Pete!" Sofia called.

"Stop, Pete!" Kat shouted.

I shook my head and walked away. I plopped down in the sand far from them. It was a beautiful sunny day on a beautiful sunny beach, and I was crying. What a weirdo! When I finally dried my eyes and flung away the mucus strings, the twins were gone.

Chapter 22

I walked back. I passed the swim spot. I made it to where we dropped our bikes.

Only my dad's bike was there. I pedaled along the path and went through the green tunnel. When I came out, the twins were waiting. I stopped my bike. We looked at each other.

"We don't want to be on the outs with you," Sofia said.

"And 'on the outs' means what exactly?" I asked.

"You know, not speaking, in a fight," Kat explained.

"Well, I don't want to be on the outs either," I said.

"Even-steven, then," Sofia said. "Come on." Sofia started to walk her bike along the path back to the main road. I hesitated. She turned back, "Well, come on."

I followed her. So did Kat. And that was it, I guess. The fight was over. No one talked for a bit. Then, Sofia opened up. "It's hard for our mom and dad. My dad's a bayman, crabs mainly, like Mayor Ooger, sometimes oysters. But, sometimes the bay doesn't give enough."

"It's giving less and less. So many big shipping tankers go up the Delaware River a few miles that way," Kat said, pointing. "Who knows how much pollution they dump in the water?"

"And there's always regulations on how many crabs or oysters you can take and what size," Sofia added.

"Last summer was good," Kat said. "He worked at Meta-Gro at night. We had plenty of money. But this summer? This is a rough summer. Some days we skip lunch or pirate it. But don't tell our parents."

"Of course not," I said, promising myself not to blurt that out like I did with Gram.

"Sorry for calling you...those names," Sofia said.

"Yeah, sorry," Kat added.

"I accept your apologies," I said.

Things were quiet—just the breeze and a gull calling overhead. I noticed in the distance what I thought was a woman painting: a chair and an easel.

Sofia broke the silence. "Don't get mad, Pete, but I never saw a boy cry like that. Not without being hurt, you know, like a fish hook in your finger or like Stuart Quackenbush. Remember when he broke his arm playing basketball, Kat? He cried."

"Most folks around here yell back at somebody," Kat said. "They don't just cry."

"Well, I do."

"How come?" Sofia questioned me.

"I have some issues."

"Like what?" Kat asked.

"Like... issues." I guess there was no hiding it now. I figured I might as well tell the girls the truth. "I can be... really sensitive sometimes. I get nervous and upset, when things don't go the way I planned it gets me stressed, and I just, well, sometimes, I just cry. I have autism. That's the way it is for me. Everyone who has it is a little different."

"I've heard of that," Kat said. "Asperger syndrome, right?"

"No," I clarified. "Doctors don't use that phrase anymore. It's just called autism or ASD, autism spectrum disorder. That's me."

Sofia let out a long sigh. The twins studied me. Sofia whispered something in Kat's ear, probably deciding to tell me this friendship is over. That was the way it always went at home. I guess there were other island kids who'd spend the rest of the summer with me.

No way. I blew it.

"I suppose..." Sofia started.

This was it.

"...we all have something different about us."

"Yeah," Kat said. "So what?"

"Yeah, so you have ASD. So what?" Sofia said strongly. "Okay?"

"Okay," I said.

We could still be friends? This was amazing. I felt warm and fuzzy in my stomach, which I realized was probably hunger. Or maybe not. We watched the woman painting on the beach.

"Hey-o, speaking of lunch," Kat said with a smirk. "Petey-boy's right. Let's not skip it. Let's pirate lunch."

Pirate lunch? I had no idea what Kat was talking about.

Chapter 23

"Thar she blows," Kat said pointing to the artist. "Our first victim."

I quickly learned that the lady painting was Shauna Clancy, an artist from New York City who came to Johnson Island to paint—this was her third summer. Her bay landscapes sold well. Being a mainlander tourist, she was the perfect person to pirate, the twins explained.

"She's taken a lot from the island, so we should take a little bit from her," Kat said. We pulled up on our bikes and approached Shauna Clancy.

"Just follow along, Pete," Sofia whispered. "You'll see how it's done."

"Yeah," Kat added, "don't talk. Understood?"

I raised my hand. "Question."

"What?" said Sofia.

"How are you going to 'pirate' her? We don't have a plank, or a peg leg, or a parrot, or a treasure map, or any pirate paraphernalia that—"

"Shut up, dum-dum," Kat hissed. "You'll blow it." She turned. "Hello, Mrs. Clancy!"

"Hello," Mrs. Clancy responded.

"How's the painting going?" Sofia said. "Looks beautiful."

"Well, the breeze is making the paint dry a little too quickly today."

"Oh, we know how you feel," Kat said. "Our day isn't so good, either."

"Really? Who's your friend?" Mrs. Clancy asked.

"This is Pete," Sofia said.

"Hello, Pete," Mrs. Clancy said.

"Hello, matey." I thought that would go well with the pirate plan. The twins gaped in disbelief.

"He's new," Sofia said.

"And he likes pirates," Kat said. "Anyway, we had some trouble today, too. You see, Pete here lost the money his grandmother gave him. You know Gram Mulligan, right?"

The artist nodded. "I do."

"This is her grandson," Sofia continued. "He's new, so we took him swimming, and he left his lunch money in his bathing suit. All gone, now. Whoosh, out to sea. And he's starving and he's too embarrassed to go back and tell Gram Mulligan. So sad."

"Oh dear," Mrs. Clancy said.

"We gave him half of our lunch," Kat lied, "but look how big he is. Not enough for him."

"So not enough," Sofia said.

Mrs. Clancy studied me. Her floppy beach hat blew in the breeze. "Is this true, Pete?"

I knew the girls said not to talk. But I knew I had to play along, too. I wasn't too worried. My pirate voice was spot-on. "Shiver me timbers," I said. The girls looked at me in horror.

"Pirates," Sofia said. "He's kinda obsessed."

Mrs. Clancy grunted skeptically. "Well, I hate to see a pirate-obsessed boy starve."

The girls smiled.

"But I don't have any money."

The girls frowned.

"I do have the rest of my lunch. The Bay Breeze B&B always packs me too much. You're welcome to it, if you'd like it."

"Arrr, ye sure?" I said, pun intended.

Mrs. Clancy winked and said, "Aye, matey, I be sure. Help yourself. It's in the box."

We thanked her for the tiny feast. Sofia offered to return the lunchbox to the Bay Breeze, and Mrs. Clancy said okay. We left and rode away.

Once out of sight, my "hearties" and I split, three ways, a bunch of grapes, a half of a ham and cheese sandwich, and a Tupperware container full of carrot sticks.

"Why'd you act like a pirate?" Sofia scolded me.

"Me? You ladies put forth the idea. You said we were pirating."

They sighed in frustration. "Ugh, he's such an idiot sometimes," Kat said.

"He doesn't know," Sofia defended me. "When we say pirate lunch, it means to get lunch by not paying for it, like tricking someone, like pirates used to sink ships and steal their stuff."

"We don't do all the 'Blow me Down, scallywag, Davy Jones' Locker' stuff!" Kat said.

"Oh," I said. "Like Mayor Ooger at Meta-Gro. I get it."

"Good. Because I'm still hungry," Kat said. "So batten down your hatches, we got more booty to pirate!"

Our next stop was the Bay Breeze Bed and Breakfast. We entered the quaint one-story building and tapped the bell that said, 'ring for service.' Introductions were quickly made. Patsy and David Crockett thanked us for returning the Tupperware by offering homemade chocolate chip cookies. Still fresh, the chocolate chips were soft and delicious. Sofia's plan all along. This pirate lunch was getting better and better.

As I ate, the Crocketts talked. I learned that they had both been born on the island. They fell in love in seventh grade and knew that one day they would get married. David was a bayman, but that life didn't always make ends meet on Johnson Island. So, when Patsy inherited this big house, she created the Bay Breeze B&B. The Crocketts each wore very faded jeans and T-shirts. Seemed like everybody wore that.

"Good summer so far?" Sofia asked as she munched the cookie.

"Well, things are okay," Patsy said. "Had a few on the Fourth of July. These last weeks were slow. We're almost sold out for Bay Day, but that's it really. Since Meta-Gro closed, it's getting worse and worse."

"I keep telling Mayor Ooger," David said. "The island can't just focus on crabs and oysters to keep us afloat. We need to advertise more. The town council needs to sell Johnson Island as a getaway resort. A place for fishing and boating."

"Or kayaking," Sofia agreed.

"Or swimming on the beach," Kat added.

"Or watching movies," I blurted out. "An island film festival! And we only shows movies that have to do with water or islands, right? You could fix up the old Palace, then bam! A trip back in time. Watch a movie the old-fashioned way, at the Johnson Island Film Festival!"

They looked at me like I was insane

"Sure, Pete. Great idea," Sofia said. "We should go. Thank you for the cookies."

Go? I was on a roll. "You could show Jaws, 1975. You'd have to show Jaws, 1975. The sequels, maybe. That'd be a hoot. Pirates of the Caribbean, 2003, would be fun. Oh, and for something classic, Key Largo, 1948, with Humphrey Bogart and Lauren Bacall."

"Oh, you'd have to have Humphrey Bogart," Sofia said sarcastically. "And Lori Bacall."

"I know, right? It'd be great. Did you say Lori or Lauren? Because her name is Lauren Bacall. Everyone has a problem with names around here. Like really, I go by—"

"Let's go, Pete," Kat grabbed my elbow. "Now."

I kept right on talking. "You guys could sponsor it! You could sell these cookies. They're so good. Ooh, you could make super-buttery popcorn, too! Johnson Island Film Fest... Be There!"

"But The Palace is a dump," David said skeptically. "It's condemned."

"I'd give any idea a try," Patsy said, "but it'd cost a ton of money just to fix it up."

"Obviously," Sofia said, pulling my arm toward the door. "Sorry, he gets twee-mangled when he has too much sugar."

"Twee-mangled?" I asked.

"Oh," David nodded. "We get you," he winked.

"I'm twee-mangled?"

"You are," Sofia said. "Thanks for the cookies."

She yanked me out the door and dragged me to our waiting bikes. Sofia scolded me as we rode. "A film festival? Really? That's a terrible way to bring people to the island."

"I don't know," I said. "I think a film fest would be fun."

"Why would people come here to watch movies?" Kat asked. "You know how hard it is to get here? One ferry runs twice a day! And on Sunday only once. You can get on the island, but you can't get off until Monday."

"Why?"

"Church, dum-dum! We're a godly community, and all," Kat explained. "On Sunday night at five, everything shuts down for church," Kat stopped her bike. "You know that."

Oh, yeah, I did know that. Gram and I had been going to church every Sunday night since I showed up on Johnson Island. "I guess you're right." I still thought it was a good idea, and maybe we could save The Palace. I knew Gram would like that.

Chapter 24

Speaking of church, one Sunday night in August, I sat in the pew of the New Testament Memorial Church. I was so bored.

The congregation was in the middle of singing all six verses of 'How Great Thou Art.'

Gram nudged my arm and glared, which was her way of saying, "Start singing, Pete!"

I mumbled along, still bored, when I heard something funny. The twins sat a pew in front of me and to my right. Sofia tried not to giggle. Then I heard it again. Kat was singing, "How great Thou fart. How great Thou fart." I almost burst out laughing, but my hand covered my mouth just in time. My whole body shook. No one near Kat had caught on yet. Hilarious!

That was how everything was on Johnson Island. You were bored, then something exciting or funny happened. You thought someone was mean, then they turned out nice.

"What's so funny?" Gram whispered.

"Nothing," I said, repressing my urge to laugh.

"Humph." She went back to singing.

Finally, the hymn ended. Everyone sat. The twins nodded at me with goofy grins. They were great. After our fight on the beach, I was more aware about lunch and money. I brought a big lunch when Gram offered to pack one. When she didn't—which meant her funds were running low—I used the spending money my parents had given me to treat them. At first, the girls said no, but I talked them into it. We hit all the island's spots—Claudine's Seafood Restaurant, Cookie's, and The Fisherman's Café. Those were all the spots. Mayor Ooger's wife owned the last one, so we got extra tartar sauce.

The service continued: scripture readings. My mind wandered. So far, despite thinking I would hate it, I really liked Johnson Island. Every morning after weeding and a swim lesson (I was almost there), the twins and I were up for a day of fun and adventure.

We played basketball or kickball (my favorite). We fished in Teddy's tiny rowboat where I kept saying "'You're gonna need a bigger boat.' Jaws, 1975," until they threatened to throw me overboard. Billy organized island-wide water pistol fights with his aqua-armory. One time, when we were hiding together, he said something strange.

I whispered, "Be prepared for anything, sir. Those twins are diabolical, especially Kat."

And Billy said, "Yeah, I know. But, you ever notice, Kat's hair is soft as caterpillar fur? And boy, her leg's broke for sure, don't you think?"

"Question." I raised my hand. "What are you talking about?"

"Nothing. I mean, if you've ever noticed, she's got soft hair and she's got nice, you know... she's nice is all I'm saying! I'm just stating a fact, if you notice, Kat's like—never mind."

"I have another question," I whispered. "Do you like Kat?"

"What? No! I mean I don't dislike her. Sort of, I guess, if I was gonna go gal-ing, which I'm not, I'd go gal-ing with her, if she wanted to. Hey-o, you're not gonna mention this to anyone? This is just between us, right?"

"Of course, I don't even know what gal-ing means."

"Found you!" Sofia screamed. Then the twins super-soaked us until we were wetter than sponges in the bottom of a bucket.

Sometimes we visited the Rec Center, where there was a gym and a side room with more board games than a Target aisle. Every game was tattered and torn, as if it had been won and lost thousands of times—taped boxes, wrinkled cards, ripped boards, oddball pieces like buttons and a fancy salt shaker for chess. In Monopoly, the race car piece had been replaced by a tiny hand-carved crab boat. It had even been painted silver by its creator—Mayor Ooger at age thirteen.

One week when it rained for five days in a row, we played an epic Monopoly game. I was Ooger's crab boat. The twins, me, and Tim Meeks were the last players standing. I had hotels on Boardwalk and Park Place, but somehow Time Meeks won! He should have never been the banker. I was pretty sure he palmed five hundred-dollar bills when no one was looking. The twins were right. He was a cheater. When we were alone, Sofia said, "That kid's as crooked as an S-hook."

"Obviously," I responded, not knowing what in the world she meant. I felt like half the time people spoke, I didn't know what they meant. Turns out, there was a reason. Gram told me that the island was so isolated, the islanders developed their own unique expressions. Most were related to fishing or crabbing or life on the island. So 'twee-mangled' was what happened when your lines holding crab traps gets tangled or knotted. But on the island, this also meant 'mixed-up or really confused or upset.' 'Crooked as an S-hook' meant you were 'dishonest or a cheater.' When we hung out at Cookie's and shared 'double headers,' it meant 'double dip ice cream cones.'

When Gram kept saying, 'Petey-boy, you're falling off,' it meant that I was losing weight (despite the double headers). If only my trainer, Chad, the man of sports who never saw Rocky, 1976, could see me now. Who needed those stupid planks?

During our dinners, Gram told family stories I had never heard before. Once a hurricane blew a tree into the bay with kittens clinging to it. My dad rescued them. In World War II, my grandfather pulled his wounded friend out of a burning anti-aircraft gun on the U.S.S. Houston right after a kamikaze hit. His friend lost his leg, but he lived. Once a week, my mom or dad called for a check-in. They talked mostly to Gram. She answered their questions with a "humph" or "mm-hmm," so they never found out about our post-bedtime movie nights.

After dinner, Gram and I went cruisin', and on nice nights we watched the sunset. After sundown, if it wasn't too hot or buggy, seemed like every kid on the island played flashlight tag or manhunt. Around nine-thirty, Gram and I settled in to watch a classic movie from her and my grandfather's collection. Since E.T., 1982, every Saturday was movie night with the twins.

"Hey-o," Gram whispered, nudging my leg. "Pay attention. Sermon's up."

I nodded. This was the best part of church. Old Reverend Apple, who'd been minister for over thirty years, stood at the pulpit. Her short hair and bouncy energy made her look like a lady in an advertisement for a retirement community. You could feel people sit straighter. Usually, her sermons flowed like a crab boat's wake and rippled into the congregation.

"There is no need for me to tell you," Reverend Apple said from the pulpit, "that life on this island can be hard. Can push you right down into the mud, so your toes are squished in it deep and dirty. But I also have to tell you that if you stop a minute and you wiggle your toes... that cool, wet mud feels good! Can you feel it?"

"Mm-hmm," half the congregation responded.

"And once that mud gets between your toes, that J-Island mud, no matter what you do—you can use soap, you can use dish detergent, you can use the most expensive coconut lime scented stuff they got at Bailey's—but you know what? That mud ain't coming off."

"Mm-hmm," everyone agreed louder.

"You are stained. Marked for life. But that's a good mark. That mark means you suffered, you struggled, and guess what? You survived!" She paused. "How'd you survive? If you look around, you'll see. Look up! Go on do it. Look up."

We all looked up.

"Up in Heaven, you see the Lord and your faith. Now, look side-to-side. Go on."

We did. Gram smiled at me. I noticed the twins down on the right. Kat stuck her tongue out. Sofia slapped her knee.

"And what do you see? You see your friends. You see your neighbors. You see your Johnson Island family. Now most importantly, look down. What do you see? Your shoes."

I did see my shoes.

"Now just like ol' Superman, use your x-ray vision, peek inside your shoes. There's your socks. X-ray your socks and... there they are... your muddy, dirty toes. That's you. You, yourself. That's how we mud-footers survive here."

People nodded with approval. I enjoyed the Superman allusion.

"So remember, as we get ready for another Bay Day celebration, and families come home to celebrate with us, it is these three things that make us strong: our faith, our community, and ourselves! Can I get an amen?"

"Amen!" the congregation responded.

Chapter 25

After the service was Fellowship time, where adults socialized in one room and kids in another. The cookies were heavenly! I adored oatmeal raisin. I poured myself a Styrofoam cup of apple juice. As I crossed the room, I entered an intense argument between the twins and our nemesis, Tim Meeks.

"You're a liar!" Sofia was saying.

"The fence runs all the way around, right to the dock," Kat confirmed.

"It's locked with a chain," Billy chimed in.

"Shut up, butt-chin," Tim Meeks barked, stringy red hair dangling in front of his face. "You don't know what you're talking about. None of you sissies do. I went inside Meta-Gro! Not one of you babies would do that. Never in a million years."

"No way!" Sofia scoffed.

"The chain's as thick as my wrist!" Kat added.

"Right, Mr. Meeks!" I declared. "No way." I had become the third voice in these group situations: Sofia, Kat, me. Like The Three Stooges, remake 2012.

"I got in along the side fence, through a hole," Tim Meeks said.

"How did you do that?" Sofia asked.

"Impossible!" Kat yelled.

"Absolutely impossible!" I added.

Tim Meeks smirked. "Not if you got bolt cutters, babies."

"We pulled them out of the bay a few weeks ago," Dimsy the chess king said.

"See? I ain't no liar."

"Did you actually see Tim Meeks cut the Meta-Gro fence with the bolt cutters?" I asked.

87

"Well, no, I didn't see it," Dimsy confessed.

"So how do we know, Mr. Meeks? Of course, I don't intend to be mean by stating this, but how do we really know that you cut the fence and snuck in? You have no proof. I rest my case." Suddenly, I was Atticus Finch in To Kill a Mockingbird, 1962.

"You want proof, chubbsy?" Tim Meeks glared at me.

"There's no need to bring weight into this conversation, sir."

"One, check the fence for the hole. Two, I can tell you what's in there."

A quiet hush fell. Well played, Tim Meeks. He got me there.

"Everything is overgrown. Weeds as tall as me. Bamboo as thick as baseball bats. Vines like ropes. Leaves the size of paper plates. And quiet. Dead quiet. You think there'd be birds in there? Ain't none. No bugs. No crickets. No nothing, just quiet. Only noise is a strange whistling howling sound when the wind blows. I could see beaten-down paths to the main house, but then even I got creeped out. I was just about to leave when I saw a light on."

"No way!" Sofia yelled.

"Yeah way, Tweedledee! A light in a top floor window. Then, it went out."

"No one's living there, dum-dum. You're lying!" Kat said.

"Yuh-huh, Tweedledum! Someone's squatting in there. Maybe old Bernard Crockett or Darnell Parks. You never see those old guys around. Or maybe something else is living in there. Remember, the weird letter Meta-Gro sent after they cleared out last year? Said something like 'Due to financial upheavals and unforeseen issues, we are forced to close the Johnson Island facility. Sorry for the inconvenience.' Which steamed my dad! He chucked a coffee cup into the wall! Inconvenience? Whole island outta work! The money we lost! That's pretty inconvenient."

"So what, Mr. Meeks? That sounds like a pretty standard business letter to me."

"Look, I told you a hundred times, Mulligan. You don't have to call me Mr. Meeks. Call me Tim, Timmy, Tim Meeks, Meeks! I ain't no mister."

"It's just something he does," Sofia explained.

"I know. It's really annoying, Tweedledee." He glared at me. "What makes it weird, piggly-wiggly, is the word and. It said, 'financial upheaval and unforeseen issues.' My question is what was the 'unforeseen issue?' All companies deal with financial junk, but what was the other 'issue?' Uh-huh? Am I right?"

"That could be anything," Sofia said, frustrated.

"Exactly! And I think—" he dropped his voice— "it could be an experiment gone crazy."

Everyone pondered this. I smelled a rat. It seemed to me that Mr. Timothy Meeks was using the gimmicks of a classic horror movie. He had the abandoned location, mad scientists, dangerous experiments, chained fences, No Trespassing signs. Why, the only thing he left out was the classic cliché of daring some fool to enter the place.

"So you all think I'm a liar? You think I never went in. Prove me wrong. I dare any of you to go in there. I double dog, triple dog, infinity or whatever dog dare you!"

And there it was. The dare was out. And Tim Meeks revealed himself as a fan of A Christmas Story, 1983. Who wasn't?

"Go through the hole I made. Walk around. You'll see what I mean. And to prove it… to prove it… I know! I saw a red Meta-Gro bucket in there. I dare any of you to find it and bring it back. Until you bring me the bucket, I ain't no liar, and you're all chickens."

The room was silent. Tim Meeks stared us down. We focused on anything but him.

"Not so sassy now, Sofia! How about you, Kat? You and your sis got enough guts?"

The twins fumed but didn't say a word.

"All talk, Tweedledee and Tweedledum, just as I thought. Biggest talkers are the biggest babies!" Tim Meeks turned to me. "What about you, piggly-wiggly. You man enough?"

I didn't answer. I was thinking. A red bucket, eh?

"Didn't think so, weirdo. Anyone else? Butt-chin Billy? Fitzie? I know none of you girls got the guts, except for maybe little Amelia here, who fought off a shark. Anyone else? No. Well then, you can all take back calling me a liar right now, every one of you, starting with Tweedledee and Tweedledum. Let's hear it: 'Tim Meeks is not a liar.' You can say it first."

The girls scowled. Sofia exhaled sharply. She was about to speak when I raised my hand.

"What? You taking it back first, Mister Pete?" Tim asked.

"No, I am not taking it back." I stood up. I crushed my empty Styrofoam cup and threw it in the trash, which might've been the coolest thing I'd ever done, next to what I was about to say. "Mr. Meeks, sir, I accept your challenge. Which specifically is to enter Meta-Gro and grab the bucket. I do believe I am man enough and the twins are woman enough, which is why I propose that they join me." You could hear the water lapping along the docks. It was that quiet. I assumed this was the last thing people thought I would do. I looked to the twins. "Ladies?"

Sofia stared at me with an open mouth. "Yes," she said finally, and nudged Kat.

"We will," Kat gulped.

"And, Mr. Meeks, I also propose if we do bring back the red bucket, that you, sir, can no longer call the twins Tweedledee and Tweedledum, me a weirdo or piggly-wiggly, Billy Pruitt butt-chin, or anyone here babies or sissies. Do you agree?"

"And one more thing," Kat added. "We fill that bucket with the muckiest bay water and dump it on your head!"

Tim laughed. "Oh, that sweetens the deal nice for you. But when you don't bring it back, what do I get?"

"The satisfaction, sir, of knowing that you were right," I answered.

"Nope. Ain't good enough," Tim Meeks said. "How about this? When you babies come back crying, first you say I ain't no liar. Second, I can call anyone any nasty nickname I want, forever. And third, for you three, let me see... Ah, you three do my chores for the rest of the summer. That a deal?"

"Agreed," I said quickly. "We all agree."

"That's a sucker's bet, piggly-wiggly, because you and Tweedledee and Tweedledum will never get that bucket. You don't have the guts. Especially once you see that place up close."

We shook hands.

The twins, too.

And with that, the dare was accepted.

90

Chapter 26

After a stroll down Broadway with the rest of the kids patting my back for accepting Tim Meeks's dare, I felt pretty good about myself. I felt brave, which was nice for a change. At last, most everyone headed home. The twins and I sat alone behind The Palace. We dangled our feet off the dock. I smiled at Sofia. She frowned at me and then punched my right arm.

"Ow! What was that for?"

"What were you thinking?" Sofia said. "Meta-Gro is creepy! Ooger told us not to go in there."

"I know, but—" I said, rubbing my arm.

Kat punched my other shoulder.

"Ow!"

"And Gram Mulligan, dum-dum! We can get in big trouble."

"Yes, but—"

"You're supposed to be a big crybaby!" Sofia complained. "Not making impossible bets with older kids. He'll be calling us Tweedledee and Tweedledum forever."

"But—"

"And working for him!" Kat said. "I bet his chores are gross! It's the end of the world!"

"Ladies, it's not the end of the world."

"Why not?" Kat asked me.

"Because I know where the red bucket is."

The girls stared at me open mouthed. "You do?" Sofia asked.

"Mm-hmm," I nodded confidently. "When we peeked in that time I saw it. I think it's really close to the gate, which I think is really close to the hole, from the way Tim Meeks described it."

"Pete Mulligan, you devil!" Kat said.

Both twins hugged me. It was the first time I had ever been hugged by a girl, let alone two girls. Even better, the ladies were no longer mad. They let me go.

Sofia's smile vanished. "We need to plan."

"Plan?" Kat jumped in. "Let's go right away! Tomorrow!"

"Tomorrow?" I gasped. Wait a minute. I was feeling brave, but not let's-break-into-an-abandoned-research-facility-tomorrow brave! "We can't! Not yet!"

"Why not?" Kat asked.

"Why not?" I needed to think quick, not my specialty. "Because... um... because... Sofia's right, we need to plan. In every great heist movie, they plan."

"What's a heist movie?" Sofia said.

"It's a type of movie when you steal stuff with a big elaborate plan, like Ocean's Eleven, 2001, or the original—"

"Oh yeah, George Clooney." Kat said. "We saw that. But, duh, this isn't a movie, Pete! Come on, Sofia, don't listen to him, we do it tomorrow!"

"What about equipment, supplies?" I pleaded. "Every heist has supplies?"

"Supplies?" Kat asked. "Like what?"

Great question! Come on, think, Peter! "Um, supplies, like, like... a rope, maybe."

"A rope?" Kat paused as she considered this. "Oh, yeah. In case we can't find the hole. I get you. We climb over the fence. I guess a rope is a good idea."

I couldn't believe she bought that.

"We need to plan, you goobers," Sofia said, interrupting us, "because we can't get caught in there. You want Dad to find out, Kat?"

"No way," Kat shook her head.

"How about Gram Mulligan, Pete?" Sofia said, pointing at me. "What if she told your mom and dad?"

"You are absolutely right," I agreed. "So we can't go tomorrow! No way, no how."

"Exactly," Sofia said.

Whew. I was feeling better.

"But," she said, pacing excitedly, "we need to go soon. Every kid on the island will be blabbing about the bet. We need to find the perfect story to cover us, and the perfect time to get in and get out. What if Ooger goes pirating there again? Now, think. When can we do it?"

"I say we go right now," Kat said. "Tonight!"

"Tonight?" I repeated in shock. "In the dark? Oh, no, no, no." This was worse than tomorrow! No way in the world I was going in Meta-Gro at night! Not for a second. "That's a bad idea. Right, Sofia? I don't even have the rope! We agreed we needed the rope!"

"Of course, it's a bad idea," Sofia said.

Oh, thank God.

"What would happen if someone saw our searchlights?" Sofia asked. The J-Island translation for 'searchlight' was flashlight. "Meta-Gro's too close to West Way. One person goes by and we'll be caught."

"See, Kat," I agreed. "Sofia's right. We can't do it tonight. Perfect logic."

Kat hissed at me. It wasn't that I didn't want to ever go in, but I needed some time to process. And going in at night would be crazy! I realized my shirt was so twisted around my finger, that I was cutting off my circulation. I untangled my finger and smoothed out my shirt.

"We need a time when almost everyone on the island is busy," Sofia considered, as she started up her pacing again. Kat tossed a rock in the bay. Then, I had an idea.

"What about church?" I suggested.

"I was thinking church," Sofia said. "But we're supposed to be there, too."

"What about after, during Fellowship?"

"You crazy?" Kat raised her eyebrows. "Do you know how many people are going to be around next weekend because of Bay Day?"

"I thought Bay Day was Saturday," I said.

"It is, but people who lived on the island and moved away come back and stay over," Kat replied. "You'll see. It's huge."

"Wait a minute," Sofia shouted. "That's it! Bay Day! The whole town will be distracted. Folks coming in on the ferry. People bringing their own boats. The harbor is on the other side of the island. We won't have morning chores. We get up early and go. Everyone will be busy getting ready. We'll be back before lunch at the latest."

"Are you sure?" I asked.

"An early morning swim!" Sofia exclaimed. "We'll tell everyone we're going to hit the beach, before the crowds arrive. That's our story. You think everyone will buy that?"

"Mom and Dad will," Kat said. "We've been doing that all summer trying to teach Aquaman here how to swim."

"Question." I raised my hand.

"Hit me," Kat said.

"That was sarcasm, correct?" I asked.

"Duh, Pete!" she answered. "Unlike you, Aquaman can actually swim."

"I'm almost there."

"Sure you are," Kat said, rolling her eyes. Definitely sarcasm.

"Well?" Sofia asked me. "You think Gram Mulligan will buy that, Pete?"

"Sure she will," Kat said confidently. "Old ladies aren't that smart."

"Normal old ladies aren't that smart," Sofia said. "But Gram Mulligan's a tricky one."

"She is," I agreed. "But she should believe me, as long as my weeding and chores are finished. I'll have everything ready."

"And you'll get the rope and supplies, right?" Kat asked.

Rope and supplies? What was she talking about? Oh yeah, the heist stuff. "Sure, Kat," I said confidently. "I'll get the rope and supplies."

"You've got one week," Sofia said. "Because next Saturday morning, bright and early: Operation Red Bucket is underway."

"And when it's all over," Kat cackled evilly, "we'll fill that red bucket with the grossest marshy, mud water and dump it on Tim Meeks's head!"

Chapter 27

By Tuesday, I came up with a scheme to secure my heist supplies and get away with the Bay Day swim plan. It was time to execute it. I walked in from a kickball game and found Gram on the phone. She waved to me.

I stood in the dining room near her and studied that weird letter from the Weed Science Society of America hanging on the wall: 'On behalf of the W.S.S.A. and the weed community, we hereby commend you and Johnson Island for your contribution in the fight against invasive plant species.' The fight? Crazy. Like it was a war. I couldn't believe she framed it.

"Uh-huh," Gram said into the phone. She listened. A few seconds later she said, "That soon?" There was a pause. "Humph." She put her hand over the phone. "Do you mind?"

"What?"

"Go in the living room, please. Some conversations are private."

"Okay."

I moseyed into the living room and opened the cabinet that housed Grandfather's movie collection. I enjoyed checking out the old VHS boxes that held the tapes. They had great movie poster pictures on the front, and the sides had different fonts that reflected the movie.

I saw the classic Western Shane, 1953, in big brown old-timey letters. I'd read it was a real goodie. I knew the ending was famous—a gunslinger rides into the sunset, as usual, and a kid yells, "Shane, come back, Shane." I thought we should watch that tonight. Without looking up and forgetting that she was on the phone, I shouted at the top of my lungs, "Hey, Gram, would you like to see Shane, 1953?"

"Sure," she answered, standing right over me.

I jumped. "Whoa! You scared me. I didn't hear you hang up the phone."

"I did." She smiled at me, which she didn't do that often. "You know that Shane—"

"1953," I interrupted.

"—is a real goodie."

So that was where I picked up that phrase.

Gram sat down on the love seat and handed me a fig cake. "So, have you had a good summer here, Pete?"

"Yes. I have."

She smiled again. "Glad to hear you say that."

She seemed like she was in a good mood. Now was the perfect time to ask about Bay Day. "Um, Gram, I have to talk to you about something."

"Oh," she said. "I have to talk to you about something."

"You first," I said.

"Nope. You first, Pete."

I needed to sound casual. "The twins and I were thinking about going on an early morning swim on Bay Day."

"Why so early?"

"Um, Sofia thinks it'll be good to go before the crowds arrive, like eight o'clock. What do you think? That okay?"

"Humph," she grunted. "That's funny."

Was she on to me already? Who was she just on the phone with? Tim Meeks's parents? She was as clever as a fox. "What's so funny?" I asked nervously.

Gram slowly chewed her fig cake then spoke. "Remember, in the beginning of the summer: I had to force you to go swimming with the girls. Here we are at the end, and you want to go early."

"It's not the end yet," I said.

"True... not yet," she answered. "I reckon you can go, if your yard work is up to snuff. This place has to be shipshape for Bay Day. Not one weed. That a deal?"

"It's a deal." We shook hands. So far so good. She said yes to the swim but now for the rope. Could I truly outsmart the island fox? "And one more thing..."

She raised a silver eyebrow. "Uh-huh?"

"Do you think I could look around in the shed for some old bottles?"

"Why?" She took another bite of her fig cake and chewed it slowly.

"Well, Sofia and Kat want to decorate them and sell them to tourists Saturday. Kat said we could make a little dough ray me."

"That sounds like her," Gram smirked. "Sure you can."

Bingo! I knew the 'dough ray me' was the right touch. "Well, how about you?" I asked.

"How about me?" Gram shook her head. "I don't want to sell old bottles. Count me out."

I laughed. "No. Didn't you want to talk to me about something? Was it your private," I made finger quotes, "phone call?"

"Oh," Gram hesitated, which is something else she rarely did. "The phone, yes, it was the phone call... Reverend Apple asked me about Fellowship..."

Fellowship? Jeez Louise! She did know about the bet. She was on to me! Was she toying with me like Tom toys with Jerry?!

"Reverend Apple wanted to know," Gram paused again. "If... if... we could bring extra oatmeal cookies for the Bay Day crowd Sunday. So, I wanted to ask you... if you would help me make them?"

That was close. "Sure, Gram. I love oatmeal cookies."

"I know you do, Pete. I know."

And that was that. Everything was set.

For the rest of that week, Gram and I were pretty chummy. For the first time all summer, she helped me with the morning yard work. I guess her back felt better. She talked more, too.

While we were weeding, I prodded her for Meta-Gro info. "I mean, why would Meta-Gro build a fancy research facility here?"

"Humph, they didn't build nothin'," Gram scoffed. "It ain't no fancy factory. It's just the old Dobbs house. Meta-Gro bought a big, old house that had got rundown, sittin' in the center of a big, old yard that had got rundown. Dobbs family had money back in the day, but it run out years ago. Meta-Gro just cleaned it up a bit, put a fence around it, added a dozen or so sheds, and started planting up a storm. Humph. And now it's an ugly, weed-infested overgrown half-acre dump from water to road. Ain't much on that corner of the island anyway. Real windy. But Meta-Gro shoulda cleaned up that mess, that's for sure."

"Were you ever inside there?" I asked.

"Few times. Your grandfather worked there for a while as a nighttime security guard. I brought him dinner on occasion. Not that there was any reason for a security guard. Johnson Island was totally safe and had been for years. Only been one murder in the island's history. Still unsolved. Happened in the thirties."

Fun fact but not very helpful. Perhaps she knew about that strange letter Tim Meeks mentioned. "Did you save the letter Meta-Gro sent when they closed?" I asked, yanking a weed.

"Nah," Gram said. "Put it in the garbage where it belonged. Good riddance. Your grandpa never liked working there. He said he felt a Jack 'o my wisp, for sure."

"Question." I raised my hand. "A what of my what?"

"A Jack 'o my wisp. Mainlanders don't know nothing. It means an evil spirit, a bad feeling. He was fit as a fiddle before he took that job. Never sick a day in his life. Suddenly, heart attack. Oh, there's a Jack 'o my wisp in there."

Interesting.

Speaking of Meta-Gro, the girls told me that they had actually seen the letter. Mr. Jin saved it. Tim Meeks was right. That weird line popped off the page: "Due to financial upheavals and unforeseen issues." That mysterious and was there.

The twins also told me that the man in charge was named Dr. Lennox. Dr. Lennox liked their dad and had promised him a promotion the following year. With the thought of extra income, Mr. Jin had taken out a loan to fix up his boat and the roof of his house. When Meta-Gro left, he'd been very bitter. Dr. Lennox had never even given a hint. "Left me high and dry," Mr. Jin complained to anyone that would listen. "High and dry."

The rest of the week was busy. I helped Gram make the oatmeal cookies. We cleaned the house from top to bottom. One afternoon, when she went to mail a few letters, I ducked into the shed to try and find my heist supplies. I was hoping to find a rope, a grappling hook, machetes, hatchets; the usual gear one would need to sneak into Meta-Gro and steal a red bucket.

What did I find? A dead mouse (gross), a flashlight that needed batteries, three old-fashioned oil lanterns, tools, and boat parts. I found a rusty Swiss army pocketknife, which worked, except the blades were stuck. I oiled it up. Later, I asked Gram if I could keep it.

"What knife?" she asked.

"This Swiss army one." I gave it to her.

She turned it over in her hand. "I haven't seen this in years. Where'd you find it?"

"In the shed."

"Well, I'll be... that's the champ... I gave this to your grandfather on his first Father's Day. He said this pocketknife was his good luck charm. Took it whenever he went on the water. Got him through many a storm, he said. Funny you found it. He thought he'd lost it years ago, about the time your dad left, I think."

"I didn't know it was that special, you should keep—"

"No." She took my hand and opened my palm. "He'd want you to have it. He would have given it to you himself, if he... Take it, Pete. It's yours. He'd be bustin' if he knew his grandson was here on Johnson Island, watching his movies, using his pocketknife." She gently placed the knife in my hand. "Just don't cut yourself. You get me?"

"I get you."

Along with my grandfather's Swiss army knife, which I hoped would be lucky during our Meta-Gro mission, I took the flashlight and found batteries. I fixed up some grimy binoculars that worked once I cleaned the gunk off. And finally, I spotted a rope. It was the one that hauled me out of the bay that first night on the island.

I stuck to my cover story and found a few old bottles. But the more I thought about not having enough equipment for the Meta-Gro mission, the more I realized it didn't matter. The plan was so simple—go in, walk about fifteen feet (to my recollection), get the bucket, get out. The whole thing might take about twenty minutes, maybe forty-five. I wasn't worried at all, except for one thing. Though I had lost weight that summer, would I be too big to fit through the hole in the fence?

On Friday night, when I was supposed to be asleep, I sat in PJ's with my Operation Red Bucket supplies laid out on my bed ready to go in my backpack. I planned on adding twenty dollars to the pile when the door suddenly opened, and Gram Mulligan came in the room.

"Pete, I need to talk to—" She noticed the supplies on my bed. Her eyes narrowed. "What in God's green earth is that all about?"

Oh no! I thought she was asleep. "I can explain."

"You better, young man." She tightened the knot of her pink robe.

"Um... it's for swimming tomorrow."

"Swimming?" she scoffed. "The rope I get, but the rest of it?"

"Uh-huh," I stuttered.

"What do you need the Swiss army knife for?" she demanded.

I swallowed. "Shark attacks."

"The binoculars?"

"Bird watching."

"What about the flashlight? In the morning?"

"Unexpected solar eclipse."

"Solar eclipse!" she yelled. "Okay, smarty-pants, where are the bottles? Where's your towel? Where's your King Kong—"

"1932," I added sheepishly.

"1932 bathing suit?! Hmm? Well? Go on, tell me!"

"Um..."

"Let's hear it!"

I hesitated. I couldn't think of anything.

"Just as I thought." She shook her head. "You've run out of lies. You're not swimming! Peter J. Mulligan, you're grounded. They'll be no Bay Day for you! Go to bed!"

She slammed the door.

Chapter 28

"No, Gram!" I screamed at the closed door. "Not that! Please! I have to go tomorrow!" I had jumped up to follow her when the door flew open again.

Gram's bony hand gripped the knob so tightly that her old knuckles were white. "I can't believe you," she said angrily. "Lying! You know I hate liars!"

"Ground me any other day," I begged, "for three days, for a week, I don't care. But I have to go in the morning!"

"Why?" Gram asked. "For what? What's so important?"

"For the twins!"

"The twins?! What are they up to?" Gram shook her head. "What did they talk you into? When I get off the phone with their parents, I'll—"

"No! It's not them. It's me. I started it. I made a bet!"

With that word, she paused. She shifted her weight and let go of the door. "You made a bet? You?"

"I did."

"What kind of bet? Who with?"

"With Tim Meeks."

"Tim Meeks?" she repeated. She put her hands on her hips. "Why?"

"It was at Fellowship last Sunday. I was sick and tired of him picking on Sofia and Kat."

"What are the stakes?" I really wasn't exactly sure what she meant, so I hesitated. She clarified, "What do you win or lose?"

"If we lose, it's bad: he gets to call the girls Tweedledee and Tweedledum forever, and me piggly-wiggly, and Billy butt-chin! And we have to do all his chores for the rest of the summer."

"Did you shake on it? Other kids see it? They know about it?"

"Yes, we shook. All the kids know."

"Humph," she said, disappointed. "It's a real bet then. What do you get if you win?"

"Tim Meeks can't make up mean nicknames for any kid on the island, and we dump mud on his head."

"I get you," Gram nodded. "Is that what all this is for?" She gestured to the bed. "To win the bet?"

"I told the girls I would get heist supplies," I confessed. "We won't even need this, but I said I would get them, so I did. I didn't want to look stupid."

"So, you're not going swimming tomorrow morning?" She sat on the edge of the bed.

"No, we're not. We're getting up early to... to win the bet," I said. "Don't worry, though, it'll take like fifteen minutes, that's all,"

"And the twins can't do it without you?"

"No."

She paused. She was considering letting me go. I knew it. And so far, I didn't have to say anything about Meta-Gro, which I couldn't tell her. "Here's the million-dollar question, Pete. What do you have to do to win?"

I couldn't look her in the eye when I said, "I... I can't tell you. You have to trust me."

"And right back to skimping on the truth." She shook her head. "If you can't tell me, you can't go." She stood and turned toward the door. She was leaving. It was over. I was grounded.

I stood up and blurted out, "That's not fair! I had to trust you! You didn't tell me things this summer."

"When?" She stopped.

"When the girls pushed me in the bay! When you forced me to take swim lessons! You never told my parents about staying up late to watch old movies. Right?"

"I suppose, but—"

"Please, Gram, please! I have to. I can't let them down."

Gram sighed. "Pete, I don't like liars. But you're right, I ain't exactly been truthful with you about everything all summer." She sat on the bed. "That's why I came up here. That phone call the other day, it wasn't from Reverend Apple. It was your mom. Her and your dad are coming tomorrow for Bay Day and stayin' over for the weekend."

"They are? Why didn't you tell me?"

This time, she didn't look me in the eyes. "Well, they told me they have a big surprise for you."

101

"What surprise?"

"I don't know. They didn't say. A surprise."

Why would I worry about that? Surprises are nice. Then, it hit me. "Do you think... they're taking me home?"

Gram shrugged. "Don't know. They didn't say. Could be. To be honest, I figure it might be that."

I sunk down on the bed next to her. "But there's two weeks of summer left before Labor Day! I don't want to leave."

"That's why I didn't tell you. I didn't want you to fret," Gram said. "I don't want you to leave either."

I was stunned. I put my head in my hands. I could feel the tears coming. I didn't even try to stop them. I hadn't cried since that day on the beach with the girls. A real record for me. Now, the thought of leaving, going home, back to school. Tears and snot. Tears and snot. It was a gusher!

Gram put her arm around me. "Now, now, Pete, don't get upset. Maybe it's just a visit. Maybe they felt like a soft-shell crab sandwich. Your father hasn't been to Bay Day in years." She rose and pulled tissues from a box. She handed one to me. "Blow."

I did. It wasn't pretty.

"Listen to me," she said. "You don't know this, not being a mud-footer and all, but on Johnson Island, a bet is serious business. When your dad was your age, he lost his skiff bettin' he could swim around the island faster than another boy. He saved up a long time for that boat. You see, folks around here don't squelch on a bet. Now, I don't like it, but if you bet Tim Meeks to help the other kids, and you shook on it, well, you gotta see it through. So, against my better judgment, I'm going to trust you."

"Really?"

"Yup. You can go with the twins. You don't have to tell me what you're doing."

I took my head out of my hands.

Gram slowly put the supplies in my backpack. She smiled when she put the rope inside and zipped the top. "But there are some conditions. Things I want you to do tomorrow. Things you have to do. You have to promise."

"What things do you want me to do?" I asked, wiping my nose.

"First, I want you to get up early. I want you to win the bet. To be honest, I never liked the Meeks family, that Tim's always been one of the blue hen's chickens."

I raised one eyebrow. "Which means?"

"He's a problem child. But look, whatever you're doing, I want you to be careful, really careful."

"I will."

"I want you home to meet your parents on the Joyce Mary at noon."

"Okay."

"And this is most important, I want you to have extra fun with your whackems. As much fun as you can."

"Question." I raised my hand. "What's whackems mean?"

"It means best friends."

"Thanks, Gram," I said.

"Can you do all that? You promise?"

"I promise."

"Good." She patted my knee. "You should probably get to bed."

I put my hand on hers. "I hope I don't have to leave Monday."

"Me, too, Pete. Me, too." She squeezed my hand and smiled at me. She let go and got up. She held the door knob. "Good night." She slowly shut the door.

I blew my nose again and went to bed.

Chapter 29

As the sun poured in my room on Saturday morning, I could feel something special. Bay Day had finally arrived. The final touches—hanging banners, preparing booths, prepping food—were nearly complete. And Operation Red Bucket was about to commence. Anticipation hung in the air.

I stared out my window at Broadway. The neighbors' houses looked great, lawns particularly green (even a few weeds), and flower beds perfect. The early sun lit up the world. The morning dew made everything glisten.

At the same time, I was pretty sure this mission with Kat and Sofia could be our last adventure together. I had a bad feeling that my parent's surprise was a ferry ticket home. If I left Monday, it would leave enough time to reconnect with my A-Team, adjust to my new house, my new town, my new school. Ugh, just the thought of school twisted my stomach in a knot.

The knot tightened—leaving the island behind meant leaving Gram and the girls behind, especially Sofia. I didn't want to go. The waterworks welled in my eyes.

But before a tear could streak down my cheek, the new me—Pete, Gram Mulligan's grandson—did something different. I pushed those sad thoughts away. There would be plenty of time for crying later. I could cry on the ferry. But right now, I had two friends counting on me: two friends who taught me to almost swim, to pirate, to play manhunt and flashlight tag, who liked my monster T-shirts, and who accepted me for who I was. So even though I was upset that my J-Island summer was almost over, for one more weekend I needed to be a Bay Boy and steal that bucket!

As I dressed, I decided to pull out the one monster T-shirt no one had seen yet—The Blob, 1958. Now, the Blob, if you never saw the movie, is a jelly-like alien that sucks up a whole town as it grows bigger and bigger, absorbing everything. The white T-shirt showed a picture of the original movie poster. I loved it. From the top of the poster, the reddish-pink ginormous blob oozes down to attack a small 1950s town—gross but cool. But even cooler, the poster had the face of the teen hero who tries to save that town: the one and only actor Steve McQueen.

He was the American POW Cooler King from The Great Escape, 1963. To me, Steve McQueen was the coolest of the cool. Even his name had a ring to it. I said it out loud slowly: "Steve McQueen." I heard the 'ee' sound slapped together in the first and last name. The hard consonant 'Mc' and 'Qu' were tough on the tongue like he was tough on bad guys. Steve. McQueen. He was a Hollywood action hero for real—he drove motorcycles, romanced leading ladies, and fought directors.

Some of his best work? Well, The Great Escape, 1963, of course. In Bullitt, 1968, he's a cop that races up and down the hilly streets of San Francisco in one of film history's greatest car chases—no CGI in that one! And in my all-time favorite Western, Steve McQueen plays one of seven gunfighters who save a town of farmers from evil Mexican bandits. The title? The Magnificent Seven, 1960! They remade it in 2017, but it wasn't the same.

Steve's face on my T-shirt inspired me. I had to be like him. Lucky for me, being heroic would not involve fighting a deadly gelatinous alien from outer space. I just had to sneak through a fence and steal a red bucket. That was the kind of hero work I could handle. Hopefully.

After breakfast, which was unusually quiet, I went out the back door. Again, I was taken aback by how green and lush Gram's little yard looked. I guess this was the magic of Bay Day everyone talked about. I pulled my bike from the shed. I brought it to the gate. Gram sat on the steps of the front porch. She sipped her coffee. The mug had a picture of a red crab. Under the crab, it read: I'M ONLY CRABBY IN THE MORNING.

"Don't forget to be at the dock by noon," she reminded me. "Be careful now."

"I will, Gram."

"Good luck."

I walked my bike through the white picket fence and thought about the first time I came through this gate. Just look at the place now. All that yard work paid off—lawn cut, weeds plucked, flowers blooming, fence newly painted. To think, I started the summer calling her Grandmother. It sounded funny to my own ears. I closed the gate and gave her an action hero salute. She raised her mug and winked.

I pedaled to Sofia and Kat's place. The twins met me at their front gate.

"Ready?" Kat asked.

"I hope so."

"Nice shirt," Sofia said.

"Thanks."

"You got the rope and stuff?" Kat asked.

I patted the top of my backpack. "Yes, ma'am."

"So I guess Gram Mulligan believed your story," Sofia said.

"She did believe," I answered. "We just have to be back by noon."

"Easy-peasy, Mac-n-cheesy," Kat said as we took off. "Forecast's perfect, too. Sunny and breezy, with only a slight chance of thunderstorms late in the day. It's all coming together."

In the morning light, we quietly zipped down Broadway. We passed the church sporting a 'Welcome' sign. We passed the post office that was only open until eleven because of Bay Day. We turned and thump thump thumped over the long bridge. The marsh looked greener and thicker than ever on this spectacular sunny day.

On the west side of the island, we coasted down the street that would usually lead to Fish Hook beach. But instead of going south, we turned north and pedaled toward the Up'ards. We passed the giant water tower with the crab on it. We passed the Bay Breeze Bed and Breakfast where we pirated the Crocketts. We saw the school and the rec center and veered off left to where Meta-Gro sat. The weedy, overgrown fenced-in mess was the only thing dirty on an island that had spruced itself up for its big day.

"Okay, this is it," Sofia said

"Finally," Kat said.

We coasted down the path toward the back entrance near the dock. On either side of us, the dune grass was tall and thick. Sofia stopped. "Ditch the bikes in here," she said.

"Why?" I asked.

"So no one sees them, dum-dum."

Our bikes hidden, we walked the rest of the way on a narrow dirt path that bordered the tall, chain link fence. Inside was an impenetrable forest of bamboo and weeds.

"I'll say this for Tim Meeks, ladies. He was right. This place does look creepy, even in the morning. It seems so dark in there."

"It's just the shade," Kat said. "Shadows from the stupid overgrown plants, that's all. How could Meta-Gro not clean this mess up? It's disgusting."

Sofia was busy running her hand along the fence. "Okay, it should be somewhere along here, near the corner, Meeks said."

We searched for a while. We pulled back tall weeds and vines from a bunch of spots, but we didn't find a hole, just more solid fence. We were frustrated, and I was sweating. Already, things weren't going according to plan.

"This is taking a long time," I said.

"It's harder than I'd thought," Sofia complained.

"Is there even a hole?" Kat wondered. "You think that jerk made the whole thing up?"

"I wouldn't put it past him," Sofia said.

I tested the fence near some huge dandelions. "We should have the bucket by now, not still be looking for— Wait a minute!" I felt something sharp. "Ah-ha! Found it." I showed them a small area of fence that had been cut. On the bottom, the chain link had been pulled back and covered with some branches and leaves. Impossible to notice if you weren't looking hard.

"Okay, Petey-boy, good job." Kat patted my back. "Let's go!" She squatted down to squirm through the hole.

"Wait." I stopped her. "Let's see where the bucket is."

"Good idea," Kat agreed.

I moved along the fence from the corner, to the dock and back gate. "We talked to Ooger over here, so I think I saw it...there!" Both girls looked as I put my finger through the fence. You could see something red down a gravel path not entirely overgrown.

"That's the bucket?" Sofia looked at it and shrugged her shoulders.

"Yeah, that's it."

"Are you sure that's even a bucket?" Kat asked.

"It's red, isn't it, and small?" I answered.

"You're right," Sofia said. "Get a good look at it. I don't want to get lost once we go in."

"Right." I nodded. "That's the plan. In and out."

We stared back and forth from the corner hole to the bucket. Back and forth. Back and forth. The number of weeds and jungle inside the fence was beyond belief. It was like some old Tarzan movie from the 1930s. Those classics always had a jungle scene with guys chopping vines with machetes. If only I had one. That was how thick it was, like the place had been abandoned for hundreds of years, even though it was only ten months or so.

We went back to the corner, pushed on the fence, and the hole opened. Sofia squeezed through first. Kat squirmed in. Then it was my turn. Of course, I got stuck.

"Ladies," I said, "I need some assistance here."

I tried to bend the fence, and the girls used all their strength, too. We really could've used Tim Meeks's bolt cutters. Finally, after much pushing and squeezing, I popped in.

Chapter 30

We stood up inside the fence. Our world had become thick and green and canopied, like a mini-rainforest. Only a few random streaks of light penetrated to the ground.

"Wow," Sofia said.

"Yeah," Kat agreed.

"Now, where is that red bucket?" I asked.

"It should be straight that way," Sofia said, pointing.

We turned and began to push our way through the jungle. Weird waist-high plants brushed against us, bamboo stalks scraped us as they reached to the sky, vines dangled from everything like snakes. I hated the feeling when a leaf touched my neck. Yech.

"I don't see a red bucket," Kat said.

"It appears that I don't either," I agreed reluctantly.

"I guess we lost track of it when we turned around to help you," Sofia said.

"It's okay," I said. "Look around. We'll find it." We peered into the emerald shadows: weeds, more weeds, bamboo, vines, weeds, tall weeds, taller weeds.

"There!" Kat said. "By that shed!"

She was right, a small splash of red! We trudged along, moving aside tall pieces of bamboo that were tangled up in the serpentine vines. We had to stop every few steps because some weeds had stickers or sharp, serrated leaves that cut us. We finally got to the tiny shed where we had spotted the bucket. But there was one problem.

"Where'd it go?" Sofia said.

There was no bucket.

"It was right here, next to the door," Kat said.

109

"I thought so, too," I said. "Did we go to the wrong shed?"

We heard a scuffling noise to our right. We looked in that direction. We listened. Nothing. Wind rattled the bamboo. We exchanged looks.

Kat shrugged. "Maybe a squirrel or something."

Squirrel? I leaned toward 'or something.' I turned around again to check things out. I did not hear or see a squirrel. I swallowed uneasily. There was no way it was a squirrel.

"Let's check out the shed," Kat said, and opened the door. It creaked, of course.

"What are you doing?" I asked, shocked. "I mean, come on, there could be anything in there." I had to convince the girls not to go in. "We shouldn't— I mean, we know the bucket's not in there, so why would we—?"

"Come on." Kat cut me off. "It'll be fun." She stepped inside.

Sofia followed her. I had no choice. I stepped in next, very slowly. Oh boy. Wild weeds grew through the shed's floorboards and broken windows. Stacked along the walls were bags of fertilizer and white and blue buckets labeled with chemical compounds we didn't understand. There were also tools on the walls: clippers, rakes, shovels, hoses, pruners.

"This is weird," Sofia said.

"Quite a lot of chemicals," I said nervously. "More than Batman, 1989, with Michael Keaton and Jack Nicholson. Lots of green chemicals in that movie." I was talking to talk. Movies calmed me down. "Remember, Sofia? The Joker origin? He falls in the vat."

"Sure," Sofia answered.

"Are you just agreeing to agree?"

"Yup," Sofia said dryly.

Kat took a pruner. "Ha! Let's use these! We'll cut right through those sticker vines now."

We each grabbed one. Armed with pruners, we stood back in the doorway. We scanned the landscape, up and down, high and low, for any glimpse of red.

"There! The bucket!" Sofia found it. "That other shed. Come on."

We cut our way to it. It took longer than we thought. Each of us getting stuck at least once. No matter how carefully we stepped, our feet got tangled in the ground vines. Even when we went slow, it was like walking in thick snow. We reached the spot. But again, no bucket.

"I could have sworn it was right here!" Sofia said.

"Me, too!" Kat said angrily.

"I guess it's too easy to get lost in this mess," I said.

110

"I know it was by this shed! I know it!" Sofia said. "We went straight. Look." She turned to our freshly cut path and she was right. It did look straight.

"Hmm." I rubbed my chin.

"Over there!" Kat yelled. "I see it!"

Kat was right. You could see it. Near the main house.

"Don't worry about the dumb stickers! Come on!" Kat ran with high steps as fast as one could run. Sofia and I tried following her, but Sofia's shirt got tangled up by some sharp thorns. I stopped to help her. I cut the sticker branches then tried to carefully pull them from her shirt.

"Jeez Louise! These are sharp," I said.

"I know," Sofia agreed, sucking the blood from her finger. "Thanks, Pete."

"Of course, milady." I mean how could I not help? It was the gentlemanly thing to do.

When we caught up, nursing cuts on our legs, Kat waited by the door of the main house.

"Well?" I said out of breath, "Do you have it?"

"Almost," she said.

"Where is it?" Sofia asked.

"Don't ask me how, but it's in there." I followed Kat's finger to the front door where a tilted Meta-Gro sign hung, overgrown with leaves and covered in green moss. The door was half-open. The light from outside spilled inside across a dirty hardwood floor, and about ten feet in, just at the edge of the light, half visible and half in shadow, was the red bucket.

I swallowed hard. "Hold on. How'd it get in there?"

"I don't know, dum-dum."

"I feel like there's more than one bucket," I said.

"I feel like someone is moving the bucket," Sofia said. I turned toward her. She was looking behind us into the weedy jungle. I did the same.

"Someone?" I gulped. "Or something?"

"No way," Kat shot back.

"Didn't Tim Meeks say he saw a light on?" Sofia reminded us.

"Do you think someone is playing a joke on us?" I asked. And if they were, it wasn't very funny. Funny was the last thing I was feeling.

"You know what I think?" Kat smirked. "It's so simple. Tim Meeks found out we were going in, and he's messing with us right now."

Really? Kat thought that. There was no way.

"Yeah, that's what's going on," Sofia agreed. "That makes total sense."

111

Total sense?! Maybe total nonsense!

"He's just trying to freak us out, so he wins the bet," Kat said.

"I don't know, ladies." Clearly, I was the only rational person left in our party. "Tim Meeks would have to be awfully quiet to be moving the bucket without us noticing."

"How could we hear anything with all the noise we make stomping through this stuff?" Sofia replied.

"That's my point exactly!" I said. "How could Tim be quiet enough to sneak around?"

"It's right there!" Kat pointed. "Let's go in the house and get it!"

"What do you think, Pete?" Sofia asked.

"Is it really that bad being called Tweedledee and Tweedledum?" I said. "I can live with piggly-wiggly, it's not the worst nickname."

"What?!" Kat exclaimed. "You want to give up?"

"We tried, right?" I explained. "We snuck in. We almost had it. But going inside. I think it's a really bad idea."

"You mainlander scaredy-cat!" Kat hissed. "The bucket is right there! And I'll bet Tim Meeks is in there, too, hiding in some corner, laughing at us."

"I'm not so sure," I said.

"Stay out here if you want," Kat said, "but I'm going in. Come on, Sofia."

Sofia put her arm on my shoulder. "She's right, Pete. We've come this far. I'm going with her. You coming?"

I wanted to say "No! Absolutely not! Uh-uh!" in the worst way! But I considered: we had come this far. The bucket was right there.

But, the house was full of shadows, and this was a classic horror movie blunder! You never go in the scary house! Never! But even as I thought that, I looked down and noticed my Blob, 1958, T-shirt. What would Steve McQueen do?

I knew the answer. Jeez Louise! Stupid heroes!

"You're right," I said to the girls. "We've come this far. If you ladies are going, I'm going in, too." I hope that sounded as if Steve McQueen had said it.

"Great," Sofia said. "It's just a prank. You'll see. No big deal."

"You can't scare us, Tim Meeks!" Kat yelled.

And with that, we stepped through the door and into the house. Weeds blanketed everything. We took a few short steps.

Kat picked up the bucket. "Finally." She smiled. "No more Tweedledum! I can't wait to see Tim Meeks's face when we dump a bucket of island muck on his weaselly head."

Suddenly, there was a strange howling sound. The door slammed shut! We jumped!

"Jeez Louise!" I said. "What was that?"

"The wind!" Sofia reassured me. "I heard it."

I stepped back in the direction of the door. My eyes hadn't adjusted to the dark yet, so I felt around for the knob. It creeped me out when I touched leaves. Finally, I got the door knob.

I pulled. It would not open. I yanked harder, leaning backward with all my weight, which is a considerable amount. It didn't budge. "It wasn't the wind," I said.

"What do you mean?" Kat asked.

"Stop kidding, monster movie guy," Sofia said.

"I'm serious," I gulped. "I can't open the door."

Chapter 31

"Step aside," Kat said, marching past me.

She pulled. Nothing. Sofia pulled. Nada. We all pulled as hard as we could. Zilch.

"See," I said. "Coming in here was a bad idea. I tried to tell you."

The twins scowled at me.

"Relax, dum-dum. Old doors get blown in by the wind all the time."

"Uh-huh," I said, shaking my head. "And get stuck so you can't open them?"

"Doors get stuck all the time on Johnson Island," Kat assured me. "Every house is old and uneven. Right, Sofia? What about our bedroom door?"

"It's true. It's the worst. Sticks all the time. Let's just calm down."

"Whatever." I folded my arms. We looked around the room.

"This place is dark," Kat said.

"Seriously," Sofia agreed. "The windows are covered in vines. I can't see much."

"Oh, I forgot," I said, taking off my backpack. "My heist supplies! I have a flashlight."

"Now, you're talking, Petey," said Kat.

All that work getting those supplies and tricking Gram finally paid off. I pulled out the light and flicked it on. We could see... a little. It didn't really look like a factory or research facility. Gram was right. It looked like a simple three-story Johnson Island house that had been converted into a lab. A stairwell, covered in shadows, ran up to a second floor. On the first floor, wire shelves lined the walls, filled with plants, watering stations, soil, small shovels, and empty stools.

I easily imagined workers sitting and tinkering with the plants. There were clipboards and electrical outlets with laptops. Above each growing station there were fluorescent lights and different switches, I guess to control what kind of light was given to each plant.

Speaking of plants, there were all sorts, with labels that were hard to read in the dim light. Since they had been left unattended for so many months, the plants spilled out of their containers and stretched onto the floor, covering it in a carpet of green leaves and vines. It was weird they hadn't died, despite no light or water. They had grown.

"Let's just get out of here and win this bet," said Kat holding the bucket.

"Right," I said. "In and out. That was the plan, remember? In and out."

"Go that way," Sofia suggested. "Maybe there's a back door."

I aimed the flickering beam.

"You put batteries in that thing?" Kat asked.

"Sure," I said.

"Why's the beam so bouncy?" Kat asked.

"I don't know."

"It's you, Pete," Sofia said.

"What? Me?"

"Give the searchlight to me," Sofia said. "You're shaking it."

Oh. She was right. My hands were trembling. I hadn't noticed. "Here."

Sofia took the flashlight. We clustered together around her and found a back door. We pulled again. It was no use—it didn't budge. Same thing for two weed-covered windows we found. Maybe they were painted shut.

"Now what?" I asked.

"I don't know yet," Sofia said, biting her lip. She was getting nervous, too. "Kat, what do you think?"

"Remember that time we came with Dad? Wasn't there a fire escape?"

"I don't remember."

"I'm pretty sure there was," Kat said, nodding. "Let's go up and find it. We'll climb out a window. No problem."

No problem? Sure. There wasn't anything scary at the top of that dark staircase, right? Of course not. Jeez Louise!

"Sounds good," Sofia agreed.

Good? No, no, no. It sounded bad. Very bad.

We returned to the spot near the front door. We looked up the stairs.

"Ladies first," I said politely. I hated that I was such a yellow-belly.

"Are you serious?" Sofia said.

"Out of the way, dum-dums," Kat said, taking the lead and the flashlight from her sister.

"One of the blue hen's chickens," Sofia whispered to me.

"Oh yeah, she's crazy."

"That's right," Sofia said, surprised. "How'd you know?"

"Gram Mulligan."

"You're a regular mud-footer now." She patted my shoulder.

"Come on, wimps," Kat grumbled.

Slowly, step-by-step, we crept up the stairs, stepping on small overgrown weeds. I tried to be quiet and not make the leaves rustle or the floorboards creak. Kat paused. Sofia and I banged into her.

"Gimme some space!" Kat said. "Why are you guys acting so weird? It's just a bunch of dumb, overgrown plants."

We had reached the top of the stairs. We saw a long, dark hallway with three different doors (closed, of course) and at the end of the hall, a staircase.

"Do you remember which room had the fire escape?" I asked quietly.

"We were here once, Pete," answered Kat.

"Should we check each room?" Sofia asked.

"I guess," I said. Not that I wanted to. Anything could be behind those doors!

"Then let's start with door number one," Kat joked in a loud voice.

Chapter 32

We entered the first room. It's windows were covered in thick, green foliage. Kat pruned away while I wandered by more lab tables with different species of plants and stacks of chemical jugs. Without noticing, I twisted my shirt around my finger tighter and tighter.

"No fire escape here," Kat said.

"Great," I said sarcastically. But something caught my eye. I recognized a word on a chemical jug. "Hey, look at this." I lead the girls to the label.

"What?" Sofia asked.

"Botanica," I read aloud.

"What's Botanica?" Kat asked.

"That's the weed killer company my Gram wrote to," I said. "They make Trimcut and all those different weed killers and fertilizers and things."

"Sure is a lot of it," Sofia said.

"Well, none of it is working." Kat gestured to a plant that sat in a bowl of orange liquid. Next to it, a half empty jug. "This guy is sitting in a tub of that junk, and he looks fine."

"Gross," Sofia said. "That does not look healthy."

"For plants or humans," I added.

"Yeah," Sofia said.

"Let's go," Kat said.

We moved down the hall and opened the next door. This room had lab tables and plants and stools and stuff and one more thing—no windows at all.

"Nothing," Kat said.

I could see her breath. "Why's this room so cold?" I asked.

"Who cares?" said Sofia.

I wondered how those plants could grow in freezing temperatures like that. I touched one and it seemed perfectly normal.

"You want us to leave you behind, dum-dum?"

"No, siree," I said, hurrying to the exit with the girls. That was the last thing I wanted. Kat shut the door behind us.

The last room was near the stairs that ran to the third floor. The stairwell was narrow and looked even darker than the main set of stairs. I peered up. I felt my heart beat faster. Keep cool, Pete, I thought. One more room to go. I was sure we'd find the fire escape. We wouldn't have to go up there. I hoped. I remembered my T-shirt—be Steve McQueen cool, Steve McQueen cool.

The third room was the same as the others at first glance, but it had what looked like small cylinder propane tanks with triggers pointing at the plants. We bunched around one plant and inspected the tank.

"What is this stuff?" Sofia asked.

"I guess they must spray the plants with it," I said.

"Let's see!" Kat grabbed the handle.

"Kat! Don't!" Sofia warned.

Kat did. She pulled back and whoosh! It wasn't a spray, but a small burst of flame. The tiny plant shuddered under the fire.

"Look what you did!" Sofia smacked Kat's shoulder. "You'll burn the whole place down."

The tiny plant was on fire!

"We have to put it out!" Sofia's eyes searched the room for a way.

"Wait," I said.

"What?" she asked.

"Look."

The flames slowly sizzled and poof! They went out. And nothing happened to the plant. Nothing! It was unburnt. It was green and healthy. We were stunned.

"Did you just see that?" Sofia asked.

"Indeed, I did."

"I'm doing it again." Kat pulled the trigger. The flames shot out. The leaves were on fire. Then in a few seconds, the flames went out with no lasting impression. We stared at each other.

"Wow," Kat said.

"Meta-Gro is growing fire-resistant plants?" I whispered. "And plants immune to weed killers. And plants that grow in ice-cold conditions. What is going on here?"

"I don't know, but I want to get out," Sofia said. "This must be the fire escape window." She went to the window and pulled aside the vines. "Get the pruners."

We followed Sofia's lead and started cutting and pulling. But as much as we cut, it didn't seem like we were getting any closer to the window. The leaves hurt my hands, too.

"How much is here?" Sofia moaned.

"The more we cut, the more there is." I tossed vines and leaves to the floor.

"Watch where you throw that, dum-dum," Kat said angrily. "You're tripping me. Ow!" Kat fell. "My feet are tangled!"

"Sorry, Kat!" I said. "Let me get your—whoa!" I tripped and hit the floor, too. From there, I saw a clump of weeds above Sofia. "Sofia!" I called. "Look out!"

The huge knot of weeds and vines dropped from the above the window on top of her. She fell on top of Kat and me. The three of us struggled on the ground. The more we fought it, the more we kept tying ourselves up.

"Get off!" Kat screamed.

"It won't!" I called back.

"No, Pete! You get off of me!"

"Sorry. I'm just trying to get out!"

"You're so heavy!"

"I've lost ten pounds since June!"

"Doesn't feel like it!"

"Stop moving!" Sofia yelled.

"I can't! It's around my neck!" I said.

"Me, too!" Kat said.

"Me, three!" Sofia said.

The more we kicked and pulled, the tighter the whole mess became.

"Help!" I called.

"Someone!" Sofia shouted.

"Help!" We all yelled desperately.

Even our faces were being covered by the weedy vines slowly growing over us like snakes. I squirmed and struggled, but somehow the vines twisted even tighter. I felt like I was in Raiders of Lost Ark, 1981, the weeds slithering everywhere like the deadly asps in the Well of Souls scene.

"I hate snakes, Jock! I hate 'em!" I barked out in my best Harrison Ford impression, quoting that famous movie line. Why? I don't know! I was freaking out!

"Snakes?!" Sofia panicked. "Where?"

"No, it's from a movie—grrk!" A thick vine was in my mouth now. I tried to spit it out. This was getting serious! Thorns punctured my skin! The weeds squeezed tighter and tighter!

Out of nowhere, a light came on, and we heard someone say: "Hold on! Hold on! I have you!" It was a man's voice. His figure loomed over us. Who was he? A Meta-Gro security guard? An evil gardener? A hideous plant-man ready to devour us?

His hands reached for us!

"Stay back!" I screamed. "I have a white belt with a yellow stripe in karate!"

Huge hands grabbed at the plants, and quickly the man untangled the whole knot.

"Easy does it. I have you. I have you," he said. We were free. "Everyone all right?"

"I'm all right," Kat said, out of breath from the struggle.

"Me too," Sofia nodded.

Maybe they were all right, but I was not. I'd almost been eaten by a plant!

"Hello," the man said. "I'm Dr. Lennox."

Chapter 33

Within a minute, the girls were standing. I was Karate Kamp-stancing and ready to unleash a deadly hammer fist on anything green that moved. I think it was called a 'hammer fist.' It had been a long time. Regardless, no plant was eating me without a fight!

"Pete, what are you doing?" Sofia asked.

"Um, we were almost eaten alive by plants, Sofia! Plants!"

"Calm down, dum-dum," Kat said. "They don't have teeth."

"Am I the only one freaking out, here?" I said, breathing heavy and scanning the plants for an attack.

"Yes," Kat said. "You should thank Dr. Lennox."

"You're perfectly safe now, young man," Dr. Lennox explained.

I took a gander at Dr. Lennox. My first impression was that he looked like a crazier version of Doc Brown from Back to the Future, 1985, if you can imagine that. They both had intense eyes and long wild hair sticking up all over the place.

"Come, come," he said dusting me off. "Let me help you. No harm done, I hope."

But the comparison ended there. Dr. Lennox's shaggy hair and bushy beard had not been trimmed in a long time, and his smudged glasses hadn't been wiped off in an even longer time. I didn't know how he could see through them. He was tall and thin and wore a wrinkled white lab coat that hung loosely on him. He leaned forward like a sunflower on a rainy day.

"I am dreadfully sorry for the deplorable conditions of this lab," he said.

The girls carried on a conversation with the doc, but I was still breathing heavy and trying to come to terms with being almost devoured by a daffodil!

Sofia apologized for sneaking into Meta-Gro.

Kat told him about the bet for the red bucket.

"Isn't that delightful?" Dr. Lennox laughed, but not in a surprised way.

I could've been the main course for a carnation!

"We have to go," Sofia said. "It's Bay Day, and people are expecting us."

"Of course, of course," Dr. Lennox said. "Bay Day. I remember. I believe I attended last summer. Expecting a big turnout, are you?"

"Maybe the biggest," Kat said, picking up the bucket.

I could have been a lily's lunch! A dandelion's dessert!

"The biggest crowd?" the doctor repeated. "Excellent, that is excellent for us. And you. I mean, the island, is it not? Just excellent, for business. All those people attending."

"Yeah, it's good for business," Kat sassed. "Especially since you Meta-Gro guys almost ruined the island!"

"Kat, don't be rude," Sofia scolded. "Right, Pete?"

"What?" I said, finally snapping out of the whole eaten-by-a-plant thing. "Um, sure, I guess you shouldn't be rude."

"No, no," Dr. Lennox said. "Of course, of course. I understand, young lady. It wasn't my plan. No, no. I did not want to shut things down. As you can see, we haven't given up. Not at all. It's those Meta-Gro people. Yes, of course, not us."

"Who else, Dr. Lennox?" I said, paying attention now.

"What's that you say, young man?"

"You said that we haven't given up," I repeated. "Is someone else working with you?"

"Did I say we?" the doctor asked.

"You did," Sofia said.

"I heard it, too," Kat agreed.

"Well, of course, I meant me, you see," Dr. Lennox apologized. "But I suppose a we might slip out occasionally because of the plants. The plants and I working together. We are a we, I suppose. Slip of the tongue. Wait a moment! Kat and Sofia? Is your father Mr. Jin?"

"Yeah," Kat answered.

"Oh, I remember him. A good man. Spoke of you girls often. I'm awfully sorry Meta-Gro pulled out. I had big plans for your father. Big plans, you know. And who is your friend here?"

"I'm Pete Mulligan," I said.

"Mulligan? How serendipitous? Your grandfather was a night watchman."

122

"You are correct," I nodded.

"How is he? He was sick, was he not?"

"He passed last year."

"Dreadfully sorry. Another good man lost. We need good people in this world. Not many good ones left. Your grandmother? Ah, the serendipity is wonderful. How is your grandmother?"

"Fine, I guess."

"Wonderful, then she'll see. Wonderful."

She'd see what? What did he mean? What was wonderful? I really wanted to go. Gram was right about this place. It gave me the heebie-jeebies.

"Have you been working here since the place closed?" Kat asked. "It's almost a year."

"I have," Dr. Lennox said proudly.

"How?" Sofia asked.

"Soldiering onward. Mustn't quit when you are on the cusp of something big."

"But what do you eat?" Kat wondered. "We've never seen you. No one has. Not in the grocery store. Anywhere. Everyone thinks this place is abandoned."

"Well, it is abandoned. Except for me. But I'm fine here," Dr. Lennox smiled. "I'm a vegetarian. I grow everything I need."

Vegetarian? Did that mean he only ate salads? I felt even more uncomfortable. Who in their right mind would eat salads for breakfast, lunch, and dinner? Gross.

"Why, my plants and I are doing quite well together. Quite well," Dr. Lennox said as he gestured to the various greenery near us. "I mean, you may think it strange for me to consider myself a partner with the plants, but do you know for how many thousands of years plants and humans have co-evolved together? We have been eating plants and making drinks from plants for millennia. We are much more similar than we are different."

Kat raised an eyebrow. "Really?"

"Guys, we should get going," I said, gesturing toward the door. "Ladies first."

Dr. Lennox ignored me. "Why, of course, of course. Did you know certain trees produce aspirin? Artemisia annua is used against malaria. Tea leaves cure diarrhea."

Which I almost dropped in my shorts when a plant tried to eat me!

"All these occur naturally: all you need is light, water, and fertile soil. Plants are our natural allies on this planet. Our natural allies. But not everyone feels this way." Dr. Lennox began climbing up the stairs. "Come with me. I'll show you! Come!"

I elbowed Sofia and looked at the stairs going down. She got my hint. "Kat, we should really get going," she said quietly. "Pete has to get back, remember?"

"Not until noon," Kat whispered back. "Come on, dum-dums, I want to see what these Meta-Gro jerks were doing. Five more minutes." She started up the stairs and called, "Right behind you, Doc!"

Sofia and I paused at the bottom of the stairs. We exchanged looks. Sofia shrugged. I couldn't abandon a friend. Reluctantly, we followed her to the third floor, stepping over weeds on the stairwell. Dr. Lennox had really let this place go.

We heard him above us, explaining to Kat, "You see, young lady, greed changed agriculture. That's what started it. Who wouldn't want plants to grow five times faster and in sterile soil? So, voila! Human scientists created synthetic fertilizers. But, in the rush to grow quickly, a plant cannot fully develop its own immune system. So, voila! Human scientists created pesticides and fungicides, chemicals to protect the farmer's investment. The chemicals protected the plants by killing disease and insects. But, as we have discovered, the chemicals affect humans, as well. It never would have happened if we'd let things stay natural, but oh no! Corporations want things fast and cheap. But fast and cheap is not nature's way!"

I noticed that, though tall, Dr. Lennox was very thin. We made it to the third floor. More lab tables and plants. Dr. Lennox ambled slowly between the workstations.

"Did you know that thousands of workers are killed by pesticides each year?" Dr. Lennox continued. "Scientific evidence may link birth defects and Parkinson's disease to pesticides. Can you imagine our own food, grown in our own country, giving us Parkinson's disease?"

"The government should do something about that," Kat said.

"Bah! The government doesn't care!" Dr. Lennox scoffed. "Corporations like Meta-Gro buy off the world's governments. They hire men like me to work on transgenic plants."

"Question, sir," I raised my hand.

"Are you raising your hand? Like school, eh? Delightful. What is your question?"

"What is a trans-pathetic plant?"

"Trans-genic, my boy. Transgenic. A transgenic plant is a plant that has been changed by altering its DNA. I have become very good at it, you see. We can improve our plants' nutritional quality, we can alter a plant to

124

make it resistant to insects, we can make it resistant to disease, we have even made crops that are resistant to weed killers."

Hmm. Like in those rooms downstairs. That little plant was probably growing in Trimcut weed killer.

"But unfortunately, or fortunately, depending how you look at it," Dr. Lennox continued, "there is always a risk of cross-fertilization."

"What do you mean?" Sofia asked. "Cross-fertilization with what?"

"Why, weeds, of course! Happens all the time. Accidents. Happy accidents, sometimes. You see, not only are the vegetables resistant to weed killers, so are the weeds. There are weeds resistant to all known weed killers. Some weeds, now out of control, are destroying whole ecosystems out there, whole islands, you see?"

"Islands?" Kat repeated.

"Mostly in the Pacific region. They're here, of course. Assembled right here."

"What?" Sofia said. "Who is here?"

Dr. Lennox gestured to different plants as we strolled by them. "See for yourself. The world's deadliest weeds. A rogue's gallery that would make any flower tremble: Mikania micrantha, 'the mile-a-minute vine,' destroying the Palau Islands in the South Pacific; the Asiatic tearthumb, untouchable without gloves due to the razor-sharp triangular leaves."

The girls and I exchanged looks. We had met Mr. Tear Thumb on the way in, and he hurt.

Dr. Lennox continued, "The leafy spurge, bamboo, Japanese knotweed, bindweed, the bitter dock—why, that one can survive in soil for a century. One plant produces 30,000 seeds! Amazing!"

"We should probably get going," Sofia interrupted.

"Of course, you should, of course. Bay Day is very crowded, I mean, will be very crowded. But don't you want me to tell you what Meta-Gro wanted me to grow?"

"I do," Kat said, winking at Sofia and me.

Sofia and I glared at her, but she did not get the hint. We followed her and the doctor to the far end of the room to a closed door. Dr. Lennox opened the door. It was his office. He walked in, and just as I was thinking, "Do not go in there, Kat!" Kat strolled in right behind him. I nudged Sofia. She knew I didn't want to enter. I noticed she seemed paler than usual. I bet she felt the same way.

Sofia whispered. "But we can't leave her alone with him." We followed them.

The room was bigger than I had thought it would be, with still more plants growing on every surface. A large desk in the corner was littered with papers, three laptops, and a small, potted rose bush. The doctor was already sitting behind his desk. He gestured at three empty stools pushed against the wall.

"Sit, my friends, sit," Dr. Lennox said.

I side-stepped toward the door, hoping Kat would get the hint, but she didn't. She pulled a stool over and plopped right down. Great.

Chapter 34

Sofia and I sat down next to her. I felt like we had reached the part in the movie when the villain revealed his evil plan. I knew my imagination was running away with me. But I couldn't shake the feeling that the good doctor wasn't so good.

"So?" Kat asked.

"A curious mind, just like your father. Wonderful. You see, Meta-Gro wanted seeds for vegetables. Super vegetables. Carrots, corn, and potatoes that would be immune to any R.E.D."

"What's an R.E.D.?" Kat interrupted.

"Random Environmental Disruptor—diseases, insects, temperature changes, infertile soil. Anything that would halt growth or production. And at the same time, Meta-Gro wanted to create the vegetable full of M.N.V., which, before you ask, young lady, stands for Maximum Nutritional Value. Imagine a single baked potato that contained an entire day's worth of protein! Canned corn that helps you grow taller! There's only one way to do that."

"How?" Kat asked.

"Genetically modify the plants."

"With what?" Sofia said.

"Human DNA."

Oh boy, that did not sound good. I said, "Excuse me, sir, I've seen a lot of movies, and I'm pretty sure that's one of those things science isn't supposed to tamper with."

"Not at all, Peter Mulligan. Not at all. It's being done. And companies don't even need to report doing so," Dr. Lennox said as he pulled the potted rose bush closer. "Fish DNA in tomatoes. Human DNA in rice. But for Meta-Gro, to get both the R.E.D. and the M.N.V.—the perfect cost-effective, engineered food that would make Meta-Gro billions—I had the brilliant idea of first splicing the DNA of fruits and vegetables with the most pernicious, indestructible weeds we could find on the earth."

"Is that why you are here?" I wondered. "Johnson Island's johnsongrass?"

"Why, yes, Peter, yes! Very good." Dr. Lennox complimented me as he pulled dead leaves from the rose bush. "This island is well known in the weed community. That is why we chose it."

Weed community? Where did I hear—Jeez Louise! Could it have been Gram's letter? That's why Meta-Gro came here?

"But also, your island's history in the bay," Dr. Lennox continued. "We used your aptly named island's famous weed as the genetic base, you see? And we've gone a little mad, I suppose. I mean, I have, I must confess." He shuffled papers and found a pair of clippers. He roughly snipped a beautiful red rose from the bush. "We started with the weed first. We created a perfect specimen and then combined it with the vegetable seeds already modified with human DNA. That led to my most brilliant discovery: how all plants communicate with each other."

"How do they communicate with each other?" Kat asked. "Do they talk? Use telepathy?"

"My, you are a wonderfully curious girl." He smiled at Kat. "They communicate on a bio-molecular level once they've shared genetic information, you see? Other scientists realized a dodder, a parasitic plant, was exchanging information with its host plant, a sugar beet. But they weren't exactly sure how the plants were communicating, but I…I alone have figured it out."

Dr. Lennox plucked a red petal from the rose and dropped it on his desk. He paused. For dramatic effect I supposed, but none of us knew what to ask next. "Do you want to know what the dodder plant was telling its host?"

We nodded.

He ripped off another petal. "It was telling the beet to lower its defenses. It was controlling it. It was taking it over."

"Like mind control?" I asked.

"Precisely, in its way. Isn't that amazing?"

"Not for the beet plant," Sofia said.

"Possibly," Dr. Lennox said. "But I am not so sure. You see, I believe that plants are far superior to humans and animals. They were here before us, and they will be here long after we make the earth uninhabitable due to our greed and violence. And in the plant world, it is the weed, the glorious weed, invader and ultimate survivor, that is the most superior."

As he spoke, he ripped more red petals from the rose that pooled on his desk like blood. "Unfortunately, a side effect of our DNA tampering was that we made them even more powerful. More powerful, in fact, than us. And we can't stop them."

"Can't science undo things?" Kat asked.

"Not this," Dr. Lennox said. "Oh no, not this. What's done is done, and what will be, will be, of course. You can't stop a boulder once it's rolling down a hill. I didn't push the boulder. No, not me. I'm just going along for the ride."

Sofia tapped my knee. "We should go," she whispered.

"Agreed," I answered.

She tapped Kat. "I know. I got it," Kat winked.

Dr. Lennox continued talking and shredding that poor rose. "For if there is one thing science has taught us, it is this: evolution is inevitable. Case in point, the dinosaurs."

"Well, I think we'll be going," Kat said, picking up the red bucket.

Dr. Lennox ignored her. "We must choose. Those not evolving into something new will be left behind, of course." He rubbed his hands together. Nothing was left of the rose.

We stood.

"We'll show ourselves out," Sofia said.

"To be on the edge of the cutting edge!" he ranted. "That is the key, you see!" He swept the red petals off the desk and onto the floor.

We took a step backward. "Thanks for the tour," I waved.

"Goodbye," Kat said as we slowly put our stools where we found them.

"The only way to survive is to adapt, and the only way to adapt is to combine and— Goodbye?" His rant ceased. "Where are you going?"

"We're leaving," Sofia said.

"Leaving? Oh, I'm afraid you can't leave," he said. "Not just yet."

Suddenly, the weeds, the plants, the greenery everywhere in the office, except the rose bush, began moving, uncoiling, unwinding, growing larger and larger.

"Jeez Louise!" I said.

"Go!" Kat shouted.

We turned to the office door, but vines had already covered it. Kat pulled. Sofia pulled. I pulled.

"You can't leave!" Dr. Lennox shouted from behind his desk. "We need your help!"

Finally, with all of us tugging, the vines snapped, and the door flew open.

"Go! Go! Go!" Sofia said.

We ran!

"Wait!" Kat stopped. "The bucket! I put it down to open the door!"

"Forget it!" Sofia ordered.

"But the bet!"

Sofia grabbed Kat's arm. "You're not going back!"

"But—"

"Shut up and run, dum-dum!" Sofia yelled.

She didn't have to tell me twice.

Chapter 35

Green vines stretched along the floor behind us like snakes as we sprinted through the lab. We could see Dr. Lennox standing in his office door watching with his arms outstretched.

"You can't go! Not yet!" he yelled, pointing in our direction. "We have work to do!"

Then, it hit me. The way he was pointing. The way he said we have work to do. "Oh my gosh!" I said. "I think he's controlling the plants."

"What?" Sofia asked.

"Are you crazy?" Kat said.

"Look at them!" The weeds were slowly growing, spilling out of their containers on the lab tables, creeping toward us, not as fast as we were running, but quickly enough. "See, they're following us!"

"You're right, dum-dum!"

"So was Tim Meeks," Sofia added. "It's just like he said. Something really weird happened here."

"Yeah, Dr. Lennox happened," I said.

We ran past Dr. Lennox's 'most-wanted' deadly weeds. Suddenly, I yelped as I felt something sharp pierce my ankle. I put my hand down and it came away wet and sticky; I looked down and felt my stomach drop. Blood. Turning back, I noticed the mile-a-minute weed had stretched out, its sharp thorns dripping red.

"Jeez Louise!" I blurted. "Sofia! Kat! I can't run. The mile-a-minute's got my leg!"

Kat spun around. She knelt by my ankle and whipped out her pruners. "Don't move!"

"That won't be a problem."

"Watch out!" Sofia shouted. More mile-a-minutes floated over us like cobras ready to strike. Sofia swatted at them with her pruner, fending off the evil weeds while Kat cut me loose.

"There," Kat said. "You're good. Let's go!"

"Thanks."

"Move!" Sofia hollered. We took off across the room. Sofia stopped at the top of the third-floor stairs. She waved us past her and slammed the door. We raced down the stairs, stumbling over more weeds. We made it to the second-floor hallway. Downstairs was out—the front door stuck. The three rooms stood before us.

"Which way? Which room?" Sofia asked. "The fire one?"

"We don't know anything about the ice one," I said.

"What about the weed killer room? The first one?" Kat said.

"I see we're all in agreement," I said sarcastically. "Which room had the window?"

"Forget it!" Sofia decided. "There!" She pointed to a ladder, almost hidden by shadows, that ran up the corner. "I'll bet it goes to the roof."

"The roof?" Kat asked. "Then what?"

"We'll worry about that later," Sofia answered.

"What about the window room?" I asked.

"We already know the weeds are blocking it," Sofia said. "That's why they tightened around us so fast. We didn't tangle ourselves up, they were choking us. Remember when Dr. Lennox came in? He didn't untie us, like we thought. I'll bet he told the weeds to let go! That room's a dead end!"

The door flew open at the stop of the stairs. "Wait!" The doctor called from the top step. "Young Peter! Sofia! Kat! Wait! You can't go! I won't hurt you."

"Well?" Sofia said.

"The roof!" Kat decided.

"I don't think it's a good idea." I hesitated.

"Are you afraid of heights, Pete?" Sofia asked.

"A little. Well, maybe more than a little!"

"Go, dum-dum!" Kat shoved me into the ladder. "Climb! Hurry!"

"Okay! Okay!" I climbed. Sofia pushed behind me, and Kat was behind her. Up we went. Hand over hand. One rung at a time. I could do this. I could do this. Why were my hands so sweaty? "Ow!" I yelled. "What the—?"

Something pointy and sharp hit me!

"Ouch!" Kat shrieked. "That hurt!"

It had hit Kat, too.

Stupid weeds! They were shooting burrs at us. Those sticker ball things that get stuck on your socks when you run through a field, but these were bigger, like golf balls, and sharper and flew with enough force to cut us. How many could hit me before I lost too much blood? I didn't want to find out. I climbed as fast as I could and got to the top of the ladder.

"There's a handle," I called down, my voice cracking.

"Turn it!" said Sofia.

"Hurry!" Kat yelled.

At this point, Kat, furthest down the ladder, was fighting for her life. One hand gripped a rung, while her legs kicked, preventing the vines from latching on to her feet. I turned the handle. The door opened with a creak—blinding sunlight. My eyes adjusted, and I climbed onto the roof.

I reached down and grabbed Sofia. We turned back for Kat. But the plants had a solid grip on her. We each held one of her arms and pulled. We kept her from moving any lower. Slowly the weeds began to win this tug-of-war, yanking her further down the ladder.

"They're too strong!" Kat said.

"Kat! No!" Sofia screamed.

"Come on, Kat!" I yelled. I pulled with all my might. I couldn't let her go! I wouldn't! Who knew what the crazy doctor would do to her?

"Shut the hatch!" Kat said.

"No," said Sofia. "Fight it!"

"Go for help. It's too much. He's got me!"

"No!" Sofia said. "We won't leave you!"

"You have to!"

"Fight it, Kat!" I gasped, straining to hold on but feeling her slip. She was crazy. We couldn't shut the hatch! We couldn't leave Kat behind. Sahara, 1943, Humphrey Bogart didn't leave anyone behind in the desert! But we were losing. This was terrible! "Kick! Please!"

"Let go of me and shut it!" Kat ordered.

"No!" Sofia cried.

"Don't listen to Sofia! Shut it, Pete! Go get help!"

Sofia shook her head at me. "Don't you dare listen to her, Pete Mulligan! Pull!"

"Get help! Do it, dum-dum! You have to do it! Sofia won't!"

This was impossible! If I let Kat go, Sofia would kill me. If we held on and we all went down, who'd save us? No one! Then, I saw a mile-a-minute vine creeping toward Sofia!

"Do it, Pete!" Kat begged.

Jeez Louise! Kat was right. I let her go. She was pulled from us. She screamed.

"Kat!" Sofia screamed back.

On my knees, I looked down the ladder. The last thing I saw was Kat's face, covered in green leaves and vines, except for her eyes desperately looking up.

Then, I slammed the hatch.

And locked it.

Chapter 36

I fell backward. Sofia was next to me, mouth wide open.

I couldn't believe I did that! Tears stung my eyes. I covered my face so Sofia wouldn't see. Dr. Lennox had Kat! He had her! And it was my fault.

Sofia shoved me. "Are you crazy? Why did you let her go?"

"We had to!" I said. "Do you think I wanted to? More vines were coming!"

"She's my sister! Get out of the way. We have to open it!"

"We can't," I said, pulling my hands away from my eyes and grabbing Sofia's arm. "They'll come up. Dr. Lennox will get us, too. You heard her, Sofia. The only way to save Kat is to get help!"

Sofia saw my tears. She shook her head. She pulled my hand off her arm. "You're right." She stood up. "I hate it. But you're right." She cupped her hands around her mouth and screamed "Help!"

I wiped my eyes. None of this was supposed to happen. It was supposed to be simple—grab the bucket, win the bet, meet my parents. A mad scientist? Killer weeds? Kat captured? Not part of the plan! Gram warned me about this place. Why didn't I listen?

Sofia hurried to the edge of the roof, which was slightly sloped, almost flat. She screamed toward Westway and the town: "Someone! Help! Help!"

I stood and joined her. "Help us!" I yelled at the top of my lungs. It wasn't working. We couldn't even see Westway. The bamboo towered over the roof by at least ten feet. A strong breeze rattled the stalks, too, causing that howling noise.

"No one can hear us, Pete. No one," Sofia said, defeated.

"I know. What now?"

"We have to save Kat!"

"Of course. How?" I asked.

"We get back to town and we do it fast," Sofia said. "We can't open the hatch. We're too high to jump. Let's look for that fire escape."

We each checked different edges of the building. Surprisingly, it wasn't that hard to walk on the roof. And with the bamboo blocking everything, it didn't feel that high. Along the edge, I was a little more cautious. I peered down. Jeez Louise!

"Found it!" I called across the roof. "But there's a small problem."

"Your scared-of-heights thing?" she asked, coming toward me.

"Well, sort of. But that's not the problem."

"What?" Sofia leaned over. The fire escape was already covered in creeping green weeds. "Okay, that's out," she said in frustration. The weeds opened their leaves and shot a few burrs.

I shielded my face. A small sticker bounced off my forearm. "I hate those things."

"Think, Pete. What else?" Sofia asked.

"I don't know."

"There's got to be—" Her eyes rested on my backpack. "Your supplies!"

"Oh yeah," I said. "The rope!"

I ripped off my backpack, unzipped it, and took out the rope. "We can climb down," I said. My heist supplies were paying off again. "Where should we tie this?"

"Forget it," Sofia said, kneeling near the edge of the roof.

"Why?"

"Come see."

I scrambled over to her and peered down. Mile-a-minute weeds slithered everywhere below us. Some were slowly creeping up the sides.

"Jeez Louise!" I said, returning the rope to my backpack.

"Humph," Sofia grunted.

"I think we're trapped," I said. "Even if we climb down, we'll never make it back to the hole in the fence. Those things will swallow us up in a second."

"I know, I know," Sofia mumbled.

We searched for a way to escape. From up here, even though it was overgrown like a jungle, the whole layout of the Meta-Gro property made more sense. Our building was in the center of a large fenced-in area that ran from Westway to the water. Surrounding this main building were sectioned off, mini-test gardens, where Dr. Lennox must grow his super seeds.

A simple shed stood near each garden. I counted about fifteen. The sheds ran all the way to the edge of the fence near the dock. Beyond it, the blue bay sparkled. A strong breeze rattled the bamboo.

We were trapped.

"Too bad we're not ancient Chinese warriors from Crouching Tiger, Hidden Dragon, 2000, am I right?" I said.

"What?" Sofia asked.

"You never saw that movie? They have an amazing fight in a bamboo forest, jumping from tree to tree. So good! It was nominated for ten Oscars. It won four and—"

"You're not helping."

"Sorry," I mindlessly twisted my shirt around my finger. I was out of ideas. "Should we surrender? Dr. Lennox said he wouldn't hurt us."

"Are you nuts? No way! We have to think of something."

"I'm trying."

"Are you? With all your Crouching Dragon, bamboo forest, mumbo jumbo?"

"It's Crouching Tiger—ouch!" A sharp burr hit my calf. I turned. The green weeds from the fire escape inched toward us across the roof like lava oozing from a volcano.

"Wait! That's it!" Sofia said. "Pete Mulligan, you beautiful movie maniac! You gave me an idea!" She reached over the side of the roof, where more weeds were slithering up, and grabbed a thick bamboo stalk. She bent it and took two steps back.

"Yup," she muttered to herself. "Pretty bendable. This will do."

"Do what?"

"I'm going to bend back this piece of bamboo, hold on to it, jump off this roof and sort of pole vault to that shed down there. Just like in your movie! And you are, too. I hope."

"What?!" A shed stood about twenty feet away. If the bamboo didn't snap, or we didn't fall off, maybe it would bend over and we could drop onto the shed roof. If this was Crouching Tiger, Hidden Dragon, 2000, that was! Which it wasn't!

"Are you insane! That's your plan? Pole-vaulting?! We'll never make it to that shed, not in a million—ouch!" A sticker ball hit the back of my neck.

"You have a better idea?"

"Yes. Anything."

"Well?"

I thought. "I got nothing—ouch!" A full-scale burr bombardment began.

"See there?" She pointed. "The way the sheds are set up? We can use the bamboo and go from, shed to shed right over the fence. We'll go from this one, to that one, to that one."

"There's no way. I can't do that."

"Pick a thick stalk," she ordered.

"I'll never be able to hold on."

"You have to."

"I can't."

"You can. Come on, don't be a dum-dum now!"

"I weigh a lot more than you, Sofia. I'm not strong enough."

"You are."

"You know in gym, when you have to climb that rope, I couldn't even—"

"Stop it!" she cut me off. "You're not the same chubby wimp I pushed into the bay back in June. You're not that kid anymore. You can do this, Pete! You have to. For Kat."

I considered this. I wasn't crazy about being called chubby, but wimp was spot-on. I wanted to believe Sofia was right. I wanted to be that kid. I glanced down at my T-shirt. Steve McQueen stared back at me. Jeez Louise! I picked an extra thick stalk of bamboo.

"This is crazy," I said.

"Pull it back like this," she demonstrated.

"Okay." I held the bamboo and took about five steps backward.

"On three. Get a running start. Hang on. When it curves over the shed let go, okay? Don't miss the shed."

"Oh boy…" This was happening way too fast.

"One. Two. Three. Go!"

Chapter 37

I held that stalk tighter than I had held that desk at Stone Hill Elementary School all those months before. My legs flailed. My arms slipped. The bamboo bent over the shed. It was now or never. I let go!

I landed with a crash and tumbled so hard, if Sofia hadn't grabbed my backpack, I'd have rolled right off the edge of the roof. But, by God, somehow, I made it.

"I did it! I did it! Just like Steve McQueen!"

"Who?" Sofia asked.

"Steve McQueen," I explained. "He's an actor from the sixties and seventies. His best movie is—"

"Not now, Pete! We have to move. Look."

From below, green mile-a-minute weeds slithered quickly toward the shed.

"Oh, right— Ouch!"

From above, more sticker balls shot down at us from the roof.

"These things just don't give up," I said.

"And neither will we," Sofia said.

We each picked another piece of bamboo, bent it back, and jumped. This was less terrifying because the sheds were closer and there was no height drop of two stories this time. Sofia landed on her feet. I landed on my knees, which resulted in a red, scraped-up mess. I rose and grabbed the next bamboo stalk, tested it, pulled it back, and we flung ourselves forward. Again, we made it. It was a good thing the bamboo was thick and strong. Her plan was working.

"You okay?" Sofia asked.

"I'll live."

"There's the fence, Pete."

It looked awfully high.

"Pull way back this time. We have to clear it," Sofia said.

I did as Sofia suggested and pulled the bamboo as far back as I could. I ran and jumped with one last mighty heave. Unbelievably, I flew over the fence at Sofia's side. When Sofia's stalk curved near the ground, she let go—a graceful landing.

Me, not so much. I let go too late, smashed into the dock, and rolled into the water. I went under. It was deep. I panicked and felt like I was sinking. After all those lessons! No!

I kicked up. I cupped my hands. I remembered to make smooth strokes—actually, that's a lie. My strokes were fast and full of desperation! But they worked! I broke the surface. Air! I treaded water for a few seconds. I couldn't believe it! I was treading water. I kicked and swam to the dock in just a few strokes! I was swimming!

I heard Sofia screaming my name. I was touched that she was so concerned about me. I climbed up the dockside ladder trying to think of something charming to say when I realized she wasn't screaming because she was worried. The weeds had her arms and legs pinned to the chain-link fence. And they were slowly lifting her up and over.

"Pete! Help!"

Soaking wet, I ran to her and grabbed her feet. Being chubby paid off. I used my weight to pull Sofia to the ground. The weedy vines surrounded both of us, but I tore and ripped. To my surprise, it worked. We were free long enough for me to drag Sofia to the dock. The defeated vines retreated inside the fence.

"Thanks," Sofia said, out of breath.

"Yeah," I replied, equally out of breath.

"You saved me."

"Yeah," I said. "Same thing."

"What do you mean?"

"You saved me, too."

"How?"

"The lessons. I swam. Maybe six feet, to the dock. Or is it swum?"

"For real? You swam. That's great!" Sofia grinned.

"Yeah, I swam. Or did I swum? Do you remember from school? Is it swim-swam-swum, like run-ran-run? I don't know."

"You swam, you swum! Who cares? You did it!"

"I know," I beamed proudly. "I can swim."

"I can't wait to tell Kat!"

With the mention of her name, our smiles faded. "Let's go," I said.

140

The weeds followed us along the fence as we ran. Occasionally, they would reach out with a sharp tendril. Whenever a weed came too close, I stomped on it with my soggy sneaker, which was surprisingly effective. We made it back to our bikes. Seeing the third bike reminded us of Kat. My gut sank thinking of her in the clutches of the diabolical Dr. Lennox.

"We have to hurry," Sofia said, as if reading my mind.

We biked as fast as our beat-up bodies could pedal us. I pondered our situation and still couldn't really believe it. An insane doctor was controlling super weeds. We still weren't sure why, and the weeds he created were deadly and amazing. Without even realizing it, I was chewing on my shirt collar. This was a new nervous tic. Mr. McQueen would not be happy. Betcha those weeds never got nervous.

"I know this is crazy, Sofia. But I sort of admire those weeds."

"Why?" Sofia said, shocked. "They were trying to kill us."

"Consider them," I said, finally spitting the wet shirt from my mouth. "They grow anywhere. They're not afraid of weed killer. Or bugs. Or us. Or anything. I'm always afraid. They adapt, too, like Dr. Lennox said. They evolve to survive. I wish I was like that. I never adapt. I get upset or cry."

"Stop your bike, Pete."

I did. Sofia stopped hers.

"What?" I said. "Why'd we stop?"

"Pete?"

"Yeah?"

Slap! Sofia's open palm smacked my face. Hard, too. It was completely unexpected.

"Ow!" I rubbed my cheek. "What was that for?"

"Listen, you, idiot! Don't admire his weeds. They're sneaky. They're invaders. They destroy things, things trying to grow, innocent things like flowers. They're bullies, Pete Mulligan, bullies! Don't wish to be like them. You're fine just how you are, okay?"

"Okay," I said. "Let's go save Kat."

Chapter 38

From the looks of the sky, it was way past lunch time. I'd been so preoccupied with running for my life, I hadn't even felt hungry. Not wanting to waste any time, we took the shortcut back across Up'ards Bridge near the large marina lot. Big mistake. The lot was full of golf carts, bikes, and mopeds. Beyond that, it was packed with people straight down Broadway, the way we needed to go.

It was insane to think we had barely escaped a mad scientist, Kat was still trapped at Meta-Gro, and yet everyone else on Johnson Island was having a good time. We walked our bikes as quick as we could, weaving in and out of the crowd. Strangely enough, no one said a word about our frazzled looks. No one cared, the place was wall-to-wall excitement! Bay Day was in full swing.

Bluegrass music twanged from a band on a small stage. The smell of fried foods—french fries, onion rings, fried oysters and chicken—hung in the air. My stomach rumbled. Didn't it know far more pressing matters were at stake? At a table, tourists sucked the meat out of crab legs, which boiled in big pots. I heard rings clinking around old Coke bottles at the ring-toss game. A group cheered near a dunk tank as the victim splashed down in the water. A pink balloon bumped into my head. Folks laughed and talked. I had missed the arrival of my parents' ferry. I banged my bike into the back of someone's legs.

"Sorry," I called over the noise. The man turned. It was Mayor Ooger.

"Whoa!" he said. "Slow down, you two. Don't kill the tourists. We need them."

"Ooger, we need you!" Sofia said.

"We need help!" I added. "Now!"

"Where's the fire? What's going on?" Ooger said in his slow waterman talk.

Sofia rapidly explained what had happened at Meta-Gro. Ooger listened, giving us the typical island head nod and humph and mm-hmm, but his eyes, which you couldn't completely make out from behind his sunglasses, didn't seem like they were fully paying attention to us.

Sofia grabbed his hand and pulled him. "We have to go! Now!"

"I'm sorry," he said. "But it'll have to wait. Bay Day is going on. And I'm in charge. You know how much money the island will make today? Every bayman, including me, counts on it. We'll do it tomorrow or Monday."

"Tomorrow or Monday?" Sofia repeated. "This is my sister, Ooger!"

"Did you not hear the term 'mad scientist,' sir?" I added.

Without another word, the mayor called to someone in the crowd and walked away. Did that just happen? He had seemed like such a nice guy. Sofia shook her head and took off. I jogged to catch up to her. She walked her bike and squeezed her way through the crowd, back down Broadway to our houses. On our way, we ran into more of our adult friends.

We told our tale to Reverend Apple, whose Fellowship meeting after church started the whole darn bet with Tim Meeks and put Kat in the clutches of a madman. I thought at least she would help. But she patted Sofia on the shoulder and said, "I am going to say a special prayer and thank God for your amazing imaginations."

We found the Crocketts at the Bay Breeze booth, where they were selling their homemade chocolate chip cookies. We cut the line, and before we could mention one thing about Meta-Gro, they told us that if we were not buying cookies we had to get out of the line.

Even the kind New York City artist lady listened to us with only half an ear, while keeping an eye on the paintings she was selling. When we finished, she just took Sofia's hand and said, "I'm sure your sister will turn up. Probably met a boy or something."

Flabbergasted. Shocked. Exhausted. Hungry, at least I was. We half-jogged, half-walked our bikes as fast as we could to Gram's house, which was closer than the Jin house. We knew someone here would care. We flung open the front gate. We dropped our bikes and ran up the path. We climbed the stairs and crossed the porch. We ripped open the screen door.

"Gram!" I yelled. "We need your help. We're in trouble!"

"How could my buddy be in trouble?"

Jeez Louise! That was my dad's voice. He stepped from the kitchen into the living room. "Dad?" He wasn't the only one.

143

"Not our Peter. He's a good boy."

"Mom?"

"He's a fine young man, as far as I'm concerned, who will someday reach his potential."

"Dr. Carlos?!"

"Who looks so handsome with his island tan."

"Miss Nunzio?!"

"And shredded! Dude, you must've lost twenty pounds!"

"Chad?!"

"Surprise!" They all said.

"This is the surprise?" I asked Gram.

"Yes," Gram said. "It is."

"Your grandmother told us you were doing so well," Mom said. "We wanted the whole A-Team to see you!"

And there they were, all staring at me. The A-Team, on Johnson Island, looking odd to me in their summer outfits: Dr. Carlos in a pink golf shirt, Miss Nunzio in a flower-print summer dress, and Chad sporting a neon yellow tank-top, neon-yellow spandex shorts, and flip-flops.

"It's great, right?" Dad asked.

"Say hello to everyone, Peter," my mom said.

"Um... hello, everyone," I managed to get out. They all greeted me with vigorous head nods and smiles.

"Are you surprised?" my dad asked.

"Astonished, actually," I answered.

"Hey!" Sofia yelled loudly. The assembled guests gave her their full attention. "Kat remember?!"

"Oh yeah, right. We can catch up later," I said. "You have to help us rescue Kat. Now!"

"Rescue her?" Gram said. "She's looking for you."

"What?" Sofia gasped.

"Sure," Gram explained. "She came by, oh, I don't know, about ten minutes ago."

"Impossible," I said.

"She did, Pete," Gram said. "She knocked on the door. Asked for you two. I said you weren't here. She said that she'd go down to Bay Day to find you."

"I don't believe it," Sofia said.

"It's true," my dad said. "We were all here when she came in."

"Didn't you see her bike?" Gram asked.

"No. Where?" Sofia demanded.

144

"In the backyard," Gram said.

Sofia pushed her way through my parents and the A-Team and out the back door. I quickly followed her. We both stood frozen. Gram was right. Kat's bike. It was there.

"This doesn't make any sense," Sofia said.

"Why?" Gram said from the back door. The group of adults craned around her to see us.

"We were..." Sofia started.

"I mean we..." I thought aloud, biting my thumbnail.

"Did something happen?" Gram asked. "Is that why your shirt's wet, Pete? You go in the dunk tank, up there?"

"What? Wet?" I stuttered, still trying to process Kat's bike. "Dunk tank? No, I fell in the bay and was swimming because—"

"Oh, Peter!" my mom interrupted me. "You can swim? You learned to swim? For real?"

"Yes, Sofia and Kat taught me. But Kat is—"

"That's great, pal," Dad said.

"Very athletic," Chad said.

"Very therapeutic," Dr. Carlos said.

"Very healthy. Swimmers are in great shape," Miss Nunzio said.

Everyone nodded and agreed with each other. What was happening here? I glanced at Sofia, who looked equally perplexed. Why wouldn't anyone let us tell the story about Kat and Dr. Lennox?

"Hey, buddy, let's all go and enjoy Bay Day," my dad suggested.

"Yes, let's enjoy Bay Day," Mom agreed.

"I would love a soft-shell crab sandwich," Gram said.

"That sounds good," said Miss Nunzio. "I've never had a soft-shell crab sandwich."

"I would like a soft-shell crab sandwich, as well," Dr. Carlos said.

"I'm skipping the healthy stuff and having a soft-shell crab sandwich, too," Chad said.

"Would you like a soft-shell crab sandwich, Sofia?" asked Dad.

"We can buy you a soft-shell crab sandwich," my mom said, smiling.

The whole group came toward us, nodding and once again agreeing with each other, and Sofia and I were swept up in the group as it moved toward the front gate when Sofia screamed, "Wait!" Everyone froze and stared at her. "What about my sister?!"

"Here I am." And to my utter disbelief, Kat strolled casually around the corner of the house. "Who wouldn't love a soft-shell crab sandwich? I know I would. I'm starving."

Chapter 39

Sofia ran to Kat and hugged her. I stood awkwardly next to them.

Sofia gestured for me to enter the group and hug as well. The adults let out a collective "Aw!" They seemed pleased at Kat's arrival. They spoke so quickly and on top of each other I couldn't tell who said what.

"How cute."

"Yes."

"Oh, yes."

"So cute."

"The cutest."

"Yes."

"Oh, yes."

Then, it abruptly stopped. The silent adults stared at us, their eyes blinking slowly.

"How'd you get out?" Sofia asked her sister.

"It was easy," Kat said. "He brought me up to his office. We talked a little more, and that was it. He let me go."

"I don't believe it," Sofia said.

"It's true. He even walked me to the gate and unlocked it."

"Question" I raised my hand. "What about all the plants?"

"Look, I'll tell you the whole thing after I eat," Kat said, smacking my shoulder. "Okay, dummy? I got such a gnawing. Should've had a bigger breakfast."

Did she just say that? Impossible!

"Let's go to Bay Day!" my dad suggested.

"Yeah," agreed Kat. "Let's get a soft-shell crab sandwich!"

The pack of adults chimed in quickly, talking again in that sing-song way over top of each other.

"Yes."

"Delicious."

"Mmm."

"A soft-shell."

"Crab sandwich."

"I can't wait."

"Yes."

Jeez Louise! What was with this overly-enthusiastic sandwich thing?

Everyone began marching in a group to the front gate, even Kat. Sofia grabbed her arm. "Kat, wait."

"Seriously, I'll tell you everything that happened," Kat said, pulling away. "But I want to eat first. I'm really starving."

"That's good," Gram said, putting her arm around Kat's shoulder. "You know what's great when you're starving?"

Oh boy, not again.

"A soft-shell crab sandwich!" Kat and the adults said in unison.

"With tartar sauce," Kat tagged on.

"With tartar sauce!" the adults agreed together.

"Come on, guys," Kat said. "Let's go."

"Let's go!" the adults repeated.

Gram led Kat out the front gate. The adults walked through next, followed by Sofia. I was the last one to leave the yard, and as I shut the gate, I noticed Gram's flower bed. In the spot where I had weeded just a day before—bright green shoots were popping up. Funny? Those weeds never looked that green. Just as I bent down to investigate, Sofia called me.

"Come on, Pete!"

The adults and Kat encouraged me in unison: "Come on, Pete!"

"Coming!" I caught up to Sofia. We stayed a step or two behind everyone else.

"They're all acting so weird," Sofia whispered. "What is going on?"

"I have no idea," I said. "Kat, too. She even called me a dummy."

"So what? Kat calls you that every day."

"Oh, no. That's not true. She's never called me that. Never. It's dum-dum. When you've been called it about a thousand times, it makes an—"

Sofia shushed me. The adults were staring and blinking at the two of us. We smiled at them awkwardly. They smiled back.

"Let's go," my dad said.

"Let's go!" the adults and Kat repeated.

"Okay," I said.

Our stroll down Broadway became more and more crowded with

147

visitors and islanders. When Kat and the adults were busy exchanging greetings with everyone, Sofia and I had another chance to sort this out.

"You know what else is weird?" Sofia said. "Not one person has mentioned how hucky we are."

"Hucky?" I asked.

"Yeah, hucky, like smelly, gross. How we look, disgusting."

It was true. We did look bad, especially me—cuts, dry blood, mud. I sniffed my Blob shirt. "You're right. I stink. It's the bay water."

"Me, too," Sofia said. "Did you know all those people were coming to visit you?"

"No, it was a surprise. Gram told me my parents were planning something, but I thought it was going to be taking me home."

"Home?" Sofia asked.

"That's what I thought. Home early."

"Off the island?"

"Unfortunately."

"I thought you would stay on the island now, after this summer. Would you want to? Stay here, with Gram Mulligan and Kat and me?"

I didn't speak. I didn't know what to say. I knew that I didn't want to leave until the summer was over. But stay here? All the time? Live here? I hadn't thought about it. I knew that I didn't like the thought of not seeing Kat... and Sofia.

"Well?" Sofia asked. She suddenly seemed mad at me for some reason.

"Come on, you two!" Kat called back.

"Yes, come on, you two!" the whole adult group repeated at the same time.

That ended our conversation. The group stopped marching and silently waited for us to catch up. When we reached them, they circled us and somehow wormed their way between Sofia and me. Our group joined another larger group of Bay Day visitors.

Everyone around us was occupied enjoying the festivities. In front of the small stage, old people danced—not pretty. A line of kids waited for face-painting. Craft booths sold hand-made island Christmas tree decorations, like lighthouses or crab traps decorated with red bows. Crammed around folding tables, people ate fresh seafood and drank root beer. It seemed normal, but something was off. It was different than the first time we had come through. People were greeting each other over and over again by saying "Happy Bay Day!" I heard that phrase constantly. "Happy Bay Day!"

"Happy Bay Day to you!"

"Happy Bay Day to you!"

The more I concentrated, the more I felt like that phrase was the only thing I heard. My eyes met with Sofia after she had just returned the same "Happy Bay Day!" greeting to an old lady. We both knew something was up. Kat was avoiding us. When we tried to catch up to her, the adults got in our way, or Kat moved faster. Once, just as I reached her, I felt a hand on my shoulder stop me. It was Dad.

He called to our group, "Hey, gang, here it is." He pointed to a food stand sign and said, "Soft-shell crab sandwiches! Terrific!"

Kat, Gram, Mom, and the A-Team repeated, "Soft-shell crab sandwiches! Terrific!"

That wasn't the word I would use.

'Weird' was more like it.

Chapter 40

As we sat at a table eating, Sofia and I tried as hard as we could to get someone, anyone to listen to us. We could not convince one adult that we should be calling the New Jersey State Police or the Coast Guard or the United States Navy. Not one person wanted to storm Meta-Gro with pitchforks and weed killer. Nobody thought anything crazy was going on— just Sofia and myself. And we tried. We really tried. But Kat was back, and the lack of needing to rescue her seemed to make everyone feel nothing else was wrong.

The adults and Kat sat and listened to us and smiled and continued eating their stupid soft-shell crab sandwiches! And they surrounded Kat. We couldn't get anywhere near her.

Sofia nudged me. "The second she gets up to throw out that paper plate, we grab her and run. Got it?"

I winked at her. "I most certainly got it." We waited. She finished eating.

"Get ready," Sofia said.

Kat started to rise. Then, the music stopped. Folks politely applauded, and Mayor Ooger took the stage. Kat sat back down.

"Crud buckets," Sofia said to me.

Ooger spoke into the microphone. "If everyone could gather round," he said. "I have some big news. That's right. Come on up near the stage, folks. Big news."

"Let's go," my dad said. All the adults and Kat agreed with him.

"Oh, yes."

"Let's go."

"Let's."

"Yes."

Swept up, we were pushed with the crowd to the stage. Finally, we stood next to Kat.

"Okay," Sofia said, "spill it."

"Spill what?" Kat asked.

"What happened to you!" I demanded.

"Shhh!" said a group of adults circled around us, raising angry fingers to their spitty lips. We shushed. Kat faced the stage. Sofia and I were forced to do the same.

Ooger tapped the mic. "Okay." He cleared his throat. "As Mayor of Johnson Island, it is my duty and my pleasure to say to you all...Happy Bay Day!"

The whole crowd answered back in that strange, sing-song way, "Happy Bay Day!"

"Yes, indeed," Ooger answered, "Happy Bay Day to all. It is a good day so far. But it's gonna get better when you hear the news. Let me begin with an introduction. I'd like to introduce someone who was a big Johnson Island muckety-muck about a year ago, and he's back, and he's going to be real important again. Ladies and gentlemen, islanders and mainlanders, I'd like to introduce: Dr. Lennox."

"What?" Sofia said in shock.

"I don't believe it!" I exclaimed.

Dr. Lennox shuffled across the stage to the microphone. The crowd, who mostly hated the man for closing Meta-Gro, stood by docilely and politely applauded.

"Let me begin by saying that it is very nice to see you all," Dr. Lennox said into the mic.

"It is nice to see you," the entire crowd responded in unison, even Kat.

Sofia and I exchanged a perplexed look. I shrugged. "It's like we're at church," she said.

Dr. Lennox put his long fingered hands into his rumpled lab coat. "Now, as Mayor Ooger has told you, I have important news. I have a new project for Johnson Island, and I need everyone's help. Is that okay?"

Sofia said, "No!"

"It's not okay, you, madman!" I added.

But our words were drowned out by the crowd's loud, "Yes, Dr. Lennox, it's okay!"

"Wonderful, then we can get started," Dr. Lennox said.

In the ensuing pause, that briefest moment of silence, Sofia spoke up as loud as she could: "Stop! What are you doing, everyone?" The entire

151

crowd turned to Sofia, and myself, since I stood right next to her. "Dr. Lennox is crazy! He tried to kill me and my sister and Pete!"

"It's true!" I shouted so everyone could hear. "Dr. Lennox is your classic mad scientist villain who has used the island to create super weeds he controls with his mind, a la Poison Ivy, played by Uma Thurman in Batman & Robin, 1997. Needless to say, Batman & Robin, 1997, is a pretty bad movie. But not as bad as Dr. Lennox!"

A rumble of confusion spread through the crowd. I turned to Sofia. "How was that?"

"Too much," she said, shaking her head.

"Now, folks," Dr. Lennox said, and the entire crowd's attention swung back to him. "Do I look like a man scientist? Pardon me, I mean, mad scientist?"

Before Sofia and I could get to the "s" of our loudly shouted "Yes!"—the town shouted us down with a thunderous "No!"

"Thank you, Johnson Island. Thank you. Now, pay no attention to those children. They'll be joining us soon enough."

Joining them? What did that mean?

"To begin," Dr. Lennox continued. "I need everyone here to return to their homes and bring back as many shovels and buckets as you can carry. Visitors may go to Meta-Gro, where this equipment awaits you. I also need wheelbarrows, as well. We have some digging to do. Let us begin."

The crowd, except for Sofia and I, slowly moved off in different directions, almost stepping into us as they went. My family and the A-Team headed back to Gram's house, even Kat. Dr. Lennox stayed on the stage, watching and giving orders.

"Stop," Sofia said to my family. "What are you doing? Don't listen to him!"

"Mom? Dad? Gram? Come on, Gram." They ignored me. "Dr. Carlos, you're not used to manual labor involving shovels! Maybe Chad, but surely you have to stop. Please stop!"

They paid no attention to us, even Kat. We followed them and got lost in the sea of people shuffling through town in various directions.

"Come on, Kat!" Sofia said. "Snap out of it!"

"Please, Kat!" I repeated, standing in front of her. She sidestepped around me.

"What's wrong with you?" Sofia begged her sister. "Kat!"

She ignored us.

"Look at me, Kat!" Sofia stopped her sister and grabbed her face. "You have to— OW!"

"What's wrong?" I said.

"My finger. It hit something sharp, like a splinter." Sofia turned Kat's face. "Or this." Behind Kat's ear was not a splinter, but a thorn, not a small one either. Sort of near the base of her skull, it was easy to miss. A tiny red leaf grew from the thorn.

"Pull it out," I suggested. Sofia did.

Kat's head sunk and rose. She blinked groggily and rubbed her neck. "What's going on?"

"Kat!" Sofia hugged her.

"What?" said Kat, confused.

"You're back," I said.

"How did I get out of Meta-Gro?"

"Don't worry about that now," I said. "Look." A few islanders in the huge crowd turned their heads and stared at us.

"Let's pull out their thorns," Sofia whispered to me. "They can help."

"I think there's too many," I whispered back.

Then, the islanders staring at us reached out their arms and marched right in our direction, knocking into others. We backed up and bumped into more people. We were surrounded!

"Oh no," Sofia said.

"Follow my lead, ladies." I dropped my shoulders and shuffled like a zombie. "Let us... get shovels," I said mechanically.

"Yes... let us," Sofia said, imitating me.

"Dum-dums, what are you doing?"

"Shut up and play along," I whispered to Kat. Just for the record, it never felt so good to be called a dum-dum.

"Why? What the heck is going on?"

"The whole island's turned against us. Do what we do."

Kat joined in. "Me... want... shovel."

Suddenly, the folks marching toward us put their arms down and followed the rest of the crowd slowly moving down Broadway.

"That was close," I said. "Follow me. I have an idea."

Acting like zombies, I guided the twins through the crowd and headed to the one safe spot on the island with no shovels or buckets or wheelbarrows or people: The Palace.

Chapter 41

Moving slowly, we zombie-walked our way down Broadway with everyone else. We slowed down even more and separated ourselves from Gram, my family, and the A-Team. Then, without realizing it, I knocked into Sofia's parents, Mr. and Mrs. Jin. When Kat saw her mom and dad, she gasped. But her parents blindly stared at us for a second, and then returned to the mindless march for shovels and buckets. Things were going downhill fast: now people didn't even recognize us.

"There's The Palace," I whispered. Ahead of us stood the half-broken marquee. We were getting closer. "Now. Slowly. Let's go."

We turned slightly toward a house that was next to the decrepit theater. We opened the gate in the chain link fence, closed it, and moved down the narrow alley. We kept our eyes straight ahead. "Anyone following?" I whispered to Sofia.

She stole a glance. "Nope."

We made it to the back door of The Palace. Sofia turned the knob. "Problem. It's locked."

"Jeez Louise! Now what?"

"Easy, dum-dum. Kick it in," Kat ordered.

"Me? I can't knock down that door," I said. "The place is in bad enough shape. My grandparents had their first date here. I can't vandalize it."

"The whole island's in bad shape, Mr. Sensitive. Take advantage of your extra weight and knock it down," Kat repeated.

My weight really had come in handy this summer, I had to admit. But I couldn't bring myself to bash in The Palace door.

"I think it's the only way, Pete," sighed Sofia. "It's falling apart anyway. It's condemned. I know you don't want to, but I think you have to." Suddenly, her head spun toward the street. "I hear people. Hurry."

She made a good point. We were desperate. "Okay." I shoved with my shoulder. Once. Twice. Thrice. Then the door popped open. We entered. Sofia shut the door behind us and put a grimy paint can against it to keep it closed. It wasn't just the paint can that was grimy; the whole place was covered in a thick layer of dust and mold. The scent of mildew filled our noses. This gunk was worse than a hundred old pairs of sneakers left in a gym locker.

"Yech! It stinks!" Kat coughed. "Smells almost as bad as Pete."

"Me?"

"I know," Sofia agreed. "He's all hucky. He fell in the bay when we escaped Meta-Gro."

"How'd you fall in the bay?"

"Um, pole-vaulting, I guess," I said.

"Pole-vaulting?! You?" Kat laughed. "Tell me everything."

"We don't have time for this," said Sofia. "Let's get to the roof."

"Why the roof?" Kat asked.

"So we can see what's going on," Sofia said.

We got moving.

"Come on, Petey-boy, you gotta spill it," Kat begged. "You were pole-vaulting?"

"I'll tell you later."

We hurried past the old screen, which had a few long rips. We jogged down the side aisle where the musty curtains hung crooked and off-kilter. The rows ran about twelve seats across. There was no center aisle. The place was too small. But it must have been some beautiful little theater back in the day. The plush seats, the heavy curtains, the intimate seating; it fit a hundred people—maybe.

We carefully opened the door to the lobby. Luckily, sheets of plywood covered the glass doors under the marquee outside. We could see a little of the street through the thin gaps between boards, but we were hidden.

Behind the concession stand, I found a dusty curtain. "Over here!" The girls caught up. I moved the curtain aside. Stairs. "This must go to the projection room," I said.

Up we climbed, and there it was, covered in dust and cobwebs, the old movie projector. "Would you look at that?" I breathed in awe.

"Yeah?" Sofia said.

"So what?" Kat chimed in.

"Ladies, show some respect. This magical machine probably projected Charlie Chaplin; The Wizard of Oz, 1939; perhaps our beloved E.T., 1982! This is a piece of history!"

"It's a piece of junk," Sofia said.

"Yeah," Kat agreed. "Focus, Pete. The roof, remember?"

So much for my cinema sentimentality. Today was all about breaking down doors and disrespecting a movie projector that should be in a museum. Oh well, we had a town to save.

"This way." Sofia stood at the bottom of a tiny stairwell. "Up here, I think. We'll be able to see Broadway from top to bottom."

She was right. Within a minute, we were on the roof. It was a flat rectangle, boxed in with a small, two-foot wall along the edge. Despite the absolute chaos of the day, here on the roof, as predicted by the weatherman, it was sunny and beautiful, with a breeze coming off the bay. Big puffy clouds rolled by, except for one dark storm cloud in the distance.

"You know, ladies," I said. "If I wasn't scared out of my mind, this would be a really nice roof. I'd love to put a lawn chair up here, watch the sunset, and eat a snack. It's a great view."

"Yeah, it's wonderful," Kat said sarcastically and pushed me.

"Ouch! What was that for?"

"That." She pointed to a hole in the roof I had almost stepped through. "The whole place could fall apart any second. Watch where you're going."

"And get down," Sofia hissed. "We could be seen. Stay low."

I ducked. "Right. Sorry. Thanks, Kat."

Avoiding the holes and boards that creaked with dry rot, we squat-walked our way across the roof and carefully peered over the edge.

Chapter 42

On the right side of Broadway, people lumbered, away from the square, toward their homes and the Low'ards. On the left side, people were returning with shovels and buckets and empty wheelbarrows. They moved so slow.

"Why are they listening to Dr. Lennox? Everyone hates him," Kat said.

"They're like zombies," Sofia said.

"Not zombies," I said, "wombies."

"Wombies?" Kat repeated. "Say what?"

"Transgenic weed-controlled zombies. Combine 'weed' and 'zombie'—you got yourself a wombie. Makes sense, right?"

"Why not call them zomweeds?" Sofia asked.

"Nope. No way," I shook my head. "There's no ring to zomweeds. That's terrible. They're wombies, alright? It has to be wombie. Let's agree it's wombie. Right now." The girls were quiet. "Good."

Kat shook her head. "Whatever they are, why are they listening to—"

"They're wombies," I interrupted. "I thought we agreed."

"Okay, why are the wombies listening to Dr. Lennox?" Kat asked.

"Don't you remember his lecture at Meta-Gro?" I said.

"He said a lot of crazy things," Sofia observed.

"I stopped paying attention," Kat confessed.

"That one weed, remember? It took over the beet plant. He must have figured out a way to take people over using weeds. That thorn in Kat's neck. Everyone in town must have one."

"Yeah, that makes sense," Sofia agreed. "I'll bet he made the weeds move the red bucket to trick us inside the Meta-Gro house. He needed to test it out, and he did it on you, Kat. Then, the weeds must have gotten to everyone during Bay Day."

157

"It's possible. Look." I pointed to the yards across the street.

The weeds, like the ones in Meta-Gro, were spilling out of the flower beds and gardens, all the places we weeded every day. They towered over the lawns and yards. They were climbing up and covering fences and trees and walls, festooned from house-to-house like green leafy Christmas lights. Even the water tower was half green. Is that how these weeds kept coming back so fast? Had they been growing under our noses all summer? Were they waiting for Dr. Lennox's orders to attack?

We sat back down on the roof out of sight. Sofia and Kat looked at me.

"Okay, I get it," Sofia said. "The town is overgrown, everyone has been turned into mindless wombies except us, but what's with the shovels? Is he planting something?"

"Yeah, where are they bringing the buckets and stuff?" Kat asked.

"The binoculars!" I said. I took off my backpack and spilled my heist supplies: flashlight, rope, binoculars, Swiss army knife, and a twenty-dollar bill.

"What's the money for?" Sofia asked, as she grabbed the binoculars.

"To celebrate Tim Meeks getting bucket-dumped," I said. "Lunch at Cookie's, my treat."

"Can I have the Swiss army knife?" Kat asked.

"Why?" I said.

"Next time a bunch of weeds are choking me—I'm fighting back," Kat answered.

"But it was my grandfather's."

"So?"

"Let it go, Kat," said Sofia. Then, carrying the binoculars, she crawled away from us, along the edge of the roof to the other side.

"Come on, Pete." Kat held out her hand.

"It's really important to him," Sofia said. "Right, Pete?" Sofia leaned down, not to be seen from the street, still crawling along the edge.

"It's really important to me that I don't die," Kat countered.

Humph. The knife was important, but not as important as the twins, especially now.

"Sure, Kat. Keep it," I said. I put the knife in her hand.

"Thanks, Pete."

"Be careful. It's really rusty. Hopefully you won't need it."

"Oh, she's gonna need it," Sofia called. "Come over here and look."

On the other side of the roof, Sofia peered through the binoculars. She faced north toward the Bay Day stage and the marina. We made our way to her by carefully crawling across the roof, sticking to the edge. I peeked over the side for a second and saw wombies all over the street in front of The Palace.

"What is it?" Kat asked.

"See for yourself." Sofia handed Kat the binoculars.

"No way," Kat said, stunned.

"What? Tell me."

"Here." Kat gave me the binoculars.

I looked. A pile of dirt had formed near the marina. The wombies were filling buckets with the dirt and dumping them into boats. "I don't believe it!" I said. "Dr. Lennox is taking the weeds off the island! Did you see how low the boats are sitting in the water? They must be loaded with soil. He'll be able to leave any minute! How'd he fill them so fast?"

"Take it easy, dum-dum," Kat said. "All crab boats sit low in the water. It makes it easy to lean over and pull up the traps. Our dad has one. It's a bay workboat. They call it a deadrise."

"Deadrise," I repeated. "Fitting name for wombies." The girls didn't react. "You know, rising from the dead? Like zombies but—"

"We get it," said Sofia dryly. "The thing is what are we going to do?"

I focused the binoculars on a crab boat. Kat was right. The front rose up from the water where a small cabin housed the controls and steering wheel. From there the crabber's big open deck swooped down. The sides dropped to within a foot of the waterline. From bow to stern—I learned a few nautical terms—the whole thing was almost the length of a school bus.

"Jeez Louise," I said. "Once there's enough dirt, Dr. Lennox will be able to take tons of plants off the island."

"I know. We have to get help!" Sofia replied.

"We'll call the Jersey State Police," Kat suggested. "They have a helicopter."

"I don't think so," I said, looking through the binoculars. "At least not with a cellphone. Check out the dock." I had noticed that wombies on the dock were tossing their cellphones in the bay. I saw smashed phones scattered on the ground. "Dr. Lennox is way ahead of us."

"Let me see!" Sofia didn't even wait for me to take the binoculars from around my neck. She ripped them out of my hands and didn't even notice the strap was choking me as she looked. "He's right, Kat."

"Um, do you mind?" I gestured to the strap around my neck.

"Oh, sorry, Pete." Sofia pulled them over my head.

"Don't panic, dum-dums," Kat said. "What about a house phone? Easy. We break into the closest house, call the—"

"Forget it!" Sofia said. "He thought of that, too. Here."

She gave the binoculars to Kat, who swung them across toward the Low'ards.

"What is it?" I asked.

"The phone lines are down." Kat pointed. "They should be running up from the bay over there, but they're not. He's thought of everything."

"From A to izzard," Sofia said.

I raised my eyebrow.

"That means from A to Z," Sofia explained.

"We're on our own?" I asked.

"Looks that way," Kat said.

We slumped on the roof, the magnitude of that thought weighed us down.

"What happened to Dr. Lennox?" I asked the twins. "He must have gone crazy sniffing too many weed killers and chemicals."

"I hate that guy!" Kat said.

"Wait, that's it! The chemicals!" Sofia cried out. "The weed killer. There must be something in Meta-Gro to stop the weeds."

"Are you kidding?" Kat said. "You saw those rooms—fire resistant, cold resistant, Trimcut resistant."

"But there must be something. Right, Pete?" asked Sofia.

"I guess he must have had some way to stop them—before he went crazy. He said plants cross-fertilize all the time. Maybe that's another reason why Meta-Gro chose Johnson Island. There'd be no chance of the new seeds getting out into the world. We're surrounded by water."

"Unless you fill boats with dirt, and ferry them straight to the mainland," Sofia said. "So what do we do?"

"I have no idea." I removed my glasses and rubbed my eyes.

"I got nothing," Kat agreed.

We sat quietly and listened to the steady shuffle of wombies on the street below.

"I guess we could try to get out those thorns," I suggested. "Get enough islanders back on our side, maybe we might... but there's just so many of them."

"And they travel in big packs," Kat reminded me. "By the time we plucked one thorn out, ten wombies would be on top of us."

Sofia spoke decisively. "We don't have a choice. We have to sneak back into Meta-Gro. There's got to be a chemical, lab notes, something to help us figure out how to stop them."

"Oh, no. No way," Kat said. "That's all the way across the island. We'd never make it, right Pete?"

160

"It does seem highly improbable, Sofia."

"We have to," Sofia insisted. "For Mom and Dad, Kat. And your parents, Pete. And did you forget, Gram Mulligan is down there, too?"

That stung. She was right. I knew it was about as impossible as the first Mission Impossible, 1996, which had the best score and spy theme music ever! I could hum that the whole way to Meta-Gro to stop myself from freaking out.

I made up my mind. I'd stick with the twins no matter what.

"Okay, Sofia. You're right," I agreed. I reloaded my supplies into the backpack, minus the Swiss army knife. "We'll take it slow. We'll walk like wombies. We'll blend in. We can do this."

Chapter 43

Without thinking, I stood to put the backpack over my shoulders.

I heard a monotone voice shout, "Up... there!" I turned, and a block away, a wombie in yellow spandex pointed at me. "There... they are!"

Jeez Louise! Why was I so stupid? I guess Dr. Lennox told the wombies to find us. He did say we'd be joining them soon enough.

"Get down, dum-dum," Kat scolded.

"I'm sorry. I wasn't thinking."

"Movie theater!" the wombie called. "On top of...the movie theater."

Wait a minute! That voice? Yellow spandex? I peeked over the edge. It was Chad! He pointed again, "Up there! Movie theater!"

Other wombies repeated, "Movie theater! Movie theater!"

"Let's go. Now!" Sofia ordered. We ran across the roof. For a split second, I felt my foot not hit solid ground. Air, it seemed like. Then, I fell.

"Pete!" Sofia screamed.

The fall didn't seem to last forever, like in the movies. My face crunched flat down before I even knew what was happening. In fact, once I had collected myself I realized that I was still on the roof, except for my right leg, which had punched a hole through the rotten wood. Bracing myself with my hands and left foot, I carefully pulled my dangling leg out of the hole. But the pressure caused more wood to splinter and break and fall.

"Sofia! Watch out!" said Kat, pulling her sister back. Out of the corner of my eye, I saw the girls scramble away just as more roof dropped.

My feet and hands found solid beams, but the rest of me: nothing. "Oh no," I gulped. Below me, I saw the red theater chairs covered in fallen debris. The splintered wood looked sharp, too, and it was right underneath me. It was a long way down! I was balanced by hands and feet over a hole as big as my body, like that yoga move downward-facing dog or... my God!... a plank!

"Ladies!" I yelled. "Help!"

"Don't move, Pete!" Sofia said.

"Obviously!" I screamed. "But I can't stay like this for long. I'm not good at planks! I hate planks! I hate 'em!"

"Hang in there, Petey-boy," Kat said. "We'll think of something."

Oh, the irony. Wombie Chad had forced me into a situation where a plank was the only thing keeping me from falling and breaking my neck. I was having one of those Star Wars, 1977, "Use the force, Luke!" voice-over moments. As my arms shook from the strain I heard Chad's voice echo in my mind: "Keep up with those planks... planks... planks." That was the echo effect. "You never know when you're gonna need to plank... plank... plank." Curse you, Mr. Chad! Curse you! My head rose slightly. "As I mentioned before, hurry ladies!"

"Pete, we need the rope!" Kat said. "Where is it?"

"Jeez Louise! In my backpack!"

"Can you get it?" Kat asked.

"No, dum-dum!" I screamed. What was she thinking? I couldn't even move, let alone balance on one hand and take off the backpack!

"Kat," said Sofia. "Get by his feet. But go slow. The whole roof is ready to go."

Kat carefully crawled behind me.

"Whatever you're scheming—hurry! My arms are shaking!"

Sofia crawled in front of me. "Calm down, Pete."

"Calm down? Do you see how far that is? If I fall, I will break a leg or an arm or both legs and both arms. Something is breaking, for sure, if—"

Sofia put her hands on top of mine. "Look at me, Pete." Her hands were so soft. My eyes met hers. "Here's what you're going to do. You're going to shimmy."

"Shimmy! What is this, Dirty Dancing, 1987? I can't shimmy."

"What are you talking about?" Kat asked.

"Jeez Louise! You guys never saw Dirty Dancing, 1987? What's wrong with you two?"

Sofia squeezed my hands. "Focus, Pete Mulligan! You're not dirty dancing."

"1987!" I added compulsively.

"You're going to shimmy your hands and feet," Sofia continued. "Actually, I mean scooch. You're going to scooch."

"So scooch, no shimmy? I'm so confused. What happened to shimmy?"

"Forget the shimmy!" Kat yelled from behind me. I tried to turn my head, but Sofia squeezed my hands again.

"Your hands and feet, Pete. You are going to scooch them over a little bit at a time, okay? Over there, to solid roof. You get me?"

"I don't know, Sofia. I'm afraid to move."

"I know you are," Sofia said. "But don't worry, Kat is going to guide your feet. I am going to guide your hands. You won't fall, okay? If you slip, we'll hold on to you."

"Well, we'll try," Kat added. "It'll be really hard to do, considering how much you weigh and all. So, try to not fall."

Of all times to hit me with a fat joke!

"Don't listen to her," Sofia shot back. "But we have to hurry. Your arms are really shaking."

"Your legs, too," chimed in Kat. "You really are bad at planks."

"Thanks for the confidence boost," I grunted sarcastically.

"Here we go," Sofia said. "Left hand scooch. Just move it a little. You can do it."

"Oh boy, oh boy, oh boy." Arms trembling, sweat dripping on my glasses, I scooched my left hand an inch. "I did it!"

"Atta boy, dum-dum," Kat said. "Now your left foot! I got you." I scooched my left foot, Kat helping me. "You did it. Now, quicker."

"See," Sofia said. "Easy-peasy. Now, bring your right hand to your left." I scooched. "And your right foot." I scooched again.

"I get it!" I said.

"Follow the rhythm," Sofia said. "Left hand, left foot, right hand, right foot." I followed the beat, scooching along while the twins guided my trembling hands and feet.

"Almost there," Sofia said encouragingly. "Get ready, Kat!"

"I am," Kat answered.

I inched closer and closer to solid roof, leaving the hole to my right.

"Left hand, left foot, right hand, right foot... and... you... are... clear!" Sofia said. "But don't just plop down and—"

I stopped listening to Sofia after clear! I couldn't hold that plank another second. "Thank God," I exhaled. I collapsed, dropping my straining arms and legs, plopping down (exactly what she had said not to do) with my full weight.

I should have listened. The spot of roof, where I dropped near the twins, creaked loudly! The roof buckled and lowered an inch, cracking like we were on top of a frozen pond that wasn't so frozen! Oh, no.

"No one move," Sofia said.

We didn't.

There was another creak.

"Okay," Sofia whispered. "You first, Kat. Very, very slowly."

As gently as possible, Kat crawled back to the edge of the roof. The wood creaked beneath Sofia and I, as if it would break apart any second.

"Oh boy," I said quietly.

"Go, Pete," ordered Sofia.

I swallowed. Then, I did the same as Kat, inching on my hands and knees like a baby. The roof groaned like Gram Mulligan's stairs. Good thing I dropped a few pounds this summer. After a tiny bit more, I finally reached Kat. "Your turn, Sofia."

Sofia followed. At first it seemed like she was going to make it easily, but after a foot, every time she placed her knee or palm down, rotten wood creaked like it would collapse any second. She needed to go a little further. She was almost there, but the cracking noises grew louder and louder.

"Hurry!" I said. "Hurry!"

Then, the roof gave.

Sofia jumped with her arms out. Kat and I grabbed her. A gaping hole opened behind her like a trap door and chunks of wood crashed onto the seats below. We peered through the hole.

"Whew, that was nippity-cut," Kat said.

"Tell me about it," I agreed. "Whatever that means."

"It means it was a close call," Sofia answered. "Let's go. We have to get to Meta-Gro."

"Wait," I said, raising my hand.

"What?" Sofia asked.

"Thank you."

"You're welcome," the twins said at the same time.

As we raced back down the stairs, I made a mental note. If I survived and things returned to normal (highly unlikely), I would have to thank Chad, my Obi-Wan Kenobi of exercise. He was right. A plank had saved my life.

From the projection room, we could see wombies filling the theater.

"Behind the concession office," Sofia said. "I saw a window."

She was right. We slipped out the window. Well, maybe 'slipped' wasn't an honest word. I guess I flopped out. Either way, we were in the alley and wombie-free for the moment.

"Let's get to Meta-Gro," Sofia said.

"Piece of cake," I said weakly.

"Don't worry, dum-dum, the wombies run even slower than you."

"Isn't that comforting," I replied.

Chapter 44

As soon as Sofia poked her head out of the alley, a wombie groaned, "There!"

"Go!" Kat ordered.

We bolted across Broadway. I knocked over a fisherman pushing a wheelbarrow. "Excuse me, sir," I said without thinking.

"Move it, dum-dum," Kat said, pulling my arm.

The fisherman zeroed in on us, and Dr. Lennox's mindless minions took up the chase.

"Cut between yards," Sofia said. "Like manhunt."

We zigged and zagged between houses, tearing open gates and climbing over fences. At least Kat had been right. The wombies did run pretty slow. But she neglected to realize that they were—everywhere! And no matter how much my mind hummed the Mission Impossible, 1996, soundtrack, I was freaking out!

To make things worse, the weeds were growing more and more. The island neighborhood we ran through looked like it had been blanketed by a U.S. Army camouflage net.

We hopped a chain link fence covered in thorny weeds. We cut through a small yard with a clothesline. But suddenly, a wombie family jumped out of a shed.

"Turn around!" Kat shouted.

We backtracked, then started going sideways, sticking to backyards and alleys. We headed toward the bridge that crossed to Meta-Gro. We paused behind Reverend Apple's church.

"So far so good," I panted.

"Wombie-free for now," Sofia said, out-of-breath. "But we have to keep moving. The bridge is close." She looked around the corner. "Oh, boy."

Kat and I peered over her shoulder.

"Jeez Louise!"

"You've got to be kidding me," Kat said.

A huge wave of weeds, blocking the way to the bridge, slithered right at us.

"Go back! Go back!" Sofia yelled.

The green devils gave chase. It was the sharp-edged, mile-a-minute weed. Curling under our feet, we dodged and jumped as the weeds forced us away from Meta-Gro and back to the edge of the island. My lungs burned. Our legs bled from a million little cuts. This was a manhunt game for real, and it never ended.

"Which way do we go?" Sofia asked between breaths. "They keep cutting us off."

"Keep running," I gasped. "They're everywhere!" A vine dropped from above, just missing me. I screamed! Steve McQueen would be so ashamed of me.

"We're running out of island," Kat said. I could hear the worry in her voice. "We're near the Joyce Mary dock, to the left of The Palace!"

"We're going in circles," I said. "Maybe we sh—"

That was when it happened. They got us. We were swallowed up in a tidal wave of weeds.

"Pete! I'm stuck!" Sofia shouted.

"Me, too!" Kat screamed.

"Sofia! Kat! No!" I yelled.

"Kat, the knife!" Sofia hollered.

"Hurry, Kat, cut us out!" I called.

"I can't move my hands, dum-dums!"

I twisted around and saw her hands roped up over her head. I rolled violently back and forth across the dock fighting. The serrated leaves and thorns tore at my skin.

Then it hit me: this was the dock where I had arrived on Johnson Island back in June. This was the spot where Sofia and Kat took my stuff, told me to wave goodbye to my parents, pushed me in the bay, and with Gram helping, pulled me out with the rope. Who would have thought this was how my summer would end?

Then, a weedy voice whispered in my head and said: "It's no use, Peter Mulligan. We have won."

Dr. Lennox's voice—in my mind. That was impossible! How?

"My lovely Arabidopsis, my rockcress plant, is on its way. With two more little thorns for your friends."

Two more? Why not three? Did that mean he got me already? I reached to check for a thorn behind my ear, but a slithering vine grabbed my arm. Then, my other arm.

"No!" I yelled.

"Pete!" Sofia shouted.

"Help!" Kat cried.

I fought to untangle myself.

"Your minds will be mine," Dr. Lennox hissed.

He was in my head, but I wasn't a wombie. Why?

"You will work for us."

Maybe the thorn wasn't in deep enough or something. I had to get free before he controlled me like that beet plant!

Arms pinned and desperate, I flipped and flopped with all my weight. Without realizing it, I rolled over the edge of the dock. The weeds slipped, then held me. I dropped but didn't touch the water. I dangled over the side, my weight straining against the vines.

"Stop!" Dr. Lennox ordered in my head. "You must come up. Come now. Not in that."

"Pete!" the twins yelled.

"Not in that," Dr. Lennox repeated in my mind.

That? That what? Did he mean the water? Did he mean the bay? I felt the vines tighten as if in response to my thoughts. Maybe I was right! I renewed my struggle, pushing my weight toward the water lapping below. It seemed like the closer I got to the water, the weaker the weeds became.

"Let's go for a dip!" I called out in my bravest action hero voice.

"Do not!" Dr. Lennox warned.

"Come on!" I wiggled, bouncing my body up and down.

"No!"

"Hasta la vista, baby!" My face was inches from the water. "Terminator 2: Judgement Day, 1991!"

"Stop!"

"You can't swim, can you?" I yanked my right arm free. It broke the surface of the water, splashing me. The squeezing vines loosened.

I plopped into the bay. If the plop was anticlimactic after all that, the doc's reaction wasn't. Dr. Lennox's voice screeched in my head like he was in pain. If he controlled the weeds, he must feel what they felt. And that screech sounded like a scream to me. I had hurt him. I mean, the water had. That was it! The bay water! For whatever reason, the weeds hated it! I reached behind my ear. A thorn! I pulled it out. Dr. Lennox's voice was gone.

"Pete, they're taking us away!" Sofia yelled.

Treading water, I looked up. The weeds were dragging Sofia and Kat backward.

"Not so fast!" I beat the water with my hands, splashing upward and some water hit the girls.

"They stopped!" Kat said.

"It's the water! Try to get to the water!" I called.

The girls fought harder, rolling back and forth, struggling to untangle themselves, while I beat the water up onto the dock. Suddenly, Sofia flipped and fell over the edge into the bay. The weeds recoiled from her and turned toward me. But they stayed back as I climbed the dock ladder. I ripped the weeds covering Kat, my dripping clothes lowering their resistance. We jumped off the dock together.

The weeds slithered to the wooden edge but did not come closer. Exhausted, we kicked and paddled ourselves away from the dock until the weeds were out of sight.

Chapter 45

We quietly swam across the harbor until we found some rowboats. We hid between two, holding onto the gunwales. We needed a breather.

"It seems like they don't like bay water," I said.

"Thanks, Pete," Sofia said.

"Yeah," Kat said. "Thanks for— Hey, you were swimming! When did that happen?"

"He finally figured it out earlier when he fell off the Meta-Gro dock," Sofia answered.

"How'd you fall off the dock?"

"The pole-vaulting thing," I said.

"Pole-vaulting? You have to tell me!"

"Not now, Kat," Sofia cut her off. "So, Pete, what do you think? Meta-Gro's out. What do we do?"

"I have an idea," I said. "Which way to Billy's house?"

"Billy Pruitt, who likes Sofia?" Kat teased.

"He doesn't like Sofia, dum-dum," I said. "He likes you."

Kat's face changed. She went pale. "What did you say?"

"Nothing. Never mind."

"We know the way to his house," Sofia interrupted.

We climbed into a rowboat and rowed around to the back of the island and made it behind Billy Pruitt's place. Luckily, he had a dock that led to his backyard. From a distance, we could see that weeds were everywhere but none of the big, scary plants.

"Ugh," whispered Kat, "the sticker ball ones. I hate those."

"Quiet, there's Billy," I said.

We sat still in the water and watched Billy come out of the house with the same blank expression everyone else had. He was a wombie,

170

alright. We watched him trudge to the shed, which was not too far from the dock. Wombie-like, he came out of the shed with a wheelbarrow and set it down. Then he trudged back into the shed.

"He must be part of Operation: Weed Escape," Sofia said.

"Looks that way," I agreed. "No sign of his parents."

"Maybe they're near the marina," Kat said. "Shh, there he is."

Billy came out again, this time with a shovel. He placed it in the wheelbarrow and shuffled back toward the shed.

"We can assume he has a thorn behind his ear like Kat did," I said. "We need to surprise or distract him long enough to get the thorn out before Dr. Lennox can figure out we're here."

"Can we do that? Isn't Lennox controlling everyone?" Sofia asked.

"Yeah, but I don't think he can have total awareness of every single plant and human at every single second. I think he must have to switch focus. I'll bet there's a little bit of lag time, and right now we can assume he is focused on loading the boats with dirt."

Sofia nodded. "And looking for us near Meta-Gro on the other side of the island."

"So, what do we do?" Kat said.

"Maybe we can distract Billy. His mind is focused on getting shovels for the dirt. Maybe if we get him to feel something that's not weed-related, we can pull the thorn and Dr. Lennox won't know."

"How do we distract him?" Sofia asked.

"I don't know," I answered.

We thought quietly. Kat broke the silence. "Hey, were you lying before?"

"About what?"

"When you said that Billy liked me," Kat said. "I always thought he liked Sofia."

"He never said anything to me, Kat. You were the one who said that," Sofia shrugged.

"Billy told me," I said.

"What?" Kat said, excited. "When? What did he say?"

"It was your weird J-Island talk, but I think it meant he liked you."

"You think?" Kat asked. "Give me the details, Pete. Now. What'd he say exactly?"

"Um, he said that your leg is broke."

"Really?" Sofia grinned.

"That's good, though, right?" I asked.

"Yeah, Pete," Sofia said, "It means he thinks she has nice legs."

"What else did he say?" Kat asked.

171

"'I wish I could go gal-ing with her.'"

Kat considered this. "Gal-ing, really?"

"Yeah." I noticed the hint of a smile on her lips, but that was all.

"Dum-dum, if we don't die and I find out that you just made that up, I'm gonna kill you."

"It's true, Kat. I promise."

"Then I have an idea," Kat said.

We slipped out of the boat and into the water. I figured the wetter the better for fighting weeds. We waited for Billy to go into the shed, then we crept up the dock.

"I got this," Kat said. She moved away from us.

"Gal-ing is a good thing, right?" I whispered to Sofia.

"Uh-huh."

"What's it mean?"

"You'll see," Sofia smirked.

Kat snuck along the side of the shed, hugging the wall. When Billy came out holding another shovel, Kat sprang forward and kissed him. I couldn't believe it. It was a long kiss. So, gal-ing meant kissing. Well, I'll be. It was working. Billy dropped the shovel. Kat's hand reached to Billy's cheek, behind his ear, and yanked out the small thorn with the tiny leaf. She tossed it in the water.

"It's out," she called to us.

"What's going on?" Billy asked, daze slowly lifting.

"Humph." Kat raised an eyebrow. "What do you remember?"

"Nothing. Like I was asleep, and I just woke up."

"You remember any dreams?" Kat asked.

"Nope. Nothing," Billy answered.

"Too bad for you," Kat grinned.

"Why?"

"Come on," I said as Sofia and I slipped by Billy and headed for his house.

"Hey, Pete. Hey, Sofia." Billy greeted us.

"Hey, Billy," Sofia said.

"Why are you guys all wet? And why are you going into my house?"

Inside Billy's room, all the rumors were true. It was an arsenal. It was the biggest collection of water guns, water pistols, water cannons, and water shooters of every make and model that I had ever seen. Better yet, most of them were souped-up with Billy's special modifications—they shot streams of water longer and farther and harder than any store-bought toy. A few were Billy's original designs made with PVC pipe and different types of water tanks that you strapped to your back like a Navy Seal or

172

something. There had to be about twenty-five to thirty of them. I was impressed.

"How did you do all this?" I wondered.

"Island life," Billy answered. "Lots of time on your hands. How many you want?"

"All of them," Sofia said.

"And your skiff," Kat said.

"Why?"

"We need to fill them with bay water," Kat said.

"Why?"

"We're going to fight the weeds, stop the wombies, and save the island," Kat said.

"Oh, okay," Billy said. "Wait! What?"

"We'll explain later, dum-dum."

We searched the house for every kind of backpack and knapsack and plastic shopping bag we could find. My plan was to fill the water pistols with bay water once we were on Billy's skiff. We stuffed the water guns into these bags. As we worked, Kat turned to Billy.

"You really don't remember anything?" Kat asked.

"About what?"

"Forget it," Kat said.

"No," Billy said. "Tell me. Did I do something? Are you mad at me?"

Kat was silent.

"Please. What was it?"

"She kissed you," Sofia said.

"What?" Billy asked, eyes wide.

"Sofia, shut up!" Kat said.

"She did? Really?" Billy asked Sofia. He turned to Kat. "You did? You kissed me?"

"Yup," Sofia nodded.

"For real. Like not a joke?" Billy asked.

"Yup," she said. "Totally for real."

"When? I don't remember."

"Humph," Kat grunted. "It doesn't count if you don't remember it, dum-dum. Forget it."

"I don't want to forget it."

Sofia tapped my arm and frowned. "Looks like the happy couple is having their first fight."

"Enough semi-romantic, pre-teen banter," I said. "We have work to do."

Chapter 46

Our first assault would be an experiment. We wanted to see what would happen if we shot a wombie with bay water. Would they snap out of it and no longer be controlled by Dr. Lennox? If so, then I had a plan on how to take back the island. If not, well, I guess we would have to think of something else.

The commando raid would take place at Cookie's, our favorite summer spot for two-stickers and ice cream. It was close to a dock, so we had quick access. Weeds covered every inch of the restaurant and everything around it from road to roof, like some garden-obsessed graffiti artist spray painted the island green. In front, we spied a group of kids and Cookie mindlessly shoveling dirt into wheelbarrows. I figured that Dr. Lennox had an ambitious yet classic plan, found in every good horror movie with a mad scientist: take his evil weeds to the mainland and take over the world. He could do it, too.

If the weeds got to the bottom of New Jersey's coast, there would be miles of fertile marshlands for them to conquer and multiply. He could create a massive green army. There wasn't much down there except a few small fishing towns. It would be easy. And from there, New York City was right up the turnpike. If he went south to Delaware, same thing—plenty of marsh and not far away was Washington, DC. We had to stop them.

"Okay, here we go," I said, making my voice deeper to sound more sure of myself.

We clambered out of Billy's skiff with as many bay water filled pistols as we could carry in our backpacks and bags. We slowly approached the wombies, who kept shoveling dirt. They hardly noticed us. Then, we let them have it! A good solid blast streamed from Billy's famous water weapons.

Cookie and the kids' heads drooped. Water dripped from their faces. With a series of clunks, their shovels dropped. Tim Meeks, of all people to save, tipped over his wheelbarrow. The group teetered back and forth.

"Are they okay?" Billy asked.

"They don't look okay," Kat answered.

"Get the thorns," I said.

We quickly moved from wombie to wombie and pulled out the nasty thorns. Then, their eyes blinked, and they wiped their dripping faces. They looked somewhat normal, except for little Amelia North. She staggered, about to fall over. Sofia caught her.

"What's going on?" Amelia asked, her princess power T-shirt dripping onto her shoes.

"We'll tell you in a minute," Sofia said.

Billy and I soaked the weeds blocking the front door. They went stiff, and we easily yanked them away. We hurried into Cookie's place, ushering our recently de-wombied friends ahead and shut the door behind. We pulled down the blinds. We were safe. I hoped that Dr. Lennox's attention was focused up near the Bay Day stage and the marina. At least for now, we were hidden and out of sight.

"What in the world is going on?" Cookie asked. "I have the worst headache."

"We'll explain in a minute, guys," Kat reassured them.

"Why's my face wet?" Fitzie wondered.

"Whoever soaked me is dead meat," Tim Meeks said, wringing out his dirty baseball cap. "This is my good hat."

"We had to do it, sir," I said. "You were a wombie."

"A what-bie, piggly-wiggly?"

"A wombie," I repeated. "Now, how many are we?"

We took a headcount. We had Tim Meeks, Cookie, Amelia North, Fitzie, Dimsy, and Vicky. Including us, that made ten altogether.

"I'm having a fluffy," Cookie said, wiping the sweat from his forehead. "Someone open a window."

"No!" Sofia said. "You can't."

"Why not?" Cookie demanded.

"Because," Sofia said, going to a window, "of this." She lifted the blind up a tiny bit, so everyone could see the weeds blocking out the light. She let it back down. Then Sofia explained the situation. The more she talked, the wider everyone's mouths grew in disbelief.

When it was over, Cookie sighed. "Anybody want an ice cream?"

"Right now?" Kat asked.

"It's just after hearing that," Cookie said, "I need ice cream."

"Yeah," Amelia said. "I want some ice cream, too."

"People," I said, "as much as I love Cookie's sweet treats, time is of the essence."

"Pete, we might as well," Sofia said. "Who knows what's going to happen out there? We could become wombies. We could be killed. We can take five minutes for ice cream, right?"

So, we paused and ate ice cream. The smell of chocolate filled the room. It was quiet, just the sounds of licking, swallowing, and scraping Styrofoam cups with plastic spoons. Everyone was thinking their own thoughts, worried about the people he or she cared about. I wondered about my parents and Gram Mulligan. Tim Meeks, of course, provided a distraction.

"So, I guess I won that bet, Tweedledum," he said to Kat.

"We had that red bucket in our hands," Sofia said. "We won the bet."

"Sure, you did, Tweedledee."

"We did, sir," I said. "It's what got us in this mess."

"What do you mean, chubbsy?" Tim Meeks sneered.

"Every time we had the red bucket in our sights, Dr. Lennox moved it to draw us in. He'd have grabbed you the day you snuck in, if you'd been brave enough to keep going, sir."

"Brave enough?" Tim Meeks repeated.

"Yeah," Kat agreed with me.

"Whatever, Tweedledum. I still win the bet! You don't have the bucket."

"Shut up, Tim Meeks!" Billy yelled.

"What'd you say, butt-chin?"

"I said shut up! Kat hates that name. She just saved your life. Show her some respect."

We were surprised to see Billy stand up to Tim Meeks. But Meeks stood right back, literally, and he was a foot taller than Billy. Tim stared down at him. "Oh yeah, butt-chin? What are you going to do about it?"

Billy stared up and shrugged. "Whatever it takes. I'm sick of you calling everyone names. We all are."

Sofia nudged Kat and whispered, "Humph, must've been some kiss. Even if he forgot about it."

Tim Meeks considered Billy. Nine sets of eyes bored into Tim, even Cookie's.

"It's true, Tim, you can be a jerk," Cookie said.

Tim glanced at Cookie, then scanned the room. He took off his cap and ran his fingers through his stringy red hair. Tim Meeks laughed. "Okay, Billy. I get you."

Everyone relaxed. For a second.

Crash! Window glass shattered. Vicky screamed!

A thick weed snaked inside toward us, the size of a Florida python!

"Watch out!" Sofia shouted.

We stumbled to the other side of the restaurant, knocking over chairs and tables. I blasted the weed with bay water. It stopped moving. "There's going to be more," I said. "It's now or never."

"All of you grab a water gun!" Billy yelled.

"Hurry! Hurry!" Kat urged.

Everyone armed themselves. I stood by the door, ready to open it. This was really happening. I swallowed hard, my throat tight. There was no time to think. "Stay together! Soak anything green! Blast the wombies in the face, then pull out the thorn. We need every mud-footer we can get. Ready?"

Nine heads nodded.

"Remember," I said in my best Scottish accent. "These... plants... may take our lives, but they'll never take... our freedom! Braveheart, 1995!"

"1990-what?" Tim Meeks snapped.

"It's from a movie," Sofia explained. "What he really means is... charge!"

Chapter 47

Picture the climax of every action flick where the good guys are about to battle the bad guys—like Guardians of the Galaxy, 2015—the heroes striding in slow motion, their eyes full of steely determination. That was us.

I flung open the door of Cookie's place, and we ran out in classic triangle formation: Billy, Kat, Sofia, and me at the point.

We reached the street that now resembled a living, writhing rain forest. Weeds and wombies faced us. Behind, Cookie and Tim Meeks and Fitzie and Amelia and the rest flanked us. In my mind, we couldn't have looked any cooler—our faces determined, our jacked-up water weapons aimed, everything happening in super slow motion, with epic background music playing. That moment seemed like it lasted forever, and the bad guys were cowering before us and we were going to win! That's exactly what it was like.

In my head.

For about ten seconds.

Maybe less.

I tend to exaggerate. Because immediately, the wombies raised their shovels! The weeds fired sharp sticker burrs! The serrated ground vines shot up!

"AHH!" We screamed like frightened kids, which we were. Even Cookie screamed. It was absolute and total panic!

I heard Kat yell, "Fight, you dum-dums! Fight!"

In seconds, we fired away—bursts of water that froze weeds in their tracks, even while sticker balls pelted our faces! We unleashed bay water blasts at every shovel-wielding wombie that got too close, sometimes ducking a rake or fist.

After I sprayed someone, I would yell, "Behind your ear!" The wombie would reach up, feel the thorn, and pull it out. I'd appraise them of the situation. Then, they were on our side. We repeated this over and over.

Soon, we had more allies—dazed and disoriented at first—some folks were immediately dragged down by ferocious vines, some, quicker to recover, joined the fight. Billy tossed them loaded super soakers, and off they went. Our numbers were growing. Some people took their rakes and shovels and turned them against the weeds.

Cookie organized a bucket brigade who filled the captured wombie buckets and wheelbarrows with bay water. We had a supply line of the plant-deadly H2O nearby to reload whenever we went dry.

We fought our way up Broadway. It was mayhem and chaos, and I lost all track of time, the twins, and the plan. I was shooting and ducking and running for my life. We were winning. The weeds were winning. I had no idea who was winning!

Out of nowhere, a root wrapped around my leg and pulled me to the ground. I was being dragged forward into the green writhing mass when Sofia saved me with a blast of water.

More folks were being freed from Dr. Lennox's control and joining us by the minute. Our numbers were growing. I thought we might actually have a chance when—

"OW!" I was hit. Hard.

"Pete!" Sofia called.

I had been struck in the gut by a stalk of bamboo that had shot out of the ground. I flew back a good six feet. I couldn't catch my breath. Another thick stalk burst from the ground and towered over me, circling like a deadly ninja staff ready to strike. Sofia fired at it, but it dodged.

It snapped down like a whip. I rolled. It missed.

A vine grabbed my legs. I couldn't roll now. "Help!" I was trapped.

"Pete!" Sofia fired again, running toward me. The bamboo bent left and her shot went wide. The stalk poised over my head as if it were relishing the moment. It came crashing down! I closed my eyes! This was it!

And then it stopped. Standing over me, blocking the bamboo with a rake turned sideways, was Mayor Ooger, his face dripping wet with bay water.

"That was nippity cut," he said.

Whew. It sure was. I freed my leg.

Another thick bamboo stalk shot from the ground and slammed Ooger. He fell back. I stood up and sprayed both stalks. They froze.

"Are you okay?" I asked the mayor.

"Yup," he said, rising to his feet. "You?"

"I am. Thanks to you, sir."

"That Jack 'o my wisp! Look what the doc's done to our island! I could tear up a crab cooker!" Ooger paused and took a breath, finally noticing what I had in my hands. "What're you shooting 'em with?"

"Bay water."

"Well, I'll be. That's it?"

"They absolutely hate it."

"That gave me a thought, Pete Mulligan. Maybe we can win this war."

Chapter 48

Now we had Mayor Ooger on our side. I felt more confident. Maybe we really could win. "What's the plan, sir?" I asked the mayor.

"Back down the block is Dorothy Joy's Gift Shop. She has water guns. Bailey's grocery store does too, I think. I'll take care of it." Mayor Ooger shouted to some de-wombied fishermen fighting nearby with rakes and shovels. "You watermen, with me!"

They followed Ooger, except for one waterman who got tripped up, caught around the ankle, and tossed over our heads into the side of a house about ten feet away. Jeez Louise! Was that guy okay? I saw his arm moving. He was hurt but still alive. I thought that I heard thunder clap in the distance, but it might have been my overactive movie imagination. Then it boomed again.

"Hurry!" Ooger shouted.

"Wow," Kat said. "Did you see that? I think the weeds are getting mad."

"Obviously!" Sofia said, pointing. "Look!"

Oh no! Racing toward us, as fast as wombies can race, were a dozen more mind-controlled folks, including my A-Team. But even worse, they were each brandishing lawn tools turned deadly! And they were headed straight for me.

Dr. Carlos whipped a weed whacker back and forth.

Miss Nunzio snapped hedge clippers at me.

Chad drove a John Deere riding mower.

And I was almost out of water.

"Don't worry, Pete." Sofia stood on my left.

"We got this." Kat said, standing on my right.

181

Kat struck first, blasting Dr. Carlos full in the face. The wombie-ized mental health professional flung the weed whacker as he reached for his face. We jumped to the side as it spun out. Sofia soaked Miss Nunzio. The out-of-her-mind social worker tossed her hedge clippers at us, but we ducked, and they sailed overhead. The girls pounced on my two A-Team members and plucked the thorns from their necks.

"I'll take care of Chad," I said. I took aim with my super soaker and had Chad's perfectly tanned and chiseled face lined up in my sights. Whoosh! I blasted him right in the kisser. The effect was wetness and anger. Chad slapped his cheeks and chest like he was psyching himself up to pump out his last set of curls at the gym. Problem was—he still sat on the lawn mower, which was now out of control.

"Chad, behind your ear," I shouted. "There's a thorn. Pull it! Snap out of it, Chad!"

No effect. Jeez Louise! I was going to have to do this the hard way. I ran toward the mower, and with a slightly above average leap, I tackled Chad and knocked him off. We tumbled to the ground. Billy took over the mower, turned it around, and used it against the weeds. Other islanders followed and grabbed the weed whacking tools, pressing our attack forward. Meanwhile, Chad and I wrestled around on the ground.

"Get off me, dude!"

"I'm trying to help! Stay still!" I struggled to pull out his mind-control thorn. Chad's long wet hair got in the way. He was so slippery, I finally gave up on trying to do it the nice way.

I pulled back my fist and punched him. It was surprisingly satisfying. And it worked.

"Dude, you just hit me in the face."

"I know. Southpaw, like Rocky, 1976, if you saw it. Now hold still." I reached behind his ear and yanked out the thorn.

"Pete, come on!" Kat shouted.

"We have to hurry," Sofia added.

I rolled off Chad and followed the girls.

"What is going on?" Chad asked. Then he screamed. It was, I couldn't help but notice, high-pitched. A large stalk of bamboo had popped up from the ground in front of him. It came down and gave him a sharp whack. "Ow! Help!"

Tim Meeks sprayed the bamboo, which went limp. "Pete, wait up!"

"Pete?" Chad said incredulously. "Will someone tell me what's going on?"

Ooger and the watermen raced past Chad, looking like soldiers, except that they held plastic water pistols of various colors—pink, blue, orange, yellow, red. Ooger yelled to them, "Move it, boys. Follow Pete Mulligan. He's in charge."

"Pete Mulligan?! In charge?" Chad asked. "What the heck is going on?"

That's the last I can report on Chad, because after that he was left behind. With the bay water bucket and wheelbarrow brigade behind, and the water gun warriors in front, half of the humans on Johnson Island stormed up Broadway toward Dr. Lennox and the Bay Day stage.

I hoped my parents, the twins' parents, and most of all, Gram, were okay.

We hadn't seen them in hours.

Chapter 49

We fought our way uptown to the stage, where we found more weeds waiting to attack.

Half of our island army held off these foes, while the rest doused and de-thorned every human we could see. Where was Dr. Lennox? Was he still controlling the weeds? It seemed like we were winning.

Yet the sky was growing darker. I couldn't tell if it was a thunderstorm rolling in or the number of weeds and kudzu vines crisscrossing over everything above me. And when I say everything, I mean everything! Like a giant green spiderweb, vines and leaves were strung overhead from water tower to telephone poles to the church steeple to rooftops. Every fence and bench, every bike and golf cart, the street, the docks, the entire island had become a ginormous jungle. When we reached the Bay Day stage, Dr. Lennox was nowhere to be seen.

"Where is he?" I asked, looking around.

"I'll bet he's by the boats," Sofia said. "Ready to take his weeds off the island."

"Let's get him," Kat ordered.

Like Tom Hanks storming the beaches of Normandy in the amazing war movie Saving Private Ryan, 1998, we charged through the green jungle to the marina. In a tight formation, we fired at every venomous vine in our way. We ducked and shot at deadly dandelions that dive-bombed us from above. We dodged and sprayed the grassy guerillas who ambushed us from below. The number of wombies decreased, and our Johnson Island infantry grew and grew.

At the marina, we found the last of the wombies, busy shoveling dirt from wheelbarrows onto the long decks of the crab boats. About fifteen deadrise crabbers were prepped like this, even Mayor Ooger's Angel Fish.

A wombie captain waited at the bridge of each boat, keys on the console, ready to go.

Our J-Island attack force spread out across the harbor front. We pumped water at any green thing that wiggled and soaked the mindless captains and shovelers—freeing everyone from plant control. Sitting extra-low in the water, each crabber was filled with at least three or four inches of Johnson Island soil. We checked, but so far, the boats were empty of weeds.

Every human was now either helping us or groggily snapping out of their daze. Hardly a weed moved, but still we pumped as much bay water as we could on them, refilling our blasters and spraying the ground like firemen putting out an inferno. We stood bloody and battered, wet and dirty, our clothes stained with green streaks, our arms and legs covered in stickers and thorns. We were a mess or, as Sofia would say, as hucky as all get out.

"I think we won," Billy said.

"Yeah," Kat said.

Maybe they were right.

"Kat, over here!" Sofia called to her sister.

"Mom! Dad!" Kat ran to Sofia. They reunited with their parents—big group hug.

Reverend Apple put her hand on my shoulder. "What was Dr. Lennox thinking?"

"We're not sure," I said to her, "but we can assume he was going to take these boats and mutated weeds to the mainland. Has anyone seen my parents and Gram Mulligan?"

"Right here, young Peter," came Dr. Lennox's calm but loud voice.

I looked up. There he was, on the roof of a weed-infested crab shack. Mom, Dad, and Gram stood vacantly next to him.

"Yes, all of us are here," Dr. Lennox said.

As if on cue, like in every dramatic bad guy movie moment, thunder clapped. It was very loud and very close. Our island army surrounded the shack, our colorful water weapons aimed and ready. Time for the showdown.

Sounding braver than I felt, I shouted, "It's all over, Doctor. Let them go."

"That's right, Doc," Mayor Ooger said. "Call it quits."

"Not yet!" Dr. Lennox coughed.

"Have it your way!" I shouted. "Super soak him, people!"

"Really?" Dr. Lennox laughed.

"Really!" Sofia called back.

The mud-footer militia raised our water pistols, pressed the triggers and—

Suddenly, weeds sprang from the ground beneath us! They entwined themselves around the guns and yanked them out of our hands! Other weeds shot up and tipped over the buckets and wheelbarrows. Bay water spilled to the ground.

The weeds snapped our water pistols in half or smashed them against thick stalks of bamboo. Rainbow-colored plastic pieces and white PVC shards rained down around us. And, just like that, in mere seconds, we were completely disarmed and defenseless.

"My water guns," Billy moaned. "All of them. Gone."

Dr. Lennox wheezed and cackled. "Did you really think three children could stop me? With water pistols? Those Mikania micrantha have been waiting for you."

"So what?" I said to him, trying to sound confident. "Your mind thorns aren't working anymore. We're all dripping in bay water. Let my family go!"

"Yeah, you're crazy!" shouted Tim Meeks.

"Yeah!" The entire town shouted to the doctor.

"In due time," he replied.

"Why are you doing this, Dr. Lennox?" Reverend Apple called up. "Last summer, you came to church."

"Why? Isn't it obviousss?" the doctor slurred. "Revenge!"

"Revenge?" echoed Reverend Apple.

Everyone assembled was perplexed.

"Revenge on who?" Sofia's dad asked.

"Why the island, of course!" screeched the doctor.

"On Johnson Island?" Mayor Ooger said.

"Yes! On you! On everyone! On the whole human race!"

"What are you talking about?" I said, feeling the first few drops of rain hit my arm.

Dr. Lennox stumbled when he took a step forward. He looked sick, his face darkening, changing color.

"We were here thousands of years before you," he ranted. "We will be here thousandsss of years after you destroy yourselves. Why wait for you to poison the planet, like you poison usss? We can take it now."

Thunder boomed. The drops of rain became a drizzle.

"Us?" Kat said.

"What's he mean?" Sofia asked me.

"Poison who now?" Mayor Ooger said.

"I'm so confused," Kat chimed in.

"The good doctor doesn't look so good," I said.

Dr. Lennox continued speaking. In his excitement, his green-tinted body began to tremble. "Since the first time our species invaded your precious fields, your farmsss, your gardensss, you have fought us. A fight to the death. But we don't die easily."

"Slow down, Doc," Mayor Ooger said, confused, "you're lookin' a little green around the gills."

The rain increased. It was a full-on summer thunderstorm.

"You have plucked us, cut us, torn us, ripped usss to pieces. You have choked us with poison to let us shrivel and die like we were nothing!"

"Us who?!" demanded Sofia.

"We are no longer nothing!" Doctor Lennox shouted. "We are no longer defenseless. We are no longer weak! We are strong! We are angry! We are standing up for ourselves!"

"Oh my God. I get it." I turned to the twins. It was suddenly crystal clear. "Don't you see? Dr. Lennox isn't controlling the weeds. The weeds are controlling him!"

Thunder boomed. The rain picked up. It came down steady—which meant—oh no!

"We are here to do one thing. Destroy you. We start with thisss husssk!"

And with that, Dr. Lennox's thin, frail body quivered, shook, and split open, right down the center, peeling in two. One side—an arm and leg, half his head and torso—dropped to the left, his other side dropped to the right, collapsing on the shack's roof with a thud. There wasn't any blood, just a weird green mist and goo.

Someone screamed.

We stood shocked and silent.

"What just happened?" Sofia squeaked.

"What did he mean by husk?" Kat whispered.

"I don't know, I—Look! He's moving," I said.

But it wasn't Dr. Lennox moving. Something was growing out of his body, rising like a flower, but what emerged from Dr. Lennox wasn't a flower.

Unfurling above him, emerged a thing—I didn't know what else to call it. A thing that was part weed and part human, something fractured in between.

Dark green stems intertwined to form the basic shape of a human, but the bottom half of the thing was a mass of strong, flexible roots. From its back sprouted thicker, longer stems uncoiling and floating in the air, like Dr. Octopus from Spider-Man 2, 2004. Green serrated leaves sprouted over the entire figure, except for its head where its sharp, piercing eyes and jagged mouths opened and closed. Yup, I said mouths. Plural. There were three.

"What is it?" Mayor Ooger asked in horror.

"Whatever it is, it just killed Dr. Lennox," Kat said.

Kat was right. It had. This thing must have been growing inside Dr. Lennox all along. That's why Dr. Lennox never left Meta-Gro for food: he didn't need human food. He no longer was human. This weed must have taken him over. Cross-fertilized with him? Planted a seed in him? Who knows? It was too gross to think about anyway.

It was the perfect plant, that perfect weed he was creating, immune to everything: drought, cold, fire, pesticides, weed-killing chemicals, spliced with DNA from the world's deadliest weeds; and from the looks of it, spliced with human DNA, too. This was the experiment inside Meta-Gro that had gone very wrong. This was the monster in the monster movie, but this monster, this Meta-Weed, was real.

The Meta-Weed raised its arm-like tendrils and every green plant on the island sprang to life. They encircled us, bounding our hands and feet and necks! They pulled at us and pinned us to the ground.

"I thought we won," Billy managed to say before a plant circled his throat.

"The bay water," I said. "It's gone. All of it washed off in the pouring rain."

"What are you going to do to us?" Kat said.

"You are nothing," the Meta-Weed hissed. "Thisss island is nothing. It is too small for our plans. We will reach the mainland and take over everything. It's all in me now, thanksss to the human Dr. Lennox. We go. You stay. Shrivel and die. Helpless."

Its vine-like arms shoved my parents off the crab shack roof. "You take thisss, Peter Mulligan." My parents fell into the green.

"Mom! Dad!" I reached toward them to help, but the vines around me tightened. I turned my head enough to see their faces. They were blinking, confused, like they were no longer wombies. Whew, that was good. Then, weeds encircled them like boa constrictors from head to toe. "Stop it!" I shouted at the Meta-Weed. "Leave them alone!"

"They are yoursss," the Meta-Weed answered. It turned to my grandmother, one arm-like tendril over her shoulder. "Thisss is mine."

"No! Not her. Gram!"

One of the Meta-Weed's back tendrils wrapped around Gram and lifted her up. Carrying her, the thing hopped down from the crab shack onto the dock. Its thick roots and rhizomes moved like a dozen strange spider legs. The Meta-Weed scuffled to a crabber filled with muddy soil. It slithered into the boat and placed Gram on the dock.

"More," it hissed to her. I heard Gram mindlessly toss shovelfuls of dirt onto the deck.

"No!" I yelled. "Stop! Take me!"

I craned my neck. Through the vines and leaves and rain I could just about see Gram step from the dock to the crabber. She started the engine. It pulled away from the harbor. Then the green covered me. I could hear the boat's engine. But that sound was soon drowned out by the grunts and groans of everyone else on the island fighting to free themselves from the weeds. I knew that we weren't sinking, but that's what it felt like as the weeds grew over top of us, layer after layer, drowning us. I struggled with every ounce of strength I had left, but it was useless.

Knowing it was over got me choked up. And for the first time in a long, long time, I started to cry. It wasn't about me dying, though. I was crying because I couldn't save Gram and the twins, my family, and the A-Team. I couldn't save Johnson Island.

And where had those green devils taken Sofia? She'd been right next to me when the battle went south.

It didn't matter. The weeds had won. We had lost.

I had lost.

Which brings me back to where my story began.

I was trapped.

Crying.

Alone.

It was the end of everything.

Chapter 50

The rain stopped. The thunderstorm was over. The clouds broke and streaks of early evening sunlight pierced through the weeds. I imagined that if you looked at the island from above, the entire thing would be green. I heard the Meta-Weed's getaway boat slowly chugging through the marina. Gram! I had to save her, somehow! I struggled one more time to escape, and this time, my fingertips touched something soft and warm and human.

"Pete? Is that you?" a tiny voice asked.

"Sofia?"

"Yeah."

As I reached for her, my waterworks trickled off. "Stretch more. Can you?"

"I'll try."

At first, it was just our fingers. The weeds gave a bit. We strained until we held hands.

"Gotcha," she said.

I turned my head in her direction. Through the weeds, I could make out her eyes.

"You think this is it, Pete?" she said.

"Maybe. I hope not. It doesn't look good."

"I know."

"At least we put up a good fight," I said.

"It was a good plan, Pete. Until the rain."

"Thanks."

We sunk an inch further, or the weeds grew over us, I couldn't tell.

"Hang on to me, Pete!" Sofia said.

"I am!"

The weeds stopped moving.

"Question," Sofia said.

I smiled. "Shoot."

"Did you have a good summer?"

"Up until this point, it was the best summer ever," I answered. "Did you?"

"Yeah, I did. You know why, Pete?"

"Why?" I asked.

She didn't answer. She squeezed my hand. I squeezed back as tightly as I could.

"I never met anyone like you," Sofia said.

"No one's ever been as nice to me as you have."

"You're easy to be nice to, you know?"

We felt the vines move again. We both grunted in pain as they tightened around us. It took us a few seconds to catch our breath.

"Question," I said.

"Shoot," she said.

"If I were Billy and you were Kat, would you have kissed me like that to save me?"

"To save your life? Of course," Sofia said.

We squeezed hands.

"Do you know what would've been different?" I asked.

"What?"

"I would have remembered."

"Humph," she said.

We stopped talking but kept holding hands. We waited for the end. Then—

"Listen," Sofia said.

"I hear it."

It was Reverend Apple's voice. She was singing an old church hymn. It was a good one. One everyone knew, and everyone joined in. I could hear Billy especially. And Tim Meeks, too. The hymn grew louder and louder, and the whole situation became more and more peaceful.

So there we were. The people of Johnson Island tied down by vines and covered in weeds, the late summer sun piercing the clouds, evening light pouring down on us, singing a hymn. And me—can you believe it?— me, holding Sofia's hand. It was almost heavenly—if we weren't about to die.

It was a nice way to kick the bucket, with my friends and family singing together, nearly everyone I cared about in one place. I was resolved that this was it. I squeezed Sofia's hand and listened to her sing. Then, the vines squeezed tighter.

The singing stopped.

And tighter.

It was becoming harder and harder to breathe.

"Goodbye, Pete Mulligan," I heard Sofia whisper.

"Sofia, I—" Her hand slipped out of mine. "Sofia?" I called out in a hoarse whisper. No answer. I gasped out, "Sofia? Anyone? Help..."

Then, without warning, the vines stopped moving. They froze.

I could breathe, just barely. The plants didn't feel angry anymore. Had it been the singing? Was it that I stopped fighting? Was it my feelings for Sofia? I didn't know.

"My vines stopped," I called out. "Sofia! Kat! Mom! Dad! Ooger! Anyone!"

"It stopped!" More muffled voices echoed around me.

Then, a shadow was above me and the weeds stretched apart. The sun blinded me for a second. After I blinked, I saw who was standing over me: Sofia and Kat.

"I had to rescue my sister first," Kat said.

"How'd you get out?"

"One bonus to skipping lunches is that I'm skinny, dum-dum," Kat said.

"And she had your grandfather's Swiss army knife," Sofia said, helping me up. "Why do you think they stopped?"

"I don't know." I listened for the boat with Gram and the Meta-Weed, which I couldn't hear. "Unless..." Then it hit me. "It's too far away. The Meta-Weed is out of range to control them. It's the only thinking weed."

"Then we better hurry. We have to catch up with Gram Mulligan," Sofia said.

"We'll take the fastest crabber on the island," Kat said. "Come on!"

As folks struggled to free themselves without a Swiss army knife, we ran as best as we could—over, under, around, through—the weeds. We reached the Angel Fish, Mayor Ooger's boat. The keys sat right where the wombie had left them.

"Ooger!" Kat cupped her hands and yelled. "We're taking your boat!"

"What?" Ooger called back. "Wait!" He wasn't happy, but there was no time to lose.

Chapter 51

"Do you know what you're doing?" I asked the twins as we leapt from the dock to Mayor Ooger's boat. I took off my backpack and dropped it on the soil-covered deck.

"Are you kidding?" Kat said. "We helped our dad fish a million times. Sofia can drive."

"Get the bowline," Sofia said to me.

"The what?"

"The bowline. The rope in the front of the boat. The one holding us to the dock."

"Oh." I unhooked it from the cleat and dropped it on the dock.

Sofia started the engine and we took off, gunning through the harbor faster than we were supposed to, but this was an emergency. "Okay, Pete," Sofia said. "Only two ways to go. East or west? New Jersey or Delaware? Gram Mulligan has to follow the channel markers. Which way do you think the weed will go? Which way?"

I thought. Where did the Meta-Weed want to go? Well, Gram was the one driving. Her only relatives off Johnson Island were us. That meant New Jersey. If there was any of Gram's mind left, that's where she'd go.

"Go east," I said. "Jersey."

"You sure?" Kat said.

"It's gotta be. Maybe. I mean, I'm sure. New Jersey. Go."

"Let's hope," said Sofia, turning the boat. "Fill those buckets with bay water, Kat. You too, Pete. Hurry. We'll need it when we catch 'em."

"Aye, aye," I said, leaning over the side and filling a bucket. I heaved it onto the deck. "Listen, Sofia," I said. "What we said to each other back there—when we were holding hands."

"Ooh," Kat said. "You guys were holding hands?"

193

"Shut up, Kat!" Sofia said angrily. "Now's no time to talk about that, Pete." She ignored me as she busied herself steering the boat. "We'll do it later."

"I just wanted to ask..." I hesitated. "I know we both thought we were going to die... but... did you...?"

Sofia pushed back the throttle and the boat leapt. I fell in the dirt. The engine roared as the boat tilted up and our speed doubled, maybe tripled. She yelled over the noise. "Not now, Pete! Shut up about it! You too, Kat!"

"Whatever!" Kat hollered back.

The Angel Fish bounced over the waves as we tore across the water. Now I knew why Ooger's boat was the fastest crabber on the island. It was a deadrise, like the others, but half the length and cabinless, just a steering column where Sofia manned the wheel. In the stern, a huge Suzuki outboard engine propelled us like an X-wing fighter blasting into hyperspace.

We followed the markers. We scanned the horizon for any sign of Gram. I hoped I had made the right choice. What if they had gone west toward Delaware?

"There!" Kat cried, pointing.

I looked and saw nothing, but that might have been because so much sea spray covered my glasses. "Where?"

"There!" Kat yelled over the noise of the engine.

"I see 'em, Kat!" Sofia said. "Hang on!"

We cut across the bay. The waves were bigger here, but even I could see that we were catching up to the Meta-Weed's full-sized crabber. Ooger's boat thumped across the water and foam flew in our faces. The precious bay water sloshed around in the buckets threatening to spill.

"Hold those buckets steady, you two!" Sofia ordered.

Kat and I did our best.

"Don't worry, Pete! She'll catch 'em," Kat yelled.

"I didn't know Sofia was so good at this! Does she drive your dad's boat a lot?!"

"Not really! This is like her second time!"

"What?!" I said. "I thought you said you went fishing with your dad all the time!"

"We do! But he never lets us drive the boat!"

We flew over a wave and the whole boat shook when we smacked back down into the water. I did my best to keep my faith in Sofia, not spill the buckets, not throw up, and not get bounced out of the Angel Fish.

We were closer now. I finally had a good view of the getaway crabber. Gram drove the boat. Behind her, the large, ugly Meta-Weed stood in the middle of the deck. Its head turned.

Oh boy!

"It sees us!" I shouted.

"It looks madder than a wet hen!" Kat said.

"I'll try to get next to 'em!" Sofia shouted. "Hit it with the buckets!"

"Okay!" I picked up the first bucket. "Hey, look!"

"What?" both twins said.

"This bucket! It's red! It's from Meta-Gro! Talk about irony, right?" We hit a wave. The Angel Fish lurched. The bucket slipped out of my hands and spilled all over my Blob T-shirt!

"Pete!" The twins screamed.

"Sorry!"

"Stop fooling around!" Kat said.

"It's okay," Sofia shouted. "We still have two more. Be careful, Pete!"

"What's the big deal? We're surrounded by bay water," I said.

"Water out here isn't exactly the same as near the island, you know," Sofia said. "It might not work the same. Okay, here we go."

Sofia eased up on the throttle to match the speed of Gram's boat, which was moving much slower than ours. We pulled alongside her. Our last weed weapon sloshed around inside the buckets.

"Let her go!" I shouted to the Meta-Weed.

Its head spun my way, and a plant tendril shot out and hit me square in the face. But I held onto the bucket.

"We go! You ssstay!" it said.

Kat tossed her bucket. The bay water hit the Meta-Weed in whatever you would call its lower extremities. Its three mouths screeched in pain! The spider-like roots thrashed on the deck.

"That hurt it," I said.

"Now, Pete!" Kat yelled.

But before I could throw my bucket, the current forced our boats apart, and we were too far away.

"Keep it steady, Sofia!" called Kat.

Sofia turned the wheel and we bumped boats again. The bucket in my arms sloshed. We kept doing that, bumping and pulling apart, hitting the sides of each other's boat repeatedly. It just wouldn't lock up and stay steady, the water and the wakes were too rough. I clutched the bucket, afraid to take a chance and miss.

"Ooger's going to kill you," Kat said.

"I'm doing my best!" Sofia said.

"Gram!" I yelled.

She ignored me.

"Gram! Come on! It's me, Pete, your beloved grandson. Come on, look at me! You can fight it!"

The boats were side by side again when a long green tendril zipped out from the Meta-Weed. The sharp vine grabbed my leg and Kat's and dropped us to the dirty deck. Miraculously, I kept the bucket up and saved the bay water. Another long vine wrapped around the steering wheel and turned it.

The boats came apart again.

Sofia struggled to control the wheel, but this forced her to grab the Meta-Weed's thorny vines. I saw blood as she twisted the wheel back toward the crabber and the boats bumped again.

It was now or never.

I tossed our last bucket of bay water.

"Jeez Louise!"

I missed.

"Come on, dum-dum!" Kat yelled.

"I got it!" I said. I leaned over the side. I almost fell overboard. Kat grabbed me. I scooped water in the bucket and tossed again.

This time, I was right on target!

The water hit the Meta-Weed right in the face.

It had no effect.

Not good.

"Sofia was right," I said. "It's only the water near the island!"

"Now what?" Kat said.

Chapter 52

I had no choice. There was only one thing left to do. "Hold my glasses, Kat."

"What?" I shoved them in her hand. "Why?"

I took two steps back to make sure I had enough room and yelled, "Take your stinking paws off her, you damned dirty weed!"

With a running start, I took a flying leap over the side of the Angel Fish, landing on the Meta-Weed's crabber smack-dab between it and Gram! "That's from Planet of the Apes, 1968, you monster!"

We faced off. The Meta-Weed stood back near the stern. Gram steered the boat in the cabin. I Karate Kamp-stanced between them. Master Jeffrey would be proud. I punched and kicked the green beast as it wrapped its thorny vines around me, snaking up to my throat and lifting me off the deck. The three mouths opened and shrieked in my face! Each mouth a different high-pitched howl! I squeezed my eyes shut. "I need some help!"

"Pete!" Sofia screamed, pulling the Angel Fish close on my left. "Kat, the gaff!"

"On it!" Kat grabbed the boat gaff, which is a wooden pole with a hook on the end for grabbing lines. She swung it over her head like a samurai and smacked the back of the Meta-Weed again and again. "Get! Off! My! Friend!" This distracted it long enough to drop me. I scrambled to my feet, slipping on the mud-slicked deck, and yanked out the thorn behind Gram's ear. Her head sunk and rose.

"Pete?" she said, confused.

"Gram!" I said. "You're back!"

"What's happening? Where are we?"

"Stop the boat!" I commanded.

"What?" she asked, still in a befuddled wombie-daze.

197

"Cut the engine, Gram. Stop the boat!" I turned her toward the helm and she did. When the crabber stopped, the Meta-Weed slid backward toward the stern.

Gram stepped out of the cabin and slipped. I caught her arm.

"Take it easy," I said. "I have you." That was when I heard Sofia.

"Watch out!" she yelled.

Oh no, I had forgotten about the Meta-Weed! I turned and ducked low. But Gram didn't.

A long vine whizzed over my head, missing me but knocking Gram overboard.

"Gram!" I shouted.

She fell in the water to my right, the opposite side of the Angel Fish! There was no way the twins could reach her. It was up to me! I crawled across the dirty, wet deck to the side of the boat. But before I could dive in, Gram surfaced, thank God. She was treading water a dozen yards away, bobbing up and down in the swells. She reached an arm up and easily swam back toward me.

"Take my hand," I called, leaning over the side. But a long Meta-Weed tendril spun over her head. It plunged into the water behind her. "Hurry, Gram! It's coming!"

But when she was only a few feet away, the tendril tightened, and the Meta-Weed's vine yanked her under the water.

"GRAM!" I screamed. She popped back up. Then, the weed pulled her back under!

"Stop! What are you doing?" I shouted at the Meta-Weed, completely panicked.

"Drive us to land or she diesss in the water," it hissed.

She popped up again—coughing and gasping for air.

"Stop it! You'll kill her!"

"Drive usss or she dies." He pushed her down again. "You'll not ssstop us, Peter Mulligan."

"Not alone he won't!" I heard Sofia cry.

Then SMASH! Sofia rammed the Angel Fish into our boat! Everything lurched to one side. Our crabber sailed sideways, away from Ooger's boat. I slipped in the mud covering the deck and fell. The vine holding Gram snapped out of the water to help the weed steady itself. I scrambled to the side and saw Gram pop to the surface just past the front of the crabber. She was treading water. She gave me a thumbs up. She was okay.

I turned toward the Meta-Weed. That DNA-enhanced devil had threatened to kill my grandmother! My eyes squinted, like every tough guy in every movie I'd ever seen. I was furious! Then, I noticed something.

The Meta-Weed was teetering, unbalanced, its roots not deep enough in the deck's muddy soil to cling effectively. This was my chance. I jumped at the thing as the boat rocked in the water. With all my weight, I grabbed the top of its torso and head. I bear-hugged it, smothering its evil face against my Blob T-shirt—a shirt freshly soaked in the J-Island bay water from that red bucket I spilled!

"You just got Steve McQueen-ed!"

I felt the whole thing give. Its roots ripped out of the muddy dirt. We fell overboard. Its tendrils loosened as it tried to grab onto the crabber, but I squeezed its face tighter and tighter, like its weeds had choked me.

"How do you like it?"

In the water, we tumbled and rolled as we fought, a tangled knot of me and vines. It struggled to break free. Sharp thorns tore at my skin, my arms, my back, my face, but I wouldn't let go! Not letting go of things, like school desks, was my specialty!

We sank further and further. I squeezed harder and harder.

Then, my lungs felt tight. I needed air. Maybe I hadn't thought this all the way through. Too late now! I wouldn't let go. Without warning, the Meta-Weed stopped struggling. It loosened its grip on me. In the nick of time!

I pushed it away and swam up as fast as I could. I heard my name being screamed, in that muffled underwater way. I desperately swam in that direction. Finally, my heart thumping in my chest, my lungs about to burst, I broke the water's surface! Air!

I saw the Angel Fish—Gram on deck with the twins. Yes, they got her. My muscles sagged with relief.

"There he is!" Kat yelled, pointing at me. "Throw him the rope!"

Gram quickly knotted the rope into a loop and handed it to Sofia, who tossed it to me. "Pete! Grab it!"

I did.

"Put it under your arms," Gram called. "We'll pull you in."

Fine by me. My arms felt like they weighed a hundred pounds each. I could hardly lift them. I secured the loop around my chest. They pulled. I kicked weakly trying to help. In the distance, the getaway crabber was drifting away with the current.

"Where is it?" Sofia asked, eyes scanning the water.

"I think it drowned," I panted. "It let go of me." I spit out water. "Is this the rope from my backpack?"

"Yeah," Kat said.

"So ironic," I half-laughed and half-coughed.

"Why's that?" Sofia asked.

"My heist supplies," I said as I reached the Angel Fish. With the help of them pulling the rope, I grabbed the edge of the boat. I rested a minute, catching my breath. "I told you every good heist movie has a rope."

Sofia smiled. "I guess you were right."

"What we really could have used was a grappling hook. But where do you find a grappling hook on Johnson—"

SPLASH!

CRASH!

A huge wave hit me! But it wasn't a wave!

The Meta-Weed burst from the water. It snaked around me and howled in rage. It clung to my back.

"Pete!" the twins yelled, hanging onto the rope with Gram.

Two thick tendrils reached past me and grabbed the side of the boat. From below, snaking vines encircled my legs and pulled me down. Jeez Louise! It was going to drown me, then climb into the Angel Fish!

Kat let go of the rope and picked up the gaff. She slammed it down on the monster's back. The green beast screeched in pain. Then its vines tightened around me like a hundred little bear hugs. It was the Meta-Weed's turn to squeeze. I held onto the edge of the boat with the little strength I had left. If I let go, I was done for, and the girls and Gram would face the monster alone. I couldn't, I wouldn't, let that happen! I couldn't freak out and get twee-mangled now!

But I was so weak. The Meta-Weed yanked me underwater. I could hear distant muffled screaming from the ladies, the idling engine of the boat, the thrashing of the water, a million tiny bubbles bursting. Wait! Twee-mangled! I remembered the twins' definition: when the crab trap lines get tangled! If we could get the Meta-Weed's roots and vines tangled in the propeller...yes. Straining my arms to the breaking point, I willed myself back up.

"Kat!" I called. "The gaff! The propeller!"

"What?" Kat yelled as she swung at the Meta-Weed's circling tendrils.

"Try to twee-mangle it—grrrk!"

It dragged me under again. No! I couldn't quit now! I broke the surface long enough to catch a breath then it pulled me back down. The Meta-Weed's thrashing vines splashed. Under the water, long tendrils moved like an octopus's tentacles. The engine was to my left. If we could only tangle a vine or two in the propeller, it would be enough.

I surfaced again. Sofia and Gram pulled the rope holding me. Kat was still whacking the thing with the gaff when I caught her eye.

"The hook, Kat," I coughed out. "Twee-mangle it...the propeller." My eyes darted left to the floating vines near the engine.

Kat's face lit up. "I get you, Pete!"

She hooked a few weedy vines and pulled them toward the idling engine. Nothing happened at first. Then, the vines on my left side tightened and pulled. The Meta-Weed's head turned toward the engine. Kat noticed. It squeezed me tighter.

"Gotcha, dum-dum!" Kat yelled.

The green beast's head spun right, and tendrils shot from the water, scrabbling to hold on. One thick tendril knotted itself around the Angel Fish railing. Two others found those T-shaped cleat things you tie boat lines to.

"Gram!" I gasped. "The engine!"

Gram nodded. She slipped and slid in the rocking boat, heading to the wheel.

"Sofia, the rope!" I said. "Don't let go!"

"I won't!" Sofia braced her legs against the deck. She wrapped the rope around her hands. The engine yanked the Meta-Weed to my left again. Its knotted tendrils tightened on the cleats and railing. It would be a tug-of-war below and above the water—the engine pulled the Meta-Weed into the propeller toward the left, and Sofia pulled me toward the right!

"It's twee-mangled good!" Kat yelled. "Crank it, Gram Mulligan!"

Jeez Louise! This was it! I clung to the rope. Gram revved the engine. The rope cut into my chest and armpits. Sofia held on, her face straining. "Kat! Help me!" she grunted.

Kat dropped down beside her and grabbed the rope.

The Meta-Weed's roots and vines were tangled in the churning propellers. It was working! The engine was winning the tug-of-war. Only one problem. It wouldn't let go of my legs. Underwater, my legs, still covered in vines, lifted toward the roaring engine with the Meta-Weed.

Then, the rope gave. I moved lower in the water!

"AAAAAH!" I yelled.

"No!" Sofia grunted. The twin's faces turned red with effort, but the Meta-Weed wasn't giving up! I couldn't breathe from the pressure of the rope.

The Meta-Weed screamed, desperate to hold on to me!

I screamed, desperate to grab the edge of the boat!

The twins screamed, desperate to hang on to the rope!

Gram revved the engine even harder. Suddenly, a thick tendril on one of the cleats snapped! Then another one!

The rope slipped another foot.

"No!" Sofia yelled.

I went under. I desperately kicked my legs. I had to get back up. Suddenly, the last thick tendril holding onto the railing split. It flew past me underwater like a torpedo. The pressure stopped.

And the Meta-Weed shot into the propeller and exploded! A terrible, shredding noise! A churning, chopping mess!

The twins pulled me up. My head bobbed in the water, one arm grabbing the side of the boat.

"It's working!" Kat cried.

Frothing green goo and ripped plant pieces bubbled to the surface around us.

"Gross," Sofia said, scanning the water.

Then the engine died with a groan and sputter. A small cloud of black smoke puffed into the air. It got quiet, with only the sound of water lapping against the Angel Fish. We watched and waited. But nothing happened.

"Whew," I exhaled.

We broke into smiles.

"That was nippity-cut, right?" I said.

"Yup." Sofia collapsed into the mud-lined boat.

"We did it," Kat said. "I can't believe it."

"Let's bring him in girls," Gram said, stepping carefully in the rocking boat. "Up and over." They hauled me into Ooger's boat, which looked terrible and was taking on water.

"Pete, you alright?" Sofia asked.

"Yeah," I answered. "Gram?"

"I'll live," she said.

"Twee-mangled?" Kat laughed, slapping my knee.

"Of all the mud-footer tricks, Pete," said Sofia. "That's the champ."

"Smart idea, kid." Gram added. "Hooking him to the propellers."

"Chewed him up good," Kat said.

We peered over the edge. Bits of weed and slick, green goo were spread around the Angel Fish. The Meta-Weed's getaway crabber, which was sinking fast, had drifted quite a distance.

"It's like in a million pieces," Sofia said.

"You think it's dead?" I asked.

"Nothing is moving," Kat said with a shrug.

We turned and sat on the deck, covered in four inches of mud and gunk and water.

"Jeez Louise, we really wrecked Ooger's boat," I said.

"Yup," Kat said. "That's what happens when you ram it into another boat at full speed, right, Sofia?"

"You think he's gonna be mad, Gram Mulligan?" Sofia asked.

"Nah, you kids are heroes. You saved Johnson Island."

The three of us looked at each other and nodded. I put my arms around the twins. Gram put her arms around all of us. I think that was the first hug Gram Mulligan gave me all summer.

"So, what do we do now, Gram?" I asked.

"They'll send someone for us," she answered. "I reckon we wait."

"Wait." I repeated. "I can do that."

"It's been a long day," Sofia said.

"You can say that again," Gram said. "I'm wore out to a frazzle."

"From A to izzard," I said.

"That's right," Gram said.

Those Johnson Island expressions were really growing on me. We sat quietly for a long while, rocking in the waves. Then, in the distance, we faintly heard a boat engine.

"That'll be them," Gram said.

"Wow," Kat said.

The sun was setting; above us, a spectacular sky.

"It's beautiful," Sofia said.

"I've never seen prettier," Kat said.

"We always have beautiful sunsets on Johnson Island," Gram said.

"Mm-hmm," I said. "We do."

Chapter 53

We weren't rescued by anyone we knew, but by a passing mainland fisherman who was kind enough to take us back to Johnson Island. Once there, we were greeted as heroes. Lots of hugs with Mom and Dad and the A-Team. I thanked Chad for his insistence on planks. The island nurse checked out Gram. Fighting monsters is tough on old ladies, even J-Island ones.

"Hey-o, everyone!" Reverend Apple shouted. "How about three cheers for our heroes?"

"Hip-hip hooray!" the crowd answered.

Everyone 'hip-hip hooray-ed' us, and we all beamed from ear-to-ear. Everyone, that is, except Mayor Ooger. Uh-oh. He was putting it together.

"Girls," he asked real slow. "Where's my boat?"

There was a moment of silence. The twins and I exchanged looks.

"Sofia's a terrible captain," Kat said, gesturing to her sister. "She cannot pull up to another boat without ramming into it!"

"What?" Sofia answered. "You told me to ram the Angel Fish into the Meta-Weed's boat!"

"Ram?!" Ooger repeated, turning red.

"It didn't matter anyway, sir," I jumped in. "After the engine exploded, we—"

"The engine exploded?!" Ooger cut me off. He removed his sunglasses. His eyes bulged. "After the engine exploded, what happened? Where is she?"

Gram came up behind us and said, "There ain't no other way to say it. She sank."

"Sank!" Ooger shouted. He ripped off his baseball cap and threw it to the ground.

Gram Mulligan put her arms around us. We took a step back. "Give him room, kids. He's 'bout to bust a gut."

"I told you greenies to wait! I told you! Why'd you take the Angel Fish? Why?"

"She's the fastest crabber on the island," Kat said quietly.

"She was the fastest crabber on the island! Oh, I've got my nuff! I can't believe it. You sank the Angel Fish. You shackly-brained, muck-rotten chicklets!"

I thought he was really insulting us here, but I never did ask anyone for the full J-Island translation, so... maybe not? Maybe.

"I'm so mad, I could tear up a crab cooker!" Ooger continued, despite the whole town watching. "I can't afford a new boat. I can barely stay above water on a good month! You gonna have to pay for it. Ain't no other way! Someone's gotta!"

"Now, hold on, Ooger," Mr. Jin said. "It was your idea to let Meta-Gro come here. If you hadn't done that, this whole mess wouldn't have happened."

"Tom, they sank my boat," Ooger said. "I can't eat without a boat. Can't live."

"We didn't want to," Sofia said.

"It just happened during the fight, sir," I added.

"That monster weed wouldn't let Gram Mulligan go," Kat explained.

"And look at our town," Reverend Apple said.

"Yeah," Cookie agreed, spreading his arms. "Who cares about one boat? Do you see the island? Do you see what Meta-Gro did?"

Ooger looked around at the crowd, at the street. He picked up his baseball cap and dusted off green leaves. "You're right. I'm sorry," he sighed. "It is my fault. We've been taken advantage of here. I have. I'm a waterman. To keep our island way of life, I talked the town council, all of you, into letting Meta-Gro come here. But they lied to me and I didn't take the time to check the facts. I wanted to believe that more work and more money would be good for us, but I reckon that temptation was a mistake. I should've remembered, when you make a deal with the devil, things look good going out, skies clear and calm water, but on the way back home, that devil sea is going to sink you. You all know what I mean. I'm sorry, gang. I'm sorry."

Ooger hung his head and sat down on a bench covered in limp weeds.

"I'm sorry," Sofia said. "We all are."

"No boat, no crabs, no money," Ooger said.

I raised my hand. "Question, sir."

"Question, what?" Ooger said, scratching his head.

"Pete has a question for you, Ooger," Sofia explained.

"Oh. What is it, son?"

"Aren't you going to sue the pants off Meta-Gro? They hired Dr. Lennox. They did the research. Technically, they own all these weeds."

"Humph. That's a thought," Ooger considered. "But corporations like that have big, fancy lawyers. They got wudgets full of money. Case could last for years. It'd be nearly impossible to win." He put his cap on his head and pulled the visor down. "But I reckon we might try." He stood up. "Hey-o, mud-footers, let's get cleaning this place up!"

"Not yet!" Kat shouted. She was carrying a red bucket. Something brown sloshed in it. The crowd stopped to watch. She and Billy marched up to Tim Meeks.

"Aw, come on," Tim Meeks said, backing away. "I saved your lives three times today."

"A bet is a bet," Kat said.

"You lost," Billy added.

"No way!" Tim Meeks replied. "This is not gonna happen."

The crowd formed a circle around Tim Meeks and Kat and Billy. Tim Meeks shook his head. "Nuh-uh, Tweedledum."

"You make a bet with 'em, Tim Meeks?" Ooger asked.

"Yeah, but—"

"Son, you gonna live on Johnson Island," Ooger explained, "you got to realize, welching on a bet is like twee-mangling a box of busters. You don't do it, if you want to make the bones."

"Say what?" I asked. I got the twee-mangled part but missed the rest. Nobody explained.

"I get you, Ooger," Tim Meeks said meekly.

"Get what?" I demanded. Some of these J-Island expressions still made no sense.

"Quiet, Pete," Gram said.

Tim Meeks removed his hat. He sat down. Billy and Kat lifted the red bucket and dumped muddy sludge on his head.

The town cheered.

"Now we're square, Tim Meeks," Kat said.

"Even-steven, Kat Jin," he said.

Chapter 54

Everyone helped with the clean-up the next day. Even the Red Cross came. It was a huge deal. We might have even been on the news. But every electronic connection to the outside world had been destroyed by the weeds. Mostly, it was a fun time—the whole island working together. But looming over it all was a sinking feeling that never went away: my summer on Johnson Island was over.

After the second day of de-weeding the island, my parents and I sat on the porch together when my mom said, "Honey, your dad and I want you to know, so you can get used to the idea… we have to leave on Friday."

"Me too?"

"Of course, you too," Dad answered. "All of us."

"Why?"

"We have to be home before school starts," Mom explained. "Stone Hill Middle School starts early this year."

"Stone Hill Middle School? We're staying in Stone Hill? You said—"

"We tried," Mom said. "We really did."

"There's factors you don't understand, Peter," my dad added. "My commute, your needs, the housing market. It just wasn't—"

"I want to stay!" I interrupted. "Here. On Johnson Island. Please."

"With my mom?"

"Yes! Please."

"Fine by me," Gram Mulligan said from the screen door.

My parents' eyes shot toward her.

"Really?" Dad asked.

Gram Mulligan nodded. "Mm-hmm."

"Please!" I begged.

My dad looked at my mom. They were quiet.

"This is just... we have to think about it," my mom said. "It's such a big step, and... we'll consult with your A-Team, okay? That's fair. Is that okay with you, Peter?"

I nodded. At least I had a chance.

"Humph," Gram Mulligan grunted. "Dinner's ready."

The next day as I helped with the clean-up, I realized that my present pickle was quite the switcheroo. In the beginning of the summer, I had hoped the A-Team would stop me from coming to Johnson Island. Now, I was praying they'd let me stay. Unfortunately, it did not work out—again. Jeez Louise!

None of them came through.

My parents told me that Dr. Carlos and Ms. Nunzio both agreed that the island school was too small and didn't have enough professionals to help me. Chad said that he was impressed with my weight loss and my new-found prowess with planks, but that Cookie's and the proximity of ice cream would be awfully tempting for a guy like me. Stupid, A-Team!

But my mom and dad still hadn't decided. I still had a glimmer of hope. Middle school would be bad enough, but at Stone Hill? With the same kids who witnessed my desk-dragging freak out? With the world's nastiest ninja bullies? No, thank you. I caught myself twisting my shirt around my finger. I stopped and convinced myself that I didn't need to panic. Not yet. Besides, the twins were sure I'd be staying. I hoped they were right.

On Thursday evening, just before dinner, it was time for my parents' final verdict. Sofia and Kat waited with me in Gram's living room. We sat on her couch. Gram Mulligan leaned against the wall near the dining room. She sipped coffee from a mug that read: CRABBY UNTIL I GET MY COFFEE. My parents sat across from us. They had to let me stay. I was sure they'd let me stay. We could all move to Johnson Island. Who cared what the A-Team said?

"Buddy," my dad said. "This was a really tough decision..."

Oh no.

"...but we think it's best that you come home... you can come back next summer or even some weekends."

"Humph," Gram mumbled.

Humph was right! My cheeks warmed, tears welled in my eyes.

"We know the summer has been special," Mom said, "but you know how you can be, and the school here is really small and—"

"You know what I think?" Sofia interrupted, pointing at my parents. "You guys are stupid. This is stupid!"

"You're making a big mistake, dum-dums!" Kat chimed in.

"Girls!" Gram said. "Ain't no need for sassin'. You apologize."

"Us?" Kat said, stunned.

"Apologize?" Sofia said.

"Come on, Sofia!" Kat rose from the couch.

Sofia jumped up. They ran out the front door and slammed it.

"Ladies!" I called. "Wait!" I followed them, but by the time I had fumbled my way through the screen door to the front porch, they were already slamming the gate and running down Broadway toward their house. I'd never be able to catch them. My mom and dad came up behind me.

"Wow, they're fast," my dad said.

"I know," I mumbled.

Mom draped her arm around my shoulders. "It's for the best, Peter."

"Is it?" I said. "For who?"

After a tense dinner, I packed alone in my room upstairs. Afterward, Gram and I settled in on the couch to watch a classic black-and-white flick called To Have and Have Not, 1944, starring Lauren Bacall and Humphrey Bogart. It was pretty romantic stuff. We hadn't gotten far when my mom joined us. My dad was out cruisin' the island and catching up with old friends.

"Peter, do you really think you should be up this late?" my mom asked.

"I guess not," I said, knowing this was a hint to go to bed.

"Humph," Gram said. "Are you tired, kiddo?"

"Sort of, I guess," I answered. What did it matter? I was leaving. It was all over.

"You have a big day tomorrow, right, honey?" Mom reminded me.

Like I could think of anything else.

"Right." I rose from the couch.

I never won bedtime battles. Gram looked at me, eyebrows raised in surprise. She paused the movie.

"Good night, Gram," I said.

"Humph," Gram said. "Good night."

"Good night, Mom."

"Good night."

Defeated, I trudged up the stairs. I knew I should have stood up for myself, but what was the use fighting with my mom? I'd already lost. I couldn't focus on To Have and Have Not, 1944, anyway. I had other romantical stuff on my mind, stuff in the "Have Not" category.

"If that's how you see it," I caught Gram's voice saying, which snapped me out of my funk. What were they talking about? See what? I stopped at the top of the stairs and listened.

"It's going to be hard enough leaving tomorrow," my mom explained. "If he's overtired, he'll cry. And it's just awful when he does. After the summer, I'm sure you know."

"Suzanne," Gram said, "as far as I know, that boy cried one time, just one time, on this island. And that's when he thought he was leaving."

Then Gram played the movie. For the last time that summer on Johnson Island, I went to my room, shut the door, and got ready for bed.

Chapter 55

Once under the covers, I kept tossing and turning thinking about the "Have Not" stuff: Sofia. One memory played over and over in my mind. When Sofia and I were trapped with the rest of the town, and the weeds were slowly choking us to death, we touched fingers and held each other's hands. It was the strongest romantic hand-holding I'd ever felt in my life! It was the only romantic hand-holding, too. But that was less important. What mattered was that we had never had a chance to talk about it. I needed to know before I left in the morning. Did Sofia feel the same way? Could we be long-distance boyfriend and girlfriend?

It was late, maybe after ten or 10:30. But I didn't care. I wasn't tired. I was wide awake. I got out of bed and dressed. I had to see her. There was only one thing to do: sneak out.

Because Gram's old house creaked like a pirate ship, I carefully opened my bedroom window. As gracefully as possible (which was not very) I squeezed out the window. Feet first, then belly and body, my head last and... there stood Sofia!

"Jeez Louise!" She was on the roof.

"Shhh!" she whispered. "Calm down."

"You scared me," I said.

She gave me a look.

"Why are you on my roof?" I asked.

"Why are you climbing out your window?" she replied.

"Why are you wearing pajamas?" They were baby blue.

"Why aren't you?" she asked. "It's way past your bedtime."

We considered each other for a moment or two.

"Ah-ha!" Sofia said.

"What?"

"You're sneaking out to see me," she said with a grin.

"And you snuck out to see me," I countered.

"Funny, isn't it?"

"Indeed."

We sat down and leaned against the side of the house. The night sky was dazzling.

"The stars look so great from Johnson Island," I said.

"Yup, not much light pollution here. You should see it in the winter, on a crisp night."

"I wish I could."

"Me too."

We were quiet again. We stared at the brilliant constellations for a while. It was peaceful. But I could feel my heart beating fast. Sofia turned and looked at me.

"Listen, I... I wanted to say I was sorry for calling your parents stupid. I mean, they are, for making you leave, but I shouldn't have said it. It was pretty sassy."

"I don't care. I agree. I want to stay here," I said.

"You do?"

"I do."

"Why?" she asked.

"Because... I like it here. Everyone. The whole island. Living with Gram and..." I trailed off and lowered my head.

"What else?" Sofia asked.

"Nothing."

"You're lying," she said. "Just say it. I know what it is."

"You," I said. "I like you."

"I know," she said and smiled. "That's why I came. I know you like me, Pete. But I have to tell you something. Before you get hurt."

"Before I get hurt?" I repeated. "What? What is it?"

"But it's hard to say."

Oh no. What did that mean? My heart beat even faster. "Just say it," I said.

"It's just..."

"What? Tell me."

"I want you to know..."

"What?!"

"I like you, too," Sofia said.

Oh, thank God. I exhaled deeply. "Phew, that was nippity cut. I thought you were going to say something else."

"I am," Sofia said. "I like you, but we can't..."

My heart flip-flopped in my chest. "What?"

"We can't be like boyfriend and girlfriend or anything like that."

"Why not, if—?"

"I told you in the beginning of the summer. My dad. No boyfriends allowed. Same thing with Kat and Billy. He says we're too young."

"Yeah, but—"

"He's serious. If he found out, he'd go crazy, he'd tear up—"

"—a crab cooker, be madder than a wet hen," I finished. "I get it!"

"He wouldn't let us be friends anymore," Sofia said.

"Oh," I said. "That is serious."

"It doesn't matter anyway. You're leaving tomorrow."

"I know," I sighed. "So what do we do?"

"I don't know," Sofia said, staring right into my eyes. "This is like one of those sad black-and-white classics you made us watch with Gram Mulligan. What would they do in the movies?"

"Um, they would say something meaningful, a famous line."

"Like what?" she asked.

I thought. "Gone with the Wind, 1939. 'Frankly, my dear, I don't give a damn.'"

"What does that mean? What don't you give a damn about?"

"Anything but you."

Then, I leaned in and kissed her.

She kissed me back!

Just like a movie.

Chapter 56

I stood on the dock by the ferry.

Seemed like most of the island was there to say goodbye. There were sad faces.

"See you next summer, Pete."

"Bye-bye, Pete."

"We're going to miss you."

I shook hands and gave hugs. Boys my age lined up in bathing suits on the dock for the island tradition of sending off the ferry. I tried to keep it together. The time had come for the hard goodbyes.

Kat shook my hand then pulled me in for a hug. "See you next July, dum-dum."

"See you, Kat."

"Try to get a new T-shirt or two." She kidded me.

"I will."

Sofia stepped up and gave me a big hug.

"I'll miss you most," I said. "We'll be in touch, we'll talk."

"I know, but it won't be the same," Sofia said.

Gram wrapped her arms around us. I pulled away from Sofia and hugged Gram.

"Thanks for taking me in. It was the best summer ever."

"Me, too." She pinched my cheek. "Here's looking at you, kid."

"Humphrey Bogart. Casablanca. 1942."

"Who am I going to watch movies with now?" Gram asked.

"Us," Sofia said.

"Yeah," Kat agreed, taking Gram's hand.

"We have to go, Peter," my dad said. "We're holding up the ferry."

"Okay," I answered, not wanting to leave.

"You take as long as you like, Pete Mulligan," the Joyce Mary captain called from the ferry. "You saved the island. We can wait. You folks are the only passengers, anyways."

"Thanks," my dad said, not looking appreciative.

"Hey-o, Pete Mulligan," the captain shouted to me. "This here ferry." He winked. "You think... 'We're gonna need a bigger boat?' Well?"

"Too easy, sir. Jaws, 1975."

The captain laughed. "You get 'em every time, kid. Hey-o, you know, Pete Mulligan… 'A boy's best friend is his mother.'"

"'A boy's best friend is his mother?'" I repeated slowly. "Hmm. I think Psycho, 1960."

The captain laughed a second time. "You win again, kid. You win again." He nodded to my parents. "Movie whiz, he is. Especially the oldies."

"We know," my mom said.

After a few more goodbyes, we boarded the Joyce Mary. I sat as close as I could to the stern. My parents sat on either side of me. Everyone waved goodbye as we slid away from the dock. The Bay Boys jumped off the side and splashed into the water, cheering. I half-smiled.

Then, unexpectedly, fully dressed, Sofia ran and leapt off the end of the dock, as if she were chasing the ferry. Her face surfaced, and she waved as the boat slowly chugged away. It was more than I could take. I put my face in my hands. I felt the beginning of a cry well deep inside of me and rise behind my eyes. Would it be a simple leaksie? A long waterworks? Or an embarrassing gross-out gusher with tears and snot? Who knew? Jeez Louise! I hadn't been off the island for a minute and I was back to the same old routine.

Or was I? I squeezed my eyes. A single tear had slipped out and wet my palm when the strangest thing happened. I decided: no. Why should I cry? I knew that I would see Johnson Island again. I would visit. I would call Sofia. I would come next summer, for sure. And crying, I thought, crying wouldn't make any difference to any of that. I could be sad about it. I could miss everyone. But I didn't need to cry. I didn't even want to right now. So, I didn't.

With my palms still covering my face, I felt my mom's hand on my left shoulder. My dad's hand touched my right.

"Oh, Peter," I heard my mom say gently.

"It'll be okay," Dad said, trying to comfort me.

"I knew you should've gone to bed earlier," my mom sighed.

Gone to bed earlier? Was that why she thought I was upset? It had nothing to do with that. Nothing at all. As I lifted my head, I wiped that one, tiny tear on my pant leg. I stood up and turned around to face them, my back leaning against the ferry railing.

"First of all," I said, "I'm not crying. And if I was, it wouldn't be because I didn't get enough sleep, like everyone always thinks. I'm not wore out to a frazzle, not a bit. Actually, Gram Mulligan and I watched movies all summer, every night, way past my bedtime!"

"You didn't!" my mom said.

"I did!" I said. "And I wasn't green around the gills once!" I stopped leaning against the railing and planted my feet. I stood straighter. "I only feel twee-mangled, because I'm going to miss my mud-footer whackems, from A to izzard, especially Sofia because we went gal-ling!"

My mom looked at my dad. "What did he say?"

Dad's mouth was hanging wide open. "He's sad because he's going to miss the island and his friends, and um, you remember, Sofia?"

My mom nodded.

"He kissed her!"

"Exactly!" I said. "I don't want to be one of the blue hen's chickens, but I want you to know, since spending the summer here... I hate going to bed early. I love watching old movies with Gram Mulligan. And I love Johnson Island!"

I turned away from them and grabbed the Joyce Mary railing.

"Humph!"

Without realizing it, I was squeezing the railing so hard my hands were white-knuckled. We chugged steadily out of the marina. Looking down at the small wake, I noticed my death grip. I relaxed my fingers and enjoyed the view. We passed the fishing boats and crab shacks. The watermen worked their traps. The tall J-Island water tower stood near the church steeple like a protective big brother. I heard my parents' voices float behind me over the humming engine.

"What do you think, Suzanne?"

"Roger, you said you hated growing up here."

"I did say that I hated growing up here," my dad answered. "But we both know Peter and I are different."

"He is one of a kind," Mom said.

"So is this island," Dad agreed.

There was a long pause. I heard the boat's engine change gears. It stopped moving. Then, it reversed. We were headed back toward Johnson Island. I spun around to face my parents, who were just emerging from the cabin.

"Mom, Dad, does this mean—?"

"You can stay, Peter," Mom said.

"With Gram Mulligan?"

"Yes, with Gram," Dad said.

"This is what you really want?" Mom asked.

"Very much so," I said. "Yes." I wrapped my arms around her. "Yes! Yes! Yes!"

My dad hugged us.

"What about you guys?" I asked. "How will we do it?"

"We'll figure all that out," Dad said. "As long as you're happy, buddy."

"I am."

Sofia was swimming toward the boat. "What's wrong?" she called, treading water halfway between the ferry and the dock. "Did you forget something?"

"No!" I yelled. "I'm staying!"

"What?"

"I said I'm staying!" I yelled louder.

"You're what?"

"I'm going to— Oh, forget it!" I kicked off my sneakers. I ripped off my Oxford shirt, revealing good ol' Frankenstein. I yanked off my glasses and tossed them at my dad.

"Peter, what are you doing?" Mom asked.

"Bay Boy stuff," I said to her. "Island tradition." Then, I jumped over the railing and landed with a splash. I surfaced and swam toward Sofia.

"What's going on?" she called.

"I'm staying!" I yelled at the top of my lungs, stopping to tread water. "I'm staying!"

"Really?"

"Really!"

"Jeez Louise!" Sofia screamed, slapping the water in excitement. "That's the champ, Pete! The champ!" She turned and swam away from me at full speed. When she got closer to the dock, I heard her shout, "He's staying, Kat! Hey-o, Gram Mulligan! He's staying!"

There was a cheer. And a chant started "Pete Mull-i-gan! Pete Mull-i-gan!"

That made me smile.

I waved to my parents on the ferry to let them know I was okay.

They waved back grinning ear-to-ear.

Sofia waited for me to catch up to her.

We swam back to the dock together.

Chapter 57

It goes without saying that here, on Johnson Island, everything worked out for the best. Sure, I still get twee-mangled about stuff. I'll always be autistic, but I just feel better about it all. I live with Gram Mulligan. Now, I call her what every other mud-footer calls her. And I am officially Pete, which is easier to say than Peter, and even used by my parents now. I like it.

Speaking of my parents, they moved to a little mainland town about thirty minutes from the ferry. They visit every weekend. A lot of times during the week my mom stays over. Mom and Gram Mulligan still disagree on some things, but my mom seems happier to me.

I am a student enrolled at Johnson Island's K-12 School, and I really like my teacher. Sofia and Kat and Billy are my classmates. But on Johnson Island, you have to be friends with everyone, especially when you run into them cruisin' most nights. Gram and I have to bundle up now—it's almost December. Soon, Christmas will be coming. I can't wait to see it here. They say the watermen decorate their crab shacks with Christmas lights.

As far as Sofia and me, and the whole boyfriend/girlfriend thing, nothing yet. The twins respect Mr. Jin's boyfriend rule, so we remain just friends.

Speaking of the holidays, Gram Mulligan and I no longer watch our movies alone. Mayor Ooger and the town did sue Meta-Gro, and the judge just so happened to grow up on another island community down in the middle of the Chesapeake Bay called Tangier. He ruled fast and in our favor. We got wudgets full of bones, which means a lot of money.

Oh, and if you were curious why the weeds couldn't stand the bay water, the lawyers found something out from Dr. Lennox's notes. He picked Johnson Island on purpose to keep his seeds and weeds contained. For some reason, our shore line has an unusually high concentration of brackish water. Crabs love it and the plants were genetically modified to hate it.

But here's the best part. Aside from Ooger getting a new crab boat, cleaning up the town, and a nice payout for every family—the Jins sure were happy—Mayor Ooger spent a little bit of money on my recommendation. He renovated The Palace. And guess what we found during construction, squirreled away in the back of a closet? Two original movie posters! Real vintage ones. Godzilla vs. The Thing, 1964, and can you believe it, Jaws, 1975! Some say the greatest movie poster of all time. They look great in my new bedroom at Gram Mulligan's house.

Speaking of Gram, she was absolutely right. The Palace is like a time machine. Now, all of Johnson Island's film buffs watch movies together in those plush seats and take a trip back to the 1930s. I am an active member of The Palace Theater Preservation Society. The twins and I get to change the letters on the marquee when new movies play. Mrs. Jin is even helping me and Gram Mulligan fill out the paperwork so that The Palace can be on the National Register of Historic Places. Speaking of Gram Mulligan, we let her choose the grand-opening flick. It was Casablanca, 1942, of course. She shed a few tears during that one. Me, too.

And if you promise to keep this a secret, because if certain people find out, I could get in trouble, I'll tell you something. During the last thirty minutes of Casablanca, 1942, in the dark, Sofia held my hand.

Afterward, I was thrilled but confused. "Question." I raised my hand.

"Shoot," she said.

"What about your dad?" I asked.

"The only time he'll show up here is for Bruce Lee movies. Besides, sometimes you have to go for it, right?"

"Humph." I smiled at Sofia.

She smiled back.

"So," I said, "does... this... mean...?"

"Does this mean what?"

"Nothing," I said. Why bother asking? I knew the rule. But to me, I consider that night at the movies our official but unofficial (please, don't tell Mr. Jin, or Sofia, for that matter) date.

On the marquee right now, we are advertising our holiday film: It's a Wonderful Life, 1946. I am so excited to experience that one on the big screen. It will be the first time Sofia and Kat have seen it. It's pretty romantic. I'm sure I'll cry at the end, too. I always cry at the end. But I'm okay with it. And so is Sofia. It's who I am.

When I think about where I started, holding a school desk and crying, to where I am now, holding Sofia's hand and smiling, I think maybe

Dr. Carlos was right. Sometimes, a weirdo can be the hero. But unlike the movies, in real life, heroes never do it alone.

Without a tough grandmother, bossy twins, an eccentric island, and monstrous weeds that tried to kill me, I would never have become a mud-footer who knows that life, especially on Johnson Island, can be pretty wonderful.

AUTHOR'S NOTE

What started out as an idea for a middle grade monster story—that came after a sweaty day of weeding my family's garden—grew into much more as I wrote The Summer My Grandmother's Yard Tried to Kill Me. If you're a curious person like me, here are a few of the real-life things I learned while researching the story. You might want to learn about them, too.

AUTISM SPECTRUM DISORDER (ASD)

I hope following Pete's adventures on Johnson Island helps you appreciate and understand a little bit more about folks with autism spectrum disorder. ASD comes in many shapes and sizes. Personally, I have been a high school teacher for years and have taught many students with ASD. They have all been funny, interesting, and inspiring in their own way, just like Pete. In my classes, I like to include everyone. I like to celebrate differences. And for students with autism, it is easy to do if you look for the person underneath the diagnosis. I urge everyone to do the same.

CLASSIC MOVIES YOU MAY NOT KNOW

Interested in Pete's movie knowledge? Want to watch the classic flicks he mentions throughout the book? You should! Just because a movie is older or black-and-white, doesn't mean it isn't worth watching. As a matter of fact, those films are like time machines—you get to see life in another place and year, maybe far different from your own. A great place to start is the same place Pete did—at the American Film Institute website (afi. com). Once there, you can check out their film lists. I highly recommend

AFI'S 100 YEARS...100 MOVIES, The 100 Greatest American Films of All Time. Many of Pete's favorites are there, but not The Blob, 1958, Steve McQueen's first starring role! Not that The Blob is bad, but when you only have room for a hundred movies, you gotta be extra picky. Sorry, Steve.

INVASIVE WEEDS ARE REAL

As much as I wish this part of the story is all made up, invasive weeds are a problem. Last time I checked, invasive weeds cost America 34.7 billion dollars annually. Mikania Micrantha, the Mile-a-Minute weed mentioned in the book, can smother small plants and even trees if left unchecked. Of course, the real-life weed can't grow as fast as the monster weeds did on Johnson Island—so don't worry! But according to the Florida Department of Agriculture and Consumer Services, the Mile-a-Minute weed has been documented "as a pest in banana, cacao, coconut, oil palm, rubber, and rice plantations. Mile-a-Minute is one of the top 100 global invasive pests." To learn more about invasive weeds and the fight against them, start by visiting the Weed Science Society of America website. Yup, there really is a Weed Science Society of America!

GENETICALLY MODIFIED FOOD

This is an interesting issue. Food that has been modified in some way, even with human genes, is really happening. Of course, creating a super weed in a lab that wants revenge on humanity is pure fantasy—so you're safe for now! However, big companies do tamper with fruits and vegetables grown right here in America. Some modified foods can help with illness, others not so much. You can check out the pros and cons of genetically modified organisms or GMOs with a simple search online.

Look for more books from Winged Hussar Publishing, LLC:
E-books, paperbacks and Limited-Edition hardcovers.

The best in history, science fiction and fantasy at:
https://www. wingedhussarpublishing.com

Follow us for information and upcoming publications

On Facebook at:
Winged Hussar Publishing LLC

Or on twitter at:
WingHusPubLLC

About the Author

Harry Harvey is an English teacher in Point Pleasant, NJ.
This is his first novel.